Praise for David Gerrold
and the Star Wolf series

"David Gerrold knows *Star Trek* better than anyone, and here's his take at how it really should have been; the *Star Wolf* series is *Star Trek* done right—moral conundrums, fascinating characters, and pulse-pounding action. Highly recommended."

—ROBERT J. SAWYER, AUTHOR OF *HOMINIDS*

". . . story moves along at the speed of light."

—PUBLISHERS WEEKLY

"[Gerrold] looks at a real problem: How do you turn a jinx ship into a fighting unit? The answer to that question has often made a great story, and it does this time too. David has studied the master story tellers—Heinlein and Forrester and Conrad, and it shows."

—JERRY POURNELLE

". . . the adventure's there, the action moves along nicely, and the villain is as nasty as anyone could wish."

—ANALOG

"David Gerrold proves that he can do all the things that made us love Heinlein's storytelling—and often better."

—ORSON SCOTT CARD

"Gerrold elevates his story line above standard battle-driven fare by focusing on the intense war of wits between the *Star Wolf's* fully dimensional human crew and its unique alien adversary. He produces intelligent and entertaining hard SF that remains blessedly free of the militaristic stereotypes rampant in other examples of the subgenre."

—BOOKLIST

"Halfway into the story, we'll already know more about poor Commander Korie, and his whole accursed crew, and every compartment in their jinxed ship, than we ever learned about Kirk and the *Enterprise* in three seasons and several feature films. Equally important, that ship and those people will go somewhere, and be changed profoundly by what happens to them along the way."

—SPIDER ROBINSON

BLOOD
AND
FIRE

ALSO BY DAVID GERROLD

— FICTION —

The Star Wolf series
Starhunt
The Voyage of the Star Wolf
The Middle of Nowhere

The War Against the Chtorr series

The Dingilliad trilogy

The Man Who Folded Himself
The Flying Sorcerers (with Larry Niven)
When HARLIE Was One
Moonstar Odyssey
The Martian Child

— NONFICTION —

The World of Star Trek
The Trouble With Tribbles
Worlds of Wonder

DAVID GERROLD

BLOOD
AND
FIRE

BenBella Books, Inc.
Dallas, Texas

BenBella Books Edition

BenBella Books, Inc.
10440 N. Central Expressway, Suite 800, Dallas, Texas 75231
Send feedback to feedback@benbellabooks.com
www.benbellabooks.com
BenBella is a federally registered trademark.

Printed in the United States of America

Library of Congress Cataloging-in-Publication Data

Gerrold, David, 1944–
    Blood and fire / by David Gerrold.— BenBella Books ed.
      p. cm
    ISBN 1-932100-11-3 (alk. paper)
    1. Space ships—Fiction. I. Title.

PS3557.E69B57 2004
813'.54—dc22

2003018535

Cover illustration by Bob Eggleton
Cover design by Melody Cadungog
Interior designed and composed by John Reinhardt Book Design

Special discounts for bulk sales are available.
Please contact bulkorders@benbellabooks.com.

For Randy, Pam,
and Captain Anne Jillian Harbaugh,
with love

Introduction

"... To boldly go where no man has gone before."

What an exceptional mandate to tell stories—daring stories, stories that broke tradition—especially in science fiction television!

When that brave opening narration introduced *Star Trek* in 1966, it expressed itself as episodes that dealt with bigotry and racism, the Vietnam War, the Generation Gap, enslavement of other races, fights for equality and many other issues of the time. Under the entertaining guise of science fiction action adventure, *Star Trek* told stories that were intelligent, life affirming, entertaining and thoughtful.

David Gerrold was a part of that groundbreaking series, writing the classic script "The Trouble With Tribbles" in addition to other episodes. It was while I was story editor of the series that I met this young, brash and brilliantly talented writer.

In the years after *Star Trek* went off the air, David and I worked together a number of times on various television shows and developed a personal tie of friendship that has never faltered. When he called me in late 1986 and told me Gene Roddenberry was going to produce a new live-action version of *Star Trek* and he himself was already involved, I was elated. The elation went to the top of the scale when I was called upon to give input into the new show and ultimately to write the two-hour pilot script for *Star Trek–The Next Generation*.

Paramount and the new UPN network had guaranteed the show a full first season. Technically, the "pilot" was the premiere movie that would kick off the hour-long series episodes. Therefore, even as "Encounter at Farpoint" was being written and prepared, other scripts were already being put into work.

Some months before, Gene, David and others from the show had attended a science fiction convention in Boston. A gay fan in the audience pointedly asked if the new show would include gay characters, as *Star Trek* had been a pioneer in depicting blacks, Asians and Latinos in key roles. Gene agreed that it was time, and he hoped to do it.

David, who was working as a staff writer, went to Gene and pitched an idea. It would be a story that was a metaphor for the AIDS epidemic, taking place on a biologically infested plague ship with several of the regular characters in jeopardy. An additional point would be blood donorship. The stakes were high; the answers were not easy; the decisions were painful. Gene could sanction a story that tackled a large issue, told through personal, emotional involvement and powerful in its message. It was what *Star Trek* did best. Gene told David to go write it.

It was only later, in the development of the script, that David realized it was a perfect place to include gay characters, and he did so in four lines of dialogue so understated that anyone not paying attention could have taken the two men as mere friends.

David turned in the first draft of "Blood and Fire" just before he was scheduled to fly out of town as a guest on a *Star Trek* Cruise. A day later, on the ship, David received a telegram from Gene that read: "Everyone loves your script, have a great cruise."

Then Gene's personal lawyer, who had assumed an unofficial position on *Star Trek–The Next Generation*, read the script. Things changed. Radically.

The lawyer and several staff members actively campaigned against the script, though some of them earlier had championed AIDS as one of the issues the show should tackle. The complimentary telegram was forgotten. Gene had a new opinion of "Blood and Fire." It was "aesthetically displeasing" with its slimy bloodworms and plasmacytes as a metaphor for AIDS. That would have to change. As for the gay couple, they would have to be eliminated or become heterosexual. It seemed they, too, were aesthetically displeasing, despite the fact they were drawn as professional and well-regarded members of the *Enterprise* crew.

When David arrived home from the weekend cruise, he found a phone message from me warning him about the bear trap he was about to walk into. In a respectful but pointed memo to Gene, David argued for his vision and for the important issues the script addressed. In front of fans and staff, Gene had declared his intention to include gay characters on the new show, even if only in one episode. Where was the courage in presenting a story with ordinary characters facing an ordinary biological threat? David's final arguments were: "If not now, when? If not here, where?"

Gene laid down his decree, not to David's face, but through one of the other producers. The script would either be rewritten as he directed, or it would be shelved. David made changes, taking out one of the gay characters and giving his lines to "Tasha Yar." It was still "aesthetically displeasing." David knew he would leave the show soon, as his contract was expiring. He offered to rewrite the script one more time, but Gene told another producer not to let him do so. A staff producer-writer tried to rework the script, calling it "Blood and Ice," changing the plasmacytes to brain-eating entities that turned infected people into zombies. Didn't work. The script was shelved, and there were no gay characters depicted on *Star Trek–The Next Generation* under Gene Roddenberry's aegis.

Later, rumors started to spread that David had been fired from the show—not true. Other rumors spread that the "Blood and Fire" script had been so bad it had to be shelved—not true. David began selling copies of it at conventions so people could read it for themselves and decide. He donated the proceeds from those sales to Aids Project Los Angeles.

With his reputation being trashed at conventions in both the United States and Britain, David responded the only way he knew how—by writing a series of fine novels. Among them were *A Rage for Revenge, A Season for Slaughter, Jumping Off the Planet, Voyage of the Star Wolf* and esteemed *The Martian Child*, for which he won the Nebula and the Hugo awards.

In the nineties, David and I developed four scripts, a full story arc and an immense bible for a potential *Star Wolf* television series or series of TV movies. The book you hold in your hand is the envisioning of the "Blood and Fire" script in a different universe and with different characters, but with even more power than it would have had as a *Star Trek–The Next Generation* episode. Read it and see for yourself how compelling and exciting a story it is—and how boldly it goes where no one has gone before.

D.C. FONTANA

Scenery

With each hyperstate jump, the distance between the two ships lessened significantly. Aboard the *Star Wolf*, the distress signal from the *Norway* was expected to become not only more distinct, but more detailed. Distress beacons were supposed to use "pyramid" coding, with successive layers of detail encrypted into the signal.

As a rescue vessel approached the source and the signal became stronger, the additional levels of information would become accessible and the rescuers would have a clearer idea of what kind of emergency to expect. Decoding the *Norway*'s beacon should have provided additional information about the nature of her emergency.

Should have.

Didn't.

In this situation, the supplementary channels remained bafflingly blank. And the itch behind Korie's shoulders became a full-blown rash, so much so that even Captain Parsons had to scratch. She grumbled her annoyance. "They want help, but they won't give details. You're right, Commander Korie. This has to be a high-security operation."

"*Extremely* high security," Korie noted. "Way out here, a month deep into the south end of the rift—this is the other side of nowhere—whatever it is they're doing, they want it secret."

On the forward display, the red star was already visible as a teardrop hung against the darkness. A pinpoint flare of blue-white flamed beyond, but the spiral streamer wasn't apparent yet, only a soft pink glow surrounding the blue-white dwarf.

"We have our bearings," reported Tor. "Ready for the next jump."

"Initiate," said the captain.

The *Star Wolf* jumped. And jumped again. And one more time. Soon, the object known only as IKE-34 was a wall of flame that filled half the visible universe. It occupied a volume of space equal to the orbit of Jupiter. Against the darkness, the blue dwarf could now be seen pulling a great streamer of flaming gas out of the tip of the crimson teardrop. The line of fire curled out and around, stretching across the visible sky like a rip; as it reached the disk-shaped well of the bright blue star, it began to spiral inward, around and around, the colors shifting more and more brightly as the crimson flames were gathered into the purpling corona. And yes, the scenery *was* spectacular. Better than spectacular. Astonishing.

From this angle, below the red star's south pole, it wasn't immediately apparent that the giant was also flattened at both poles; it was impressive nonetheless. Despite the *Star Wolf*'s distance—several billion kilometers—the massive size of the star created the looming perception that they were close enough to touch it. The perspectives of space create impossible visions, and this was one of the more impossible views. That long-dead poet had been right. Enjoy God's handiwork in silence. Across the Bridge of the starship the crew worked wordlessly, but again and again their eyes were drawn to the forward display.

Eventually, the magnitude of the view became so intimidating and oppressive that Captain Parsons ordered the image muted down. "We don't need the eye of hell looking down on us," she remarked. "We've got work to do. Let's turn that off." She stepped down from the Command Deck, only three short steps into the well of the Operations Bay, but a whole other domain of command and control. She took a familiar position next to the astrogation console, just behind Tor's left shoulder. "How long to close with the *Norway*?"

"Fifty-six hours. Coming in across the pole brings us in a lot faster—but the *Norway*'s in the plane of the ecliptic—a 'Missionary Orbit.' Coming up from under, we'll have to accelerate constantly to catch up, correcting all the way in, and decelerate only in the last few hours. Tricky, not impossible."

"And if those folks are in serious trouble . . . we still might not be in time," said Parsons.

"They never should have parked so close to the star," Tor replied. "They've made the rescue operation damn near impossible."

"That may be the point," said Korie, coming up beside them. "They *wanted* to make interception difficult. By staying within the gravitational corona they're beyond the reach of hyperstate—no ship can jump in that close, neither friend nor enemy. The approach has to be made in normal space. The slow way. That gives them time to detect, scan and evade."

Parsons nodded. "Tactically, that was the right decision. In practice, it's going to kill them. This'll be another one for the textbooks. All right, take us in, Commander Tor." She turned to Goldberg at the communication station. "Lieutenant? Do you have anything else yet?"

The stout, red-headed man at the console shook his head. "Sorry, Captain. The signal is still blank."

"That's what I expected." She turned to Korie. "In a way, they're doing us a favor. When the inevitable board of inquiry asks why there were no survivors, we'll be able to point to the deficiencies of their orbit and their distress signal."

"Failure to arrive in time," murmured Korie. "That's what they'll say. Of course, we'll be excused for that—but it'll still be a black mark on our record."

"Don't sweat it," said Parsons. "If this ship can carry the burden of blame for Marathon without flinching, it can easily handle a minor embarrassment like this one." She turned away from Korie's dour expression. "All right, let's do the dance. We all know the steps." She headed back up to the Command Deck, the raised dais at the rear of the Bridge. "Oh, Mr. Korie—one more thing." She waited until Korie had joined her up behind the railing. In a more conversational tone, she asked, "Have you examined the manifest of the supplies we're delivering here?"

"Yes, ma'am." Korie waited for the captain to make her point.

"Notice anything interesting?"

"Quite a few things."

"Such as?"

"Well, there's a more-than-usual complement of biotechnical equipment and supplies, isolation gear, repulsor valves, magnetic bottles and so on."

"Your assessment?"

"It's a no-brainer, Captain. They're engaged in Class-X medical research. All that isolation gear says they're dealing with extreme toxicity."

The captain nodded. "That's my thought too. We've got a mean, ugly bear here. Train your mission team carefully." To his look, "Yes, I'm going to want you to lead it."

"Not Brik? This should be his responsibility."

"Think about it. If you were captain of a distressed vessel, how would you feel if the first person to your rescue was a Morthan . . .? And if your ship was involved in a Class-X operation and security was a major concern—would you believe a Morthan in an Alliance uniform?"

"Point taken," said Korie, embarrassed that he hadn't thought of it himself. But then, he'd been focusing on the more immediate problem—trying to figure out what the *Norway* was doing out here.

"I want you to be careful," the captain added. "Feel free to break out any of the gear in that cargo you need to protect yourselves and the *Star Wolf*."

"Already planning on it."

"And don't listen to Hall's complaints about the charge-backs."

"I never do."

"How's your itch?"

"Ferocious."

"Good. Carry on."

Korie felt comfortable with Captain Parsons—the first time he'd felt comfortable with a captain in a long time. It was a pleasant change to have his abilities not only respected, but depended upon. He nodded his assent and turned back to his headset to complete an earlier discussion with HARLIE, the starship's intelligence engine. He and HARLIE had been sorting through the appropriate procedure books and manuals for dealing with medical emergencies, especially those involving possible contamination by unknown toxic substances. When he finished that, he headed forward to the Med Bay to confer with Chief Surgeon Molly Williger.

Dr. Williger was notorious as the shortest, ugliest woman in the known universe, but few people who served with her ever noticed that; all they saw was one of the best doctors in the fleet. Williger was just finishing a routine medical check on Crewman Brian Armstrong when Korie entered. Armstrong, a side of beef with a grin, flashed his smile at Korie as he pulled his shirt back on. "Hiya, sir."

Korie nodded a curt acknowledgment. He rarely smiled. "Armstrong."

"Sir?" Armstrong began eagerly. "I'd like to volunteer for the Mission Team. Dr. Williger says I'm in good shape. I can carry things. And I'm certified for security duties—"

"I can see you're in good shape." Korie noted Armstrong's well-developed body. "But we're going to need specialists for this operation." Noting Armstrong's immediate disappointment, Korie added, "But—I haven't made any final decisions yet. I'll keep you in mind."

"Thanks, sir. Thanks Dr. Williger." Armstrong grinned again and left. Williger and Korie exchanged amused glances.

"Gotta give him credit," Korie said. "He wants to work."

"He's bored," Williger said. "And he's got this thing going with the Quillas."

"I thought he was over that."

Williger jiggled her hand in an "iffy" gesture. "Armstrong doesn't understand intimacy. The Quillas are a fascinating mystery to him." She added, "He knows how to be friendly, not close. He uses friendliness as a defense against intimacy. But apparently, the Quillas got to him anyway."

"I saw your report."

When he had first come aboard, Armstrong had enjoyed a quick liaison with Quilla Delta, not realizing that all of the other Quillas were telepathic participants. The discovery of a male Quilla—Lambda—had startled him. Later Armstrong and Lambda had become friendly, if not exactly friends. Then Lambda was killed in action—

"Armstrong hurts," said Williger. "And he has no one to talk to about it. He's taking it a lot harder than he shows. All this energy and enthusiasm is . . . denial and sublimation and overcompensation." She sighed. "And then we brought two more Quillas aboard, one male, one female, and . . . well, Armstrong is jealous—"

"Jealous?" Korie looked incredulous.

"Of the male Quilla. Of the closeness the Quillas have. How much do you know about Quillas?"

Korie shrugged. "Haven't really given it too much thought. They're a religious order, dedicated to serving others, aren't they?"

"Well, you should give it more thought than that," Williger said. "They're not just a religious order, they're a conjoined mind in multiple bodies."

"So? What does this have to do with Armstrong?"

"The Quillas had a private welcoming ceremony—and Armstrong was left out of it. How could he be included? When Quillas take a new member into the cluster, there's a whole ritual of joining—very spiritual, but very physical as well. They have to tune themselves to each other. Usually it's only a matter of a few days. This time it took over a week. Armstrong felt like they were shutting him out. On top of Lambda's death—well, he's confused and he's hurting."

Korie made a face. This was not something he wanted to deal with.

Williger glowered up at him. "I know—you don't think self-esteem issues are your concern, they're supposed to be mine. Or the Quillas'. But it *is* your concern, because he's part of your crew. Armstrong needs something to do that lets him feel essential. Right now—he doesn't." The little doctor looked to Korie sharply. "That's why he's trying so hard to be everyone's best friend. That's all he knows how to do. He needs something else to be good at."

"The problem is, he doesn't have any skills. He's not our smartest crewmember."

"I thought you had him in a training program."

Korie sighed. "He passes his tests, but his scores are always just *barely* passing. He's doing just enough to get by. I need more than that. I can't risk putting him anywhere essential. That's why I keep rotating him."

"Maybe you should trust him with a little responsibility. Maybe he'll surprise you."

"I don't see any evidence to suggest it."

"Uh-huh," Williger said sharply. "And maybe he's feeling the same thing you are, Commander. All you want is *your* chance too."

Korie glanced over at her. He did not like being reminded of the fact that he was not yet wearing captain's stars on his collar. He held back his immediate response, exhaled instead. "That's not what I came down here for, Doctor. We need to finalize our plans for the medical mission team. We need to plan their training—we have to assume the *Norway* is an extremely toxic environment."

Williger noted Korie's deliberate change of subject with a curt "Fine." Then she added, "I'm going with you. And I'll want Brian Armstrong too."

"No, you aren't," Korie said. "The captain doesn't want to risk you."

"But she'll risk you . . .?"

"I'm expendable. You're not. You'll monitor from the Bridge, or from Med Bay. You can still have Armstrong, if you want."

"I suppose this is not negotiable."

"That's correct."

"Well . . . all right." She sighed acceptance. "I tried. Listen, if the situation is really bad over there, we'll need to use the forward bay as an auxiliary receiving room. I assume you'll be docking at the nose?"

"That's the recommended procedure."

"I want enhanced scanners on your helmets, with high-med software. I'll give you Chief Pharmacist's Mate Berryman as your senior corpsman. Hodel and Easton are also certified. Take them. You won't reconsider Armstrong?"

"Not this time, no. I was thinking Bach and Shibano."

Williger frowned. "Shibano's a cowboy—and Bach hasn't been certified yet for medical missions."

Korie ran a hand through his hair. How to say this without sounding paranoid? There was no way, so he just said it. "We don't know what's over there. I need security people."

"Yeah, I heard about your itch. Half a dozen people came in asking for skin-rex lotion." Her expression was wry. "It must be catching, eh?"

"I certainly hope so."

Lambda

Armstrong sat alone in the mess room. Thinking. His cup of chocolate sat cold and forgotten in front of him. On some unspoken level, he understood what his problem was. And now, today, for some reason, he was almost ready to speak it—if not to anyone else, at least to himself.

It wasn't loneliness. It was that thing on the other side of loneliness.

He could talk to people, he could make friends, he could get people to spend time with him, and he usually didn't have any problems with women either. He'd had more than his share of sexual exercise. And even a relationship or two. So, no, it wasn't loneliness.

It was that *other* thing. About *belonging*. About being a part of something—not just a plug-in module, replaceable, discardable—but something more essential. Something with identity. He wanted to know that what he did was useful and important, and even necessary to the success of the ship. And the war.

It was a need that he couldn't explain, and he felt frustrated every time he thought about it—this feeling that he had to be something more. But there was nothing particularly special about Brian Armstrong. He was big, good-looking, a little goofy, likable, mostly capable, and just like several billion other men in this part of the galaxy. If he died right now, there would be no evidence that he was ever here, except a few records in the Fleet rolls. There would be no artifact, no object, no person, no heritage, nothing remarkable to indicate that Brian Armstrong had passed this way; nothing to say that Brian Armstrong had left the universe a better place than he found it. And despite his genial, easy-going nature, Brian Armstrong found this thought intolerable. It wasn't death he feared; it was being *insignificant*.

He just wanted to . . . make a difference. That was all.

Quilla Delta sat down opposite him. She placed one blue hand on top of his. He glanced up, met her eyes, forced a half-smile, pulled his hand away, then looked back down at his lap.

"You are not happy, Brian," she said. "That makes us sad."

Armstrong didn't answer. To answer would have meant discussing the things that he didn't discuss with anyone. If Lambda had lived, maybe he would have. He had thought about it a lot, what he wanted to say to Lambda. Lambda had seemed to know something of his confusion—

11

"Lambda is not dead," Delta said. "Everything that Lambda was, everything that Lambda knew—it still lives inside us. Only the body is gone. Not the soul. Not the spirit."

"I can't believe that," said Armstrong. "I've studied a little bit about Quillas. About massminds. I know that there's a kind of synergy that happens. But there's no way the soul of an individual can leave a body and take up residence in a networked collection of other bodies. It's just not possible."

"Yes, it is," said Delta in a different voice. A voice that Armstrong recognized in spite of himself, and he looked up with a start. "Everything that I was when I was alive I still am. I'm just living inside a different body now. I told you that Quillas are immortal, Brian. This is why I became one. Because I was like you. And I was unhappy that way."

Armstrong started to lower his eyes again, then changed his mind and looked into Quilla Delta's face. Her skin was the most beautiful shade of blue. Her eyes were shadowed with magenta; her lips were almost the same shade. Her quills were a bright red Mohawk across her bald blue scalp. She had a slim, boyish quality and yet she was as feminine as a rosebud. He thought she was the most beautiful and the most irresistible female he had ever seen. She was also the most affectionate—he knew that there were no personality differences between one member of a Quilla cluster and another, but nevertheless he still felt she was the most *affectionate*. Maybe he was projecting his own feelings, maybe not. It didn't matter. He couldn't deny her anything.

He licked his lips uncomfortably. They were dry. His whole mouth was dry. "I, um, have to go." He started to rise. But as he did, he saw that they were no longer alone. Quilla Beta, Quilla Alpha, Quilla Gamma and the two new ones, Quilla Theta and Quilla Omega.

Omega was a tall, blue man, taller even than Lambda had been. He stepped forward now. "Brian Armstrong, we know the source of your unhappiness. We are sorry for having caused you pain."

"It's not your fault," Armstrong said.

"But it is our *responsibility*. We know that you felt *distanced* when we expanded our cluster. We know that you felt shut out of our closeness. This makes us sad. Our closeness should not be a barrier. It is not a prize that we keep to ourselves; it is a gift that we share with others."

"You can't help it," Armstrong said to all of them, trying to avoid looking at Omega. "It's just the way you are. You're all one mind. And I'm not. I'm not part of you. I'm just me. So just by existing the way you are, I'm automatically shut out. It's my fault for presuming that I could ever be anything more than another John. I was stupid."

"No," said Delta. "Not stupid."

"Whatever. Listen, thanks for all the . . . attention. It was fun, okay? But like the song says . . . I was looking for love on all the wrong planets. It was a mistake. I'm sorry that Lambda's gone. I liked him. I like all of you, but uh . . . can't we just be friends now, something like that?"

Omega blocked his exit. "Lambda lives in me too, Brian. Listen. This is what Lambda wants to say to you. 'Ever since the first day you have been running from us. Your few conversations with Lambda were the only time you stopped running. It was the only time you treated any of us like a person. The rest of the time you acted like we were bodies, here only for your sexual pleasure. Did you think your callous behavior wasn't hurtful to us? Perhaps it is you who owe us an apology.'"

"Yeah, well—maybe I do. I'm sorry for treating you all like—like objects. Sex toys. Freaks. I dunno. Whatever. I was wrong. May I go now?"

"Brian—" This time Gamma stepped in front of him. "We ask only one thing. Just please stop running from us."

"Okay. I'll stop running. May I go now?"

Quilla Delta stepped in close. "We miss Lambda too," she said. "His body fit right. Almost as nice as yours. Sometimes we cry for him—for that missing piece of ourselves. Do you cry for him, Brian? I think you want to. If you do, it's all right." Without waiting for his answer, she put her arms around him and gently pulled him to her. He stiffened, but she refused to let go. He closed his eyes, but she still refused to let go. Instead she held him—and held and held and held him. Did she want him to cry? He didn't know. He didn't feel like crying now. He didn't know what he felt—this wasn't a familiar situation.

The other Quillas wrapped their arms around them, and now Armstrong felt himself being passed from body to body. He couldn't tell which of them was holding him. He opened his eyes only once and saw that he was being hugged by Omega, then closed them again until it didn't matter anymore whose arms were wrapped around him. And still they passed him around.

"Listen to me," a soft voice whispered in his ear. It sounded like Lambda again. "When you're ready to talk . . . we'll be ready to listen. Give us that chance, Brian? Please?"

Despite himself, he nodded.

And that was enough. That was all he needed to do. When they finally let him go, he felt different—and he was different. He looked from one to the other of them and realized he'd taken on a terrifying new responsibility. Honesty.

History

Contrary to popular expectations, the invention of faster-than-light travel did not create an age of enlightenment. Quite the opposite.

Imagine the human species as a vast stew of ideas, opinions, neuroses, ideologies, beliefs, religions, pathologies, illnesses, cults and paradigms—a sea of competing world-views, models of reality at war with each other; an ecology of memes, each one struggling for living space in the heads and hearts of human beings.

The introduction of cost-effective FTL access to other worlds gave each of these memes access to the living space it wanted. The result was an explosion of humanity in all directions: each ship filled with idea spores and belief cuttings and world-view seed-carriers—all those little ships filled with infectious opinions and belief systems, each and every person a host for his part of the larger energizing meme. It wasn't humanity that emigrated to the stars; *it was the memes.*

Humans live and breed for their beliefs; often they sacrifice everything for the thoughts they carry. History is a chronicle of human beings dying for their convictions, as if the continuance of the idea is more important than the continuance of the person. The ideology becomes more important to the carrier than his own ability to be human.

All the disparate models of reality, each one demanding its own space to dominate and thrive, drove their bearers outward—the memes drove men like parasites riding in their minds—and the human species spread its motes across space like a field of dandelions exploding in a tornado, creating a million new places for memes to thrive and a billion new memes to live in them.

Interstellar travel fractured and fractionated the human race. A thousand new religions. A hundred thousand new schools of scientific thought. A million new worlds, each one with its own dominant meme. Most of the memes were benign: "Love one another. Judge not, lest ye be judged. Do unto others as you would have others do unto you." Some were not: "Our book is the only true book. Our God is the only true God. Our belief is the only true belief. All others are false . . . and must be eradicated." Some were untested: "We need a place to live where we won't have the oppressions of others keeping us from being who we really are."

The problem that each of these colonizing memes ran into was *reality*. Every single world that human beings stepped out onto presented its own particular set of challenges—capping the volcanoes for geothermal energy, cracking the ice to make oceans, releasing water from the mantle to make air, mining heavy metals for industry, securing a power supply from the wind and the water and the sun, getting enough oxygen into the air, cooling the atmosphere with shadow fields, warming the seas with core taps, designing crops that could survive, dealing with hostile organisms, determining both long- and short-range weather patterns, constructing safe shelters, putting up satellites, establishing global communications, designing a working government. . . . Compared to the last challenge, of course, all the others were easy. You could always tell when a planet was viable—but nobody was ever convinced that a government was fine. *Any* government.

And as each set of memes left the pure ideological vacuum of space and collided with the hard soil of reality, the laws of evolution kicked in. Each new world worked its own conditions, and the memes were given the same choice as every other survival-oriented entity: adapt or die. Those that adapted, evolved. And, inevitably, mutations occurred. The planets themselves added their own flavors to the mix, creating new memes in the ecology of ideas. Over time, the rigors of the environment always took precedence—in every case, the flavor of the planet eventually overwhelmed everything else, becoming the dominant taste in the stew.

Human colonists—carriers of the memes—were caught in the middle, as usual. Humanity changed. Adapted. Evolved. Mutated. And redesigned itself accordingly—creating new memes and new explosions of trade and colonization. Humanity's memes drove it outward, forcing it to become something new on every planet it touched. Humanity spread throughout the galaxy like a rapidly evolving intelligent cancer.

On some worlds, a particularly seductive meme took hold—the idea that if humanity now had the power to redesign itself, then humanity *should* redesign itself. Imagine . . . a truly *efficient* and *capable* human being. Imagine a human who was "more-than" human. The "More-Than" meme was more than just "another good idea." For some, it became a cult, an obsession, an ideology—a religion. For some, it became a holy war.

Some of the More-Thans seceded from the Covenant and headed out beyond the frontier—sand not just beyond the frontier, but to the far side of the rift, a natural barrier to further human expansion. Humanity—*unimproved* humanity—would be unlikely to challenge the rift. Or so the More-Thans believed. They were wrong, but they believed it anyway.

The Morthan meme, mixed with the isolationist meme, was a dangerous combination. And those who espoused it were clearly unfamiliar with the evolutionary consequences that befell isolated populations on islands, in preserves or separated on distant planets—or perhaps they felt that because they understood the laws of nature, they were somehow immune to their effects.

Countering the Morthan meme was another one: the meme of Alliance, the idea that the human family, despite all its diversity and difference, was still evolved from the same basic stock and was therefore still a family, and that whatever new shapes or ideologies might occur across the galaxy, the fundamental relationship of a common heritage was enough of a foundation on which to build an Alliance of trade and cultural exchange.

As disastrous as the meme of isolation was to the Morthans, equally disastrous was the meme of a universal family of humanity that could include and celebrate every separate form of behavior and belief. Memes are survival-oriented. Memes tolerate only memes that are sympathetic or complementary. Memes cannot tolerate antithetical ideas.

But memes don't die, humans do.

Humans, as the carriers of ideas, as the servants of ideologies, shed their blood whenever two memes came into conflict.

And the conflict between the Alliance meme and the Morthan meme promised to be the most terrible of all.

Brik

Not all Morthans believed in the goals of the Morthan Solidarity. This did not automatically mean that they believed in the goals of the Alliance either, but there were some who had fled Morthan space and applied for asylum. Some of the refugees ended up as civilian advisors. Others, for reasons of their own, enlisted to serve in the Allied Star Fleet. Lieutenant Commander Brik was one of those Morthan officers.

Brik stood three meters tall, almost too tall for the corridors of a destroyer-class liberty ship. There was room for him to stretch to his full height only on the Ops Deck, the engine room, the Cargo Bay and his private quarters. Everywhere else, he moved in a near-feral crouch.

The more traditionally human members of the *Star Wolf* crew often speculated on Brik's motivations. To most of them, he remained an incomprehensible enigma. Why would *any* Morthan want to live and serve with human beings? If Morthans believed themselves to be "more than human," then wouldn't such a role be demeaning and degrading?

In point of fact, Lieutenant Commander Brik had not too long ago held that very view—that service with human beings *was* an extremely repugnant duty, almost a personal disgrace. But he also was smart enough to recognize that the prejudice he felt was more the voice of his upbringing on a Morthan world than a product of any direct interaction with human beings. So with great difficulty he had put aside his prejudice in favor of a more useful curiosity about the nature of humanity— an act of will power that had initially left him trembling with fury but had now subsided into just another knot in his second stomach, something he could live with. He was still discomfited by humans, but not for the reasons humans believed.

Brik's original distaste had now been supplanted by something even more uncomfortable. Honest interest. For all their faults, insecurities, inaccuracies, inabilities, neuroses, psychoses, pathologies, beliefs and other failings, humans were still . . . *interesting*. Part of Brik's interest lay in the fact that human identity represented the undeniable ancestral origin of Morthan identity. It was humans who had come up with the idea of a superior bioengineered species. It was humans who had begun the process of creating the Morthans—at least until the fifth generation, when there were finally enough mature Morthans motivated to take responsibility for their own future.

Brik had come to believe that for Morthans to control the direction of their own evolution, it was essential to understand the source material. Knowing what made humanity successful was as important as knowing where humanity could be improved. So Brik's curiosity was rooted in a very selfish motivation.

At one point, Brik had been concerned about the possibility that he might end up developing a certain degree of *affection* for his human comrades-in-arms. And for a while, he had even toyed with the possibility that this might be a useful domain of personal experimentation. However, after his single attempt at fathoming human sexuality he realized that this was probably not a fruitful avenue of research for him. The experiment—undertaken with, and at the behest of, Lieutenant J.G. Helen Bach, one of his security officers—had been a near-fatal disaster.* Near fatal for Lieutenant J.G. Helen Bach, that is. The curious lieutenant had paid for her misadventure with ten days of downtime in Med Bay.

The consequences for Brik were not physical—but shortly thereafter several salacious rumors about his physical prowess began to circulate through the ship, and although no one ever said anything to him directly, Lieutenant Commander Brik was painfully aware that he had become something of a legend among the crew. Particularly the female members of the crew. His relations with Bach had been strained ever since, to say the least.

Eventually, Bach applied for a transfer, which Korie—as acting captain—had denied. Then Brik applied for a transfer, although not for the same reasons. Not knowing how to deal with the sexual relationships, human gossip or the prurient interest of a bored crew, he felt just vulnerable enough that he recognized he could become a serious danger to the rest of the ship. He wasn't certain he could control his own deadly impulses—at least not until Korie called both Brik and Bach into conference and ordered them to find a way to work together. *Or else.* He did not specify what the *or else* would be. He did not even acknowledge the specifics of the situation. He simply said, "You two are assigned to work together. Find a way to do that. Now. You're both rational, intelligent beings. You're both mature enough to work security—the crew looks to both of you as role models for shipboard discipline. We have a new

---

* *The Middle of Nowhere.*

captain coming aboard in three days. I intend to turn this ship over with the highest possible confidence rating. You are officers trained to handle problems at your level and pass only solutions upward. If you start passing problems up to me, you won't like my solutions. I promise you." And then he added, "Fortunately, I don't like either one of you enough that I'll have to feel bad about the consequences. Is this clear? Good. Now go do your jobs and let this be the end of it. Dismissed."

Officially, the fleet preferred that crew members abstain from having sexual relationships, lest it complicate the chain of command. Unofficially, commanding officers only acknowledged personal or sexual relationships when they interfered with the smooth running of the ship. A reprimand of this type would be a serious blemish on the career of any officer on whose record it appeared. To his credit, Korie kept his reprimand off the record and his remarks were never entered into either Brik's or Bach's service log.

Once Korie had ordered Brik to comply with Fleet discipline, Brik's personal dilemma was resolved. He knew how to follow orders. He knew how to fulfill his duty. He knew how to be responsible: push all personal concerns aside; they no longer exist. End of dilemma. Bach followed his lead and their professional relationship resumed in an atmosphere of cold, crisp politesse. Neither of them ever mentioned the matter again, nor did Korie.

For his part, Brik used the episode as a confirmation of his earlier suspicion that attempts at affection with ancestral-form human beings would be a mistake. Ancestrals were irrational beyond anything he had previously conceived. In the domain of sexual relationships, they were clearly insane. Psychopathic. Criminally deranged. Not to be trusted without a keeper.

Nevertheless, when ancestral-form human beings put aside sexual matters, they were *almost* civilized. And in that regard, Brik had to acknowledge that they were obviously capable of extraordinary self control—perhaps even more self control than most Morthans. Morthans didn't have sex. Morthans didn't have hormonal storms driving them crazy. Morthans didn't have these same kinds of overwhelming physical urges. So Morthans didn't have to control them, didn't have to know how to behave appropriately toward others. Morthans were trained early how to behave—distrust everyone and everything. Learn that and you know how to survive and succeed for the rest of your life.

But humans—ordinary humans had all these other operating *modes*. They made jokes. They flirted. They *told the truth*. All of these modes were alien experiences to Brik—so alien, in fact, that he was beginning to suspect that ancestral-form humans were far more unfathomable to Morthans than Morthans ever would be to them. And for that reason, he began to suspect that the Morthan Solidarity might actually lose the war.

It was a curious thought. Morthans lose?

Militarily, Morthans were clearly superior—but interstellar space was a great equalizer. A torpedo could be launched from a small ship as well as a big one—it could destroy a big ship as well as a small one. So the advantage lay not in strength, but in speed and tactics.

Humans had speed, but Morthans had tactics.

Given that equation, the smart money would bet on the Morthans—but more and more Brik was beginning to realize that the essential irrationality of human beings made them tactically impossible to predict, and possibly impossible to defeat. And if that were so, then the *unthinkable* might actually be true—human beings might be superior to Morthans.

All those different operating modes. Humans had more different ways to be, more different ways to *think*, than Morthans did.

Very troubling.

Because if this were true, Brik could not afford to dismiss affection or sexual relationships. If this particularly uncomfortable thesis had any validity to it at all, Brik had to continue his investigations. No matter what the personal cost.

Indeed, his personal commitment to expanding his knowledge of dangerous things *demanded* that he return his attention to these investigations. The thought bothered him immensely and he inflicted severe damage on both of his workout robots while he dealt with the discomfort.

His exercises gave him a way to maintain—and beyond that, he could safely postpone any further inquiries into the matter of emotional attachments because Korie had effectively ordered him to. *"Do your job"* took precedence.

At least for now.

Preparation

For a long while, the crew of the *Star Wolf* had been resentful of Korie's treatment. They had complained—with considerable justification—that the executive officer drove them too hard. But later, after several missions and several close encounters with the enemy, after several opportunities to see how well the ship functioned in a crisis, the crew's attitude had changed dramatically. They still complained about how hard Korie worked them—but now they did so with a considerable degree of pride. Their unofficial motto was, "Yes, but he's *our* son of a bitch."

Captain Parsons had come aboard the *Star Wolf* well aware of Korie's reputation. She knew his record, she knew what fires fueled his engines. She had expected a humorless man, a grim one, a martinet—someone like his mentor, Captain Richard Hardesty, only younger and without the augments. What she found was someone much more complex.

At first, Korie seemed to her much less than she had expected. But then, perhaps she wasn't certain at all what she expected. What she found was a young man who was deceptively soft-spoken and respectful of her authority. Possibly he had grown more relaxed with his situation over the past year. And possibly the tales of Korie were somewhat exaggerated. In either case, she found him intriguing—particularly the depth of his knowledge about his starship. She suspected that he could take it apart and rebuild it single-handedly, if given enough time. And add a few improvements in the process. So far, she hadn't found any situation he couldn't handle. And she doubted she would.

She caught up with him in the officer's mess, where he was poring over a set of schematics.

"How's your team doing?"

"They've had thirty hours training, Captain. They've had the last six hours off so they can be thoroughly rested and ready when we go in."

"What about yourself?"

"I've had my sleep for this month."

"We're going to have some very long days coming up . . ."

Korie nodded, still preoccupied with the diagrams. "I can handle it."

Parsons stepped in close and whispered, "I know you can handle it.

But I don't want you playing superman *all* the time. You've got to learn how to pace yourself or you'll burn out before you're thirty."

"I'm thirty-two," Korie said.

"Then you're overdue. We've got six hours until we begin final approach. Go take a power nap—"

"I don't need—" Korie stopped himself. "Aye, Captain." He switched off the display, pulled his headset off and picked up his coffee mug and sandwich plate. He ducked through the hatch to "Broadway," the starship's main corridor. Captain Parsons watched him go, pleased that Korie was learning how to follow orders.

She'd been worried about her executive officer's strong will and independent nature. That was part of his "legend" too. It was no secret among his fellow officers that Jon Korie had earned his captain's stars three times over. That the admiral had not yet given him a ship of his own was rapidly becoming an embarrassment not only to Korie, but to everyone serving with him as well—not to mention other captains whose names had come up later than Korie's.

In fact, Korie didn't know it, but Parsons had refused this posting when she discovered her executive officer would be Jon Korie. But Admiral O'Hara had told her to put her objections aside and take the ship. It wasn't that Korie was unready for command—he'd already proven that—but there were *other* factors at work. And in the meantime Korie needed the opportunity to practice the virtues of patience and cooperation. Parsons' supervision would be a useful and important role model for him.

Parsons suspected that Korie had already figured it out. Korie's mental agility was part of his growing "legend" among those who had served with him, and it was part of the scuttlebutt around Stardock that Jon Korie could tell you how far out of alignment the hyperstate grapplers were just by tasting the soup in the galley. Parsons had not yet seen Korie demonstrate this particular skill, but after a few weeks of watching him oversee the maintenance of the vessel, she would not have been surprised. The man was the most totally dependable officer she had ever met. Almost a machine.

Neither was it a secret why Korie was so driven. Korie's wife and two sons had been on Shaleen when the Morthans attacked. They were presumed dead. Afterward, Korie had received a delayed-in-transit message from Carol indicating that they were trying to evacuate to Taalamar—but Taalamar had been destroyed by an avalanche of asteroids, launched by teams of Morthan commandos. The *Star Wolf* had been part of a massive (but insufficient) evacuation effort. In what few records survived from Taalamar, there was no evidence of the arrival of his wife and children. Emotionally, Korie had lost them, been given a nugget of hope, then lost them again.

Still, part of him prayed. He didn't want to be alone. Perhaps they had been separated. Perhaps one of the boys had gotten away. But he didn't dare torture himself with those thoughts anymore. That was planting the seeds of madness.

At Stardock, Korie routinely and methodically worked out with robots designed to look like Morthans. He pummeled, kicked, beat, attacked, bit, punched and butted the robots with his head, oblivious to his own risk of injury. Several times, the gym attendants had considered restraining or sedating him. But Korie was only one of thousands who felt the need to kick the living crap out of a Morthan, and the workouts with the robots were considered a valuable therapeutic exercise for everyone.

At all other times, Korie's demeanor was singularly professional, but it did not require a quantum mechanic to figure out why Korie was so obsessive about keeping the *Star Wolf* functioning at optimum military readiness. Whenever the ship came to port, whether Stardock or any other safe harbor, Korie had Chief Petty Officer "Toad" Hall out negotiating for upgrades, spares and additional weaponry, whatever he could find, wherever he could find it. The *Star Wolf* had even taken aboard a shipment of six defective torpedoes—rather than let them be recalled, Korie and Chief Engineer Leen intended to rebuild the units to their own specifications.

As long as Korie's obsessions were sublimated into such potentially useful outlets, Captain Parsons had no objections. Indeed, she actually enjoyed watching Jon Korie work. He was a complex and interesting man—and he had the effect of energizing everyone around him. Parsons had written the admiral that she had never been on a ship that hummed with so much directed activity, and she felt this was directly due to Jon Korie's determination, now shared by the crew, that the *Star Wolf* would outlive the blemishes on her name.

"There are a lot of advantages," Parsons had written, "to serving on a big ship, a ship like the 'Big E.' It's the biggest, the best, the boldest and the brightest. Wherever you go, you're regarded as the pride of the fleet and the hope of humanity. But the 'Big E' doesn't get sent out to the front lines because the Fleet can't take the risk of losing her. The psychological shock wave that would send across the Allied Worlds would be devastating. So it falls to the smaller ships, the liberty ships, to plow the dark between the stars and take the ultimate risks. This is where the real heroism is found—among the men and women who know that they are not going to be celebrated wherever they go, among those who are doing their jobs because they know the value of their actions to the Fleet. Despite the risks, despite the lack of appropriate reward, despite the lack of glory and fame—these are the people who are going to make the difference for all of us. What is truly remarkable about all of them is what they bring to their work—not just a sense of obligation, but more than that, a genuine affection for their duty.

"These young heroes—and heroes they truly are—have learned to love their mission. Whatever it is that energizes these people," Parsons concluded in her letter, "it is not only a source of enormous hope, I believe it will eventually prove to be the fuel for our victory over the Morthan Solidarity. I do not know if this feeling can be trained or taught, but once experienced, it can never be forgotten or expunged from a human soul."

Admiral O'Hara had replied, "Captain Parsons, thank you for your note. I intend to share your thoughts with all of the other captains under my command. I can see now that I was right to insist that you take the *Star Wolf*. I had expected that there was much you would teach her crew. I am pleased to find that you are learning as much from them. Carry on."

Probes

"Thirty seconds to horizon—" called Tor.

Parsons checked her own display. Even though she knew exactly what she would see, she had long ago gotten into the habit of confirming everything herself. "Good," she said. The hatch behind her popped open. Without turning around, she said, "We're now officially in range. Did you have a nice nap, Mr. Korie?"

"Yes, Captain, I did," he replied stiffly.

She gave him a questioning look. Was he still smarting at having been ordered to rest?

"It was an interesting experience, sleep," he said blandly. "I'll have to try it more often. Thank you for the opportunity."

Parsons allowed herself a hint of a grin, a wry expression. Korie was clearly not without a sense of humor—he could even allow the joke to be on himself. That was good to know. She nodded and turned forward, all business again. "Let's get a close look at the *Norway*. Commander Brik—?"

The Morthan Security Officer and chief of strategic operations straightened up and turned to face the captain. When he stood on the Ops Deck, he could turn toward the Command Deck and be eye-to-eye with his superior officers, so he had made his post a work station directly ahead and to the left of the captain's command chair. "Aye, Captain?"

"Launch a spread of three probes. Monitor them all the way in."

"Aye, Captain. Launch bays armed and ready. Stand by." He turned back to his console and began reading calmly off his display. "Probes are hot and green. Launching on my mark . . ." He snapped open a plastic protective cover, and flipped a red toggle. "We are armed. Three . . . two . . . one—" There was a row of buttons next to the toggle; three of them were lit. He pressed the first one, paused, pressed the second, paused again, then pressed the third. With each touch, the hard thump of a torpedo launch thudded through the ship.

Captain Parsons' coffee rippled in her mug; she replaced the cap and put the mug back in the holder in her chair arm.

At his station, Brik continued to watch his displays. "Probes accelerating. On course. Probe one has acquisition of target . . . Probe two has acquisition of target . . . Probe three has acquisition of target. Flyby in seventeen minutes. Deceleration begins in thirteen. Confidence is high, and all three units are in the groove, five by five." He punched up the next program in the series and reported, "We have acquisition of all three signals. We'll have a half-second delay at maximum range."

"Thank you, Mr. Brik." Parsons retrieved her coffee and turned her attention to the holographic display in the center of the Ops Deck. It showed the bloated red spheroid with the orbit of the *Norway* tracking around it and a separate line showing the interception course of the *Star Wolf*. Although they were now decelerating at full power to the plasma drives, they were still more than half a light second away from the other ship. In six hours, their respective trajectories would be almost matching. Less than two hours after that, they should be close enough for final approach and docking.

The physics of the problem were trivial. HARLIE could have the answer on the screen before a person finished asking the question. But the logistics of the problem were complicated by IKE-34's primary, the bloated red star. Once per orbit—once per artificial "year"—the *Norway* would have to pass through the streamer of flame being pulled out of the red star by the blue. This was clearly a "fail-safe" orbit. If something went wrong on the *Norway*, if she were disabled and couldn't break orbit or if there was no one left alive to give the order, she would be destroyed by her passage through the fire.

The *Norway*'s large orbit gave her a long "year"—more than forty-eight months—so she had clearly been on station for some time; she was just now approaching her time of passage. Within a few days at most, she would be gone. The *Star Wolf*'s timing was fortunate—or maybe not. They still didn't know what they would find aboard her.

This was the troubling factor in Captain Parsons' calculations. How badly was the *Norway* incapacitated? Could she be saved? Was she so badly contaminated that she should not be saved? If they were to make the attempt to save her, would they have time to decontaminate the ship? Assuming the contamination was of a controllable nature. Nothing was known. Everything was assumption.

The procedure books provided some useful guidelines to follow, but every situation was unique. And this one was probably off the map, out of the manuals and deep into unknown territory. Captain Parsons wasn't afraid of the challenge; on the contrary, it both intrigued and excited her—but she was also aware that a high-risk situation meant the possibility of fatalities and that was the one part of the job she could never be comfortable with. The human cost. No matter how careful the precautions they took, there were always possibilities.

Her coffee had gone cold again. She replaced the top on her mug and put it back in its holder on her chair arm.

She turned her attention back to her display. The probes continued to accelerate, racing ahead, sacrificing themselves in a high-speed interception, crossing the path of the *Norway* as close as possible, scanning her in a series of high-speed flybys, and then shooting off irretrievably into flame and distance. The signals from the probes would tell them if there was still life aboard the *Norway*.

If there was, they would continue their interception. If not, then Parsons had the option of breaking off and heading back out to space. In this case, it would mean shutting down the plasma drives, ceasing to decelerate and continuing up and out past the course of the *Norway*, away from the red giant and out beyond the gravitational corona where they could safely jump back into hyperstate—and continue on to their next rendezvous.

Parsons bent to her personal display and watched as the tracks of the probes approached the orbit of the *Norway*. There were two blips on each line—the first blip was the projection of the real-time position of the torpedo, the second blip was the time-delayed information received from the missile. At this distance, the blips on each line were less than a half-second apart.

"Receiving five by five. Thirty seconds . . ."

"Put it on the main display."

The forward view opened up, became the view from the leading torpedo. To one side was a dim pink glare; the corona of the red star. To the other side, darkness. The glare washed out everything else—all except a single pinpoint of light, moving slowly downward toward the center of the image, growing brighter . . .

"Twenty seconds."

A green target circle appeared around the moving object. Down the left side of the image, acquisition numbers scrolled up in a blur too fast to read. A telescopic lens shifted into place and the shape of the distant vessel became clear.

"Ten seconds . . . nine . . . eight . . ." Tor counted methodically. "Five . . . four . . . three . . ."

The flyby itself proved to be anticlimactic. The probes were traveling so fast in relation to the *Norway* that the starship flashed past almost too quickly to see. The display showed a quick flare of reflected light—the probe-torpedoes had aimed pseudo-white lasers as they'd passed. The three probes had bracketed the starship in an equilateral triangle. Their combined scans would provide the *Star Wolf* with a three-dimensional view of the ship, in case there was visible damage or other conditions that might affect the rescue operation. Their internal scans should also show if there was any evidence of life still aboard the vessel.

"All right," said Parsons. "Let's look at the visual first. HARLIE?"

The forward display flickered to show the probe-torpedo flyby again, this time in slow-motion. The torpedoes had passed within a kilometer of the crippled vessel, close enough to light it up as bright as daylight with their spotlights. Three separate views of the ship floated past, first one, then another, then the third. The red star was visible as background in one scan, as a crimson reflection in the others.

HARLIE repeated the images in an endless cycle, occasionally pausing or expanding them into close-up examinations. Each of the torpedoes had run multiple high-speed cameras, each with different capabilities. There were also infrared and radio-detectors, gravitational lenses, microwave and radar scanners—plus several devices so esoteric that they were simply referred to as X-modules, and their outputs were considered gifts from God.

"No apparent visible damage," said HARLIE. "Some weathering from the local coronal effects, but that's to be expected. Stand by please. I'm collating the internal scans. Preliminary infrared analysis shows the vessel is radiating heat in a manner consistent with viability, no apparent anomalies. Deep-spectrum scans show the presence of oxygen and nitrogen and carbon dioxide within the hull. Microwave scans show movement—not as much as we would expect from a fully-manned vessel, but movement nonetheless. Some anomalies here. A lot of low-level noise, higher than usual for a normal background reading. The torpedoes queried the ship's autonomous system and received no reply. Life support systems are still operative, but most of the rest of her internals appear to be inactive."

HARLIE paused for a beat, then concluded, "Even without collation, I would give high confidence to the possibility of survivors aboard the *Norway*. Conditions for the maintenance of life are present and there is evidence of movement consistent with human life. We are also detecting the presence of magnetic containment fields and repulsor lenses."

"Thank you, HARLIE," said Korie to his headset. "I want to see the raw data now, and the collation as soon as it's finished."

"The collation is ready now," the intelligence engine replied. "Which would you like to see first?"

"Let's start with the collation." Korie was already turning to the display on his workstation. He grunted to himself and his expression went grim.

When he looked up, Parsons was waiting for him. "Your estimate of the situation, Korie?"

"Proceed to final approach and use that as a go/no-go."

"I concur," said Parsons.

"I'll have to brief the mission team." Korie looked unhappy. "We'll have to go in."

"Don't take anyone who isn't Class-X certified. This is going to get nasty, isn't it?" Her expression turned grim. "How's your itch?"

Korie reached around as if trying to scratch his back. "Right there," he said. "Between the shoulders. All the way down to the bone."

Approach

From a distance, the *Norway* looked normal.

The *Star Wolf* had come up and under the other ship, referenced to the plane of the ecliptic. She had deliberately overshot the common interception point by several thousand kilometers and was now decelerating in the final stages of her approach to allow the *Norway* to "catch up" to her.

Captain Parsons had chosen this approach to allow maximum observation of the distressed vessel before final contact was made. "Let's run a seven-layer series of scans, full-spectrum, in-depth, the works," she ordered. "That'll give the Mission Team an extra hour to prepare special-need equipment. Alert Dr. Williger; I'll want her on the Bridge to help evaluate the data. Commander Tor, put out three more probes—let's get some additional perspectives. Make sure those probes are high-confidence, and let's use tactical units as well as bioremotes. Lt. Goldberg, have you been able to raise contact? No? I didn't think so. Commander Korie, let's continue the assumption of an extremely toxic Class-X situation. Strictly by the book throughout. *No* exceptions."

"Aye, Captain." Korie turned back to his headset. "HARLIE, do you copy?"

"Yes, Mr. Korie. I have already amended the checklists and procedures to be consistent with the captain's orders. There are several situations in the book, however, where the standard procedures are inconsistent with the captain's instructions. While it is unlikely that we will be confronted with such situations, I have amended the procedures for this operation in favor of caution over expediency. It seems to me that is the captain's intention. Is this correct?"

"Yes, HARLIE, that is correct. You done good."

"Thank you, Mr. Korie."

On the forward display, the *Norway* was looming huge. She was identical in structure to the *Star Wolf*, but her engines were lighter and her armaments were fewer, almost nonexistent. She bore the markings of a scientific research vessel.

HARLIE spoke then, as much for the log as for the Bridge crew. "Still no contact with the *Norway*. Her autonomic system is running unevenly.

Her intelligence engine is either unable or unwilling to respond. The ship appears to be adrift."

Parsons nodded. Like most captains, she took the lethetic intelligence engines for granted. Korie was the only officer she'd ever met who treated the machinery with the same courtesy he gave humans. Perhaps that was one of the reasons he was able to coax so many extraordinary behaviors out of HARLIE. But even if it was only just another one of the quirks that made Korie "*our* son of a bitch," Captain Parsons was willing to tolerate it.

HARLIE spoke up suddenly, "There is one interesting anomaly, Captain."

Parsons looked up sharply. So did Korie. And every other officer on the Bridge. "Go ahead."

"There are active repulsor valves throughout the *Norway*. I am not sure why."

"Let's see a schematic," Parsons said, almost in unison with Korie. They exchanged a glance. "Sorry, Captain," Korie said.

"No apology necessary," she answered. They both turned to the display on her workstation where HARLIE had brought up a simplified graphic of the *Norway*. The repulsor valves were shown as a cluster of throbbing red bubbles located just aft of the engine room.

Neither Parsons nor Korie said anything for a moment while they studied the display. Finally, the captain broke the silence. "They've divided the ship."

"That's what it looks like," Korie agreed. "People on one side. Toxic something on the other."

"Yes, but which side is which?"

Korie shook his head. "It depends on . . ." His sentence trailed off.

"If you were going to host a very dangerous experiment on board this ship," Parsons mused, "where would you put it—forward or aft? Med Bay or Cargo Bay?"

Korie weighed the possibilities. "Cargo Bay is easier to evacuate. Just open the hatch and drop everything into space. If this stuff—this *thing*, whatever it is—is that toxic, then I'd put it in the Cargo Bay. On the other hand . . . Med Bay is forward of the Bridge, you could put additional research labs in the cabins forward of Med Bay, use the Airlock Reception Bay as a decontamination section, and seal the whole thing off from the rest of the vessel. It depends on how big and how toxic this thing is and how hard it is to control. It could be either side."

They studied the display in silence for a moment, as if there were a clue in it they had somehow missed. Korie stared at the schematic of the starship. The engine room was located in the aft third. There were equipment bays behind the engine room, and the Cargo Bay was situated behind that. The repulsor bubbles were just forward of the Cargo Bay, centered on the autonomic core of the vessel, so the division of the ship was unequal, more than two-thirds back.

Either the danger was confined to the Cargo Bay and the rest of the ship was habitable. Or—it was in the forward part of the ship, which meant that the crew was trapped in the Cargo Bay. Korie pointed. "If it was in the forward part of the ship, then it got out of control and raged aftward. If it was in the aft part of the ship, then the survivors isolated it there and they're in the forward division—but then why were there no responses to our signals? And why didn't they evacuate the Cargo Bay to space the minute it broke out?"

"So you think the survivors are aft?"

"I can argue the other side equally well," Korie said. "It was aft, got into the autonomics and made it impossible for the crew to control the ship. They isolated it, but they can't evacuate it."

"What does your itch say?"

"My itch doesn't like either side of this equation. If we guess wrong—" He didn't have to complete the sentence.

"You want to flip a coin?" Parsons asked.

"No," said Korie. "Let's go with my first guess. The crew would have given themselves the larger part of the ship and isolated it in the Cargo Bay. The survivors are forward."

"It's your call."

Korie nodded glumly. "It's what I'd do. It's the *logical* thing to do."

The captain frowned. "Not everybody is as logical as you are." Then she stepped forward and called out an order to her helm and her astrogator. "Nose-to-nose docking. Set up your approach. Let's do it." She turned back to Korie. "Break out the spare repulsors from the cargo and install them forward. Let's focus them into the docking tube."

"They'll use a lot of power—"

"We'll shut down the active core-control of the singularity and depend on the passive systems to maintain."

"Can't do that for too long. Thirty-six hours max. After that, you don't have the power to reboot."

"We don't have thirty-six hours in any case. That ship is falling into a star. Let's get in, get the survivors, and get out of here. If we can save the ship, we'll tow it. HARLIE, set up the procedures."

Docking

The *Norway* was traveling "sideways," perpendicular to the star's equator, her bow pointed toward galactic south—so the *Star Wolf* would have to come up from "below" for a nose-to-nose docking. As soon as HARLIE confirmed that they were in the channel for final approach, Parsons issued a single order. "All right," she snapped. "Let's do it. You have a go for docking."

Korie was listening through his headset. "The mission team is ready," he reported.

"Good. Mr. Korie, go suit up. I'll meet you at the forward airlock for inspection. As soon as the docking tube is pressurized, you're going across."

"On my way, Captain." He was already pulling his headset off.

"Oh, Korie," Parsons called after him. "I want the log of the *Norway*." Her tone was unequivocal. "Make that a special priority."

Translation: *Make it your first priority*. Rescue of the survivors was secondary to understanding what had happened here. Rescue was important. Understanding was *more* important. "Aye, Captain," Korie said. He didn't always agree with the cold equations of space, but he never argued with them.

Korie ducked down into the Fire Control Bay, an equipment-filled chamber directly underneath the Command Deck. Five more steps aftward, down another short ladder and he was in the keel, the corridor that ran through the spine of the ship. He turned and headed forward, already thinking ahead to the mission. His frown deepened as a thought occurred to him. Did Captain Parsons know something more about the *Norway* than she was acknowledging? Did she know what they were likely to find?

No. He dismissed the thought. If she knew, she'd have briefed him. She wouldn't send a team into danger uninformed. No captain would. But it was possible she knew *something* . . . No, Korie thrust even that thought away. "Jon, your paranoia is showing again," he said to himself.

On the Bridge, Captain Parsons watched the progress of the docking procedure with deep concern. The forward display showed the nose of the *Norway*, seen head on. The image of the starship grew steadily, expanding to fill the screen. The docking collar was open in a receiving position. The mating of the two vessels should be routine. But Captain Parsons had learned the hard way that nothing was ever routine in space. Everything was potentially deadly.

HARLIE spoke then. "We are now in position for acquisition."

"Activate the repulsor fields," Parsons ordered.

"Activating the repulsor fields," Goldberg echoed. Through the keel of the vessel, a new note added itself to the symphony of shipboard sounds, a deep heterodyning sensation. "Confirmed," said Goldberg. "Fields are up. Five by five."

"We are ready to proceed with acquisition," HARLIE said. "Go or no-go, Captain?"

Parsons nodded. "Go." Then she added, "Bring us in gently."

"Working," HARLIE said.

At their respective stations, the astrogator and helm watched carefully, each ready to take control immediately if any untoward circumstance occurred that HARLIE couldn't handle. As unlikely as such a situation might seem, it had happened. And the Fleet had a tradition of never allowing its intelligence engines to work without human supervision.

The two ships thumped softly together. The connection was barely felt aboard the *Star Wolf*.

"We have acquisition," said HARLIE. "Nose-to-nose docking confirmed."

"The board is green," confirmed Jonesy from the helm. From the astrogation station, Tor added her own confirmations.

"Extend the transfer tube," ordered Parsons.

"Working," HARLIE said. A moment later, he added, "Transfer tube extended, sealed and locked. Stand by for transfer tube integrity check." He paused. "Integrity check confirmed. Confidence is high. Ready for pressurization."

"Confirm that," Jonesy said.

"And again," echoed Tor.

"Pressurize," ordered Parsons.

"Working," said HARLIE. And a moment later, added, "We have pressure in the transfer tube. Equalized. Confirmed."

Jonesy confirmed that, and so did Tor.

"All right. Good. We're ready to pop the hatch," said Parsons. "Commander Tor, you have the conn." She ducked down through the Fire Control Bay, following Korie's path down to the keel and forward to the Airlock Reception Bay.

At the nose of the ship, the airlock itself was a cramped tube, barely wide enough for two suited crewmembers at a time. Directly behind the airlock was the Forward Airlock Reception Bay. The FARB, as it was identified on the bulkheads, was a wider tube than the airlock. It was lined with suit-lockers, equipment racks and maintenance stations. Separating the Reception Bay from the airlock was a decontamination station.

At the moment, the Reception Bay was cramped with suited figures. Although the *Norway* was a pressurized environment, Class-X protection required the use of starsuits or equivalent protective gear. Korie had opted for starsuits. Again, the captain's imperative for caution had outweighed all other concerns, including comfort, mobility and expedience.

Captain Parsons had to turn sideways to squeeze past the suited figures; she worked her way forward to Korie, acknowledging nods all the way. Chief Medical Officer Molly Williger was briefing Medical Technician Paul Berryman; not that he needed additional instructions at this point, but Molly Williger preferred to leave nothing to chance and she was trying to pour forty years of hands-on experience into a twenty-three-year-old body. Berryman was wearing a portable medi-kit and a variety of scanning tools and medications.

Security Officer Helen Bach stood patiently against one wall, flanked by Fire Control Officer "Wasabe" Shibano and Daniel Easton, another crewmember assigned to security detail. Easton had worked security before and had demonstrated considerable aptitude for it; now he was checking the charges on his, Bach's and Shibano's weapons—an exercise in redundancy, because the other two would have already checked their own armaments; but the revised procedure book required security teams to triple-check each other's equipment. All of them wore additional helmet cameras. Every starsuit helmet on the ship already had a standard bank of cameras built-in, but for this mission additional high-resolution cameras and wide-spectrum scanners had been mounted on helmets, chest panels and backpacks.

At the forward end of the reception bay, Mikhail Hodel was conferring hastily with Korie. Two Quillas, Omega and Theta, were helping Korie suit up while he talked. Parsons squeezed past Easton to join them. "Status?" she asked.

"Just waiting for Mr. Korie to come up clean and green," said Hodel.

Behind her, Easton reported. "All the other boards are green. The hardware is ready. The software is clean. We have clean signals from all the remotes. Confidence is high."

Parsons nodded curtly. There wasn't much she could say that she hadn't already said. The situation was unknown, almost certainly dangerous—*extremely* dangerous. Everyone knew it. "All right," she said. "Let's do it."

"Aye, aye, Captain," Korie said, just as the two Quillas lowered his helmet in place and sealed it with a series of electronic beeps and whistles. Parsons turned aftward. Easton was checking Berryman's suit as carefully as a mother; Berryman looked as annoyed as an impatient cub. "Will you stop fussing already?" Berryman said. "No," Easton replied blandly. He yanked another strap.

Parsons followed the two Quillas aft, to get out of the way of the exiting team members. She paused alongside Molly Williger, meeting her glance with a questioning look.

"Med Bay is ready," Williger said unconvincingly.

What made Captain Parsons an exceptional captain was that she listened to a person's tone as much as their words, sometimes even more so. Now she looked at the chief medical officer, her eyes narrowing perceptively. "You don't sound optimistic."

Williger looked up sharply. "You know the stats, Captain. Ninety percent of these rescue operations are too late. Yes, there might be people still alive over there, but . . . they might also be trans-critical." *Trans-critical.* Beyond saving.

Or worse. *Infectious.*

"I'm aware of that," said Parsons. "But the rules of rescue are always operative, and those rules date back to a time even before there were spacecraft. Even if we have to put ourselves at risk, we're required to make a full and responsible effort." Then she added, "*And* we need the log. Almost as important as the rescue—sometimes even more important—we need the ship's log. In this case . . . this is probably one of the sometimes."

Williger grunted—neither agreement nor disagreement, merely acknowledgment. Like a stone dropped from a height, they no longer had a choice in the matter; they were going to fall toward their inevitable conclusion no matter how they felt about it. She turned back to preparations.

Wasabe Shibano was double-checking Korie's gear and the integrity of his starsuit. Korie ignored Shibano's attentions as best as he could while he briefed Hodel. "HARLIE can't get the log out by remote. Their intelligence engine has probably been shut down. We'll try and wake it up, of course, but we don't have the override codes if it's locked down. If that's the case, we'll go around and yank the data from below. We'll dump a copy of the core into one of our transmitters and let them decode it back at Fleet. I want to go straight to the trunk-channel under the Intelligence Bay and tap in there. The system should be on standby, but if there's no power, then I'll climb up and pull the cards manually. If the cards are missing, then we'll have to grab the orange box. That's your job. You know where the access panel is? Just behind the captain's chair?" Hodel nodded and Korie passed over a plastic card, which Hodel tucked into a holder on the forearm of his suit. "Those are the codes to disarm the self-destruct on the orange box. If anything abnormal pops up, abort the procedure. Commander Brik will be riding in your ear, so minimize the jokes, Mike."

"I've worked tougher rooms than this," Hodel said. Even through the glass of his helmet, his grin was visible. "I'll have that Morthan giggling in his shorts in no time."

"As bizarre as that image is," Korie acknowledged, "let's stick to business on this one. This is serious."

Hodel sighed. "Aye, aye, sir."

"Thanks, Mike." Korie wondered if Brik had heard the exchange. Most likely, he had. Even so, he was unlikely to comment on it. Korie didn't like Brik very much—no one onboard really did—but he did respect him, and the one time Fleet Command had offered to replace the Morthan security chief, Korie had rejected the suggestion. For all of his personal distaste, he knew the *Star Wolf* would never find a more qualified officer. He didn't know how Brik felt about him, and he didn't much care, although he surmised that Brik was at best amused and at worst annoyed by Korie's presumption of equality because they both wore the same uniform. The important thing was that they worked well together. Possibly because they were each trying to prove something to the other.

Annoyed, impatient and tense, Korie called back over his shoulder to Shibano. "Are we done yet? Or what?"

"*Jai!*" said Wasabe, in that little explosive punctuation mark of language that non-Japanese hear as "Yes," but really means, "I hear you," and sometimes also means, "but I'm too polite to say no." In Shibano's case, however, it actually meant "Yes."

Although raised in a traditional Japanese culture, Shibano had been a starship officer long enough to have achieved that state that some sociologists called *trans-human*—a condition where one's mental state was no longer local to a specific circumstance, but had become attuned instead to an interstellar scale of human behavior. In lay terms, a *trans-human* was an individual who had lived among the stars too long, someone with a million-light-year stare—someone who had traded in his or her definition of humanity for a more direct working knowledge of *sentience*.

By that definition, most of the officers in the fleet could be considered trans-human. It came with the job. Few people were born into a trans-human state, but almost all evolved into it living on a starship. But some officers were more trans-human than others. Korie, for instance . . .

Korie finished with Hodel and spoke now to HARLIE. "Status report?"

HARLIE replied blandly, "The transfer tube is fully pressurized. Integrity is confirmed. Repulsor fields are focused. Confidence is high. All mission preparations are complete."

"All right," said Korie. "On my mark. Let's go."

At the aft end of the Reception Bay, Parsons and Williger watched grimly. The interior hatch of the airlock popped open and the mission team began filing quickly into the cramped space of the airlock tube.

"Mr. Korie—" Parsons said quietly into her headset.

"Captain?" His voice came back through her earphone.

"Let's be careful out there."

Hearing that over his suit-phones, Korie smiled in recognition. It had been the watchword on Parson's first ship, the *Michael Conrad*. Maybe it could be the watchword here too. Certainly, it should be.

Hodel saw Korie's smile. He'd heard the captain's instructions, but not having the same background as Korie, he saw it as a straight line needing a topper. Ever the comedian, he poked Wasabe in the ribs and added, "Yep. Watch out for sparkle-dancers and man-eating tribbles."

"A man-eating tribble?" Wasabe asked.

"Some men will eat anything," Hodel replied blandly, reaching for a handhold.

Korie, Bach, Hodel, Shibano, Berryman and Easton lined up in three rows of two in the airlock tube. As the hatch popped shut behind them, each grabbed one of the handholds above—this was a precaution in case of sudden decompression. Not that they expected it, but it was part of the drill.

"We're green," said Korie. "Do it."

Through their suits they could hear the mechanical sounds of clamps engaging and locking—additional fail-safes on all the hatches. The deep heterodyning note of the repulsors was more noticeable *here*; an almost palpable sensation that made the hair on the back of the neck stand up in dismay.

Korie studied a display on the bulkhead. "Tube pressure confirmed here," he reported.

For a moment, nothing happened, then—

Boarding

The hatch opened slowly, revealing the interior of the transfer tube. The semi-translucent material of the tube looked solid, an illusion of air pressure. The presence of the looming red star seeped through the membrane; one side of the tube was dark, the other glowed with a brooding crimson tint. Railings extended the length of the tube to provide handholds for the starsuited crew. Exterior to both ships, the transfer tube was a null-gravity zone.

Standard procedure would have been to leap out into free fall and coast across.

But not here, not now. Not with the repulsor fields throbbing.

The fields were a physical presence, like invisible surf pushing them inexorably forward. Coming from the other direction, it would have felt like pushing through gelatin and spiderwebs and elastic; it would have felt as if the air had been *thickened*. Moving *with* the pressure was like riding a rising balloon. It was a tangible sensation. The mission team grabbed handholds on the railings and let themselves be pushed along.

The combined strength of three concentric fields was focused into the transfer tube. The power expenditure to maintain a palpable force of this strength was enormous. The *Star Wolf* had shut down all of her non-essential systems to maintain this safety barrier.

Korie had never moved through such a strong field before and it gave him a queasy sensation in his gut as the pressure worked on his internal organs. And then, abruptly, he was through the thickest part of the field and coming up to the outer hatch of the *Norway*'s forward airlock. Even so, he could still feel a residual push.

Korie turned and watched as the entire mission team came across. Lt. Bach was the last to exit the *Star Wolf*'s airlock. Korie reported, "All right. We're clear. Seal the hatch." It popped shut with a hard mechanical thump—the *Star Wolf* was secure. And as soon as the *Norway*'s hatch was opened, the mission team would be regarded as contaminated . . .

Hodel was watching a set of readouts on the arm of his suit. "Pressure is equalized to the *Norway*," he announced.

Korie acknowledged the report and turned forward to the *Norway*'s forward hatch. He held an entry card against a reader plate, and waited for the panel to turn green, silently praying that the *Norway* would recognize their authority. He didn't want to manually force the hatch, he didn't want to cut his way in. He wanted this operation to run smoothly. By the book. The panel went green and Korie whispered soft thanks to the unseen crew on the other side. "That's a good sign," he said.

"Yeah, they're only paranoid, not crazy," agreed Hodel.

"It's wartime. Everybody's crazy. The only question is whether we're crazy *enough*. All right, here we go. Bach, Easton, Shibano—" The security officers pulled themselves into position just behind Korie. They unshouldered their weapons. They raised blast-shields into position.

Korie punched the OPEN panel with his gloved knuckle. The panel flashed red and showed the word TESTING—and then the hatch popped open in front of them and they were staring into the empty airlock of the *Norway*.

They waited a moment, to see if anything would happen. Nothing did. "It's still a go," came the captain's voice.

The chamber ahead was dark and featureless—except for the lack of light, it was identical to the lock they had just exited. Korie released his grip and allowed the repulsor field to push him forward into the silent ship. The security team followed. They oriented themselves vertical to the *Norway*, moved through the airlock hatch and dropped to the deck.

When the last crewmember had entered the airlock—it was Helen Bach—they sealed the hatch and waited while the *Norway* ran its own air pressure checks. The throb of the repulsors faded behind them.

"Looks like the autonomic system is still up and running," Korie noted, as much for his team as for the listeners still aboard the *Star Wolf*: Parsons, Tor, Brik, Williger . . .

"That's good news," said Hodel. "Makes all our jobs easier."

"Mission Team, we copy that." Tor's voice came through their suit-phones.

The last panel flashed green. "All right, let's go." Korie popped the final hatch. The interior of the *Norway* lay before them . . .

It was not a reassuring sight. The Airlock Reception Bay was dark. There were two starsuits still hanging on the racks and one fallen to the deck. A scattered assortment of equipment lay about—as if someone had tried to dress in haste, without regard for procedures. Without regard for anything except escape.

"Hodel?" asked Korie.

"Already scanning." Hodel was studying the readouts on his suit arm. "Nothing yet."

Korie switched on his external speaker. "Ahoy the *Norway*! Is anyone here! We're here from the *Star Wolf*. We're here to help you! Ahoy the *Norway*!" He held up a hand for silence. The mission team held still. Listening to the silence.

"Ahoy! Anyone . . .?"

No one.

Korie gestured and the team moved forward—from the Airlock Reception Bay into the keel. It was bad news. Too many lights were out. The keel was shadowed and gloomy.

"Sir?" Hodel pointed. Korie followed the direction of his gesture.

Something in the darkness. Something that flickered insubstantially. And was gone. And then flickered again in another place. Like fairy dust or very faint fireworks.

"What is it?" Hodel asked. "What does it mean?"

"It means . . . I guessed wrong." There was a cold hollow feeling growing in Korie's gut. "We should have come in the other end." To Hodel's look, he said, "I expected them to be thinking logically. Sorry, Mike. The job just got harder." *I made a mistake.*

"Mission Team, report," said Tor dispassionately. "What are you seeing?"

"Some kind of . . . it's hard to describe. Fireflies? I'm not sure. Adjust your display. It's very faint."

"Okay, we've got it now."

Korie glanced at the small monitor panel set inside his own helmet. It showed what they were seeing on the Bridge of the *Star Wolf*. The flickers were clearer on the screen. They left tiny dark trails. But they were still insubstantial, appearing and disappearing seemingly at random. Not a lot. It was like something half-glimpsed out of the corner of the eye; when you turned to look directly, it was gone. Korie had the impression of tiny lights that were pink and gold and red, but not really.

And then there was that *other* thing—the sound of the *Norway*. It was *different*. There were none of the familiar background noises of a living ship. Korie's eyes narrowed. The air circulators were off. The coolant pipes were silent. The water and sewage systems were equally still. The silence was eerie. Even the quiet beeps from the various monitors were absent. Starships aren't silent. No matter how well designed or constructed, whether macro, micro or nano, things make noise. Liquid flows through pipes. Air moves through tubes. Everything whistles, vibrates and hums like the pieces of a massive faster-than-light church organ, striking deep chords and mechanical harmonies. This ship . . . didn't. The effect was terrifying.

"The ship is deserted?" Hodel asked.

"No," said Korie. "HARLIE detected life aboard her. They're just not at this end." He unclipped several small round probes from his suit-belt, activated them and tossed them down the corridor. The units righted themselves in midair, popped open tiny lens ports and scanner outlets, then headed deep into the *Norway*. Back on the *Star Wolf,* a control team would monitor and direct the units.

Korie waited for a confirmation from the captain. "The probes aren't showing anything alive. But there's a lot of noise in the signal."

"Your orders, Captain?"

"Get the log and get out of there."

"Aye, aye." Korie gestured the team forward.

Bach and Shibano followed close on Korie's heels. Bach swung her rifle nervously from one side to the other.

"Afraid of ghosts?" Shibano whispered to her.

"Nope. Just don't want to be one."

Korie frowned back at them. "Belay that chatter."

"Aye, sir. Sorry."

They came to a vertical intersection in the corridor, a place where ladders extended both up and down. Also diagonal access tubes opened off to the starship's farm. Korie directed Bach, Easton and Hodel up the ladder to the "north end" of "Broadway"—where the ship's main corridor terminated. He, Shibano and Berryman continued aftward through the keel.

Sparkling

The funny flickering in the air was a little more noticeable here. Berryman frowned at his scanner's readings, a growing sense of disquiet in his chest. "Sir?" he said to attract Korie's attention.

Korie hesitated, waiting. "What is it?"

"Some kind of . . . *wavicle*, I think." Half-wave, half-particle, with some of the behaviors of each. Unpredictable.

The flickers were starting to drift toward them now. They looked harmless, but clearly, they were an unknown phenomenon and had to be regarded as deadly until proven otherwise. Certainly, they were related to the condition of this vessel.

Shibano reached out and tried to grab a few of the fairy pinpoints, but they whirled out of reach like motes of dust. He grabbed again and again, but each time the sparkles eluded him. There were more twinkling pinpoints around him now, flickering in and out of existence. They were both beguiling and . . . disturbing. They danced in the air with a nervous quality.

Berryman turned slowly, trying to scan them with a hand-held unit, but the wavicles seemed to be avoiding an area defined by his scanning field. Both Korie and Berryman noticed it at the same time.

"Do you want to try turning that off?" Korie suggested quietly.

"I suppose we could try that," Berryman replied, just as cautiously. He switched off the scanner. He turned slowly, observing the behavior of the wavicles. They danced in closer . . .

Korie and Berryman exchanged a glance.

"Do you want to try and catch one?" Korie asked.

"Dr. Williger will have my hide if I don't try."

"Don't make assumptions!" Williger's voice came rasping into their helmets. "I'm more likely to skin you alive if you put yourself in unnecessary danger."

"Do you want some of these things or not?" Berryman retorted.

Williger didn't reply immediately. She was conferring with Captain Parsons. Finally, her voice came back, "If you can get one in a bottle, fine. If not—don't."

Korie said. "I don't think they like the scanning fields." To Berryman, he added, "Try turning your helmet scanners off."

"And then what?"

"And then, I think, we'll find out whether or not they're trying to get to us. Look, there's more of them than ever. They're certainly attracted to something—probably us. But the scanning fields are keeping them at bay."

"Do you think they can get through our suits?"

"They shouldn't be able to. We're Class-X certified."

"So was the *Norway*."

"Mm. Point taken."

"But if they can get through our suits," Berryman continued, "then we have to assume we're already contaminated."

"There is that too," Korie acknowledged. "But I think, in the interests of knowledge, that we need to know just what the hell is going on here. How safe is it to proceed?" Korie switched off the scanners mounted on his helmet. The wavicles swirled inward toward him, but none actually alighted on his suit. Korie and Berryman looked at each other through the faceplates of their helmets. Neither had an answer to the unspoken question.

"Is it the scanners? Or the suits? Or a combination of the two? Or something else?"

Without being told, Wasabe Shibano reached up and switched off the scanners mounted on his chest and back. For a moment, nothing happened. The wavicles continued to swirl just beyond arm's length.

"Okay," said Korie. "I think we're safe. It's the suits." He nodded forward. "Let's get the log and get out of here."

And then—as they moved, so did the wavicles. Suddenly agitated, they danced like a seizure of fireworks, like exploding fireflies—they bounced and twinkled and flickered and suddenly began alighting on all three of the starsuited figures, outlining each of them in faint sparkling luminescence.

"Oh, shit—" said Berryman, uncharacteristically.

Korie didn't say anything. But he was thinking it. *My second miscalculation. The price on this one is going to be high.*

Only Wasabe Shibano remained unaffected. He held out his hand in front of his helmet, staring at the unexpected radiance. The effect was ghostly and magical. The strange glow was reflected in his helmet pane and his eyes were wide with awe.

Korie looked at his own hands then, as did Berryman. The three of them looked at each other—in amazement as well as horror. All of them were gleaming with a myriad of twinkling points. They looked *enchanted*.

Their communicators were chattering in their ears unheard. Tor's voice, Williger's, Brik's and Captain Parsons'—"Korie! Answer me! What's going on over there! What's happening!"

"It's all right," Korie managed to say. His voice cracked. "We're . . . surrounded. But we're not being hurt—"

"Get the log and get out of there. *That's an order*," snapped Parsons. "No! Forget the log. Just get out of there. Now!"

"Our suits are holding—" Korie started to reassure them.

"But for how long?" Williger's gravelly voice cut in.

As if in answer to her question, Berryman shouted, "Oh, God—!" Korie whirled to look at him. He couldn't tell if it was a scream of fear or astonishment—but Berryman was *glowing* suddenly brighter! Shibano too! Korie looked to his own hands—the rest of his starsuit—he was gleaming as bright as the others!

He looked to them and saw—the sparkling motes were *seeping into their suits!* His own as well!

It wasn't painful—it was *interesting*. It *tingled* . . . the feeling was almost sexual. But underneath it was another thought. *Is this my third mistake? The final one?*

"Hey!" laughed Shibano. "That tickles!" He looked to Berryman and Korie. "Doesn't it?"

Berryman looked uncomfortable—not because it hurt, but because he was already wondering about the medical implications. He looked to Korie.

Korie nodded an acknowledgment. "It's an odd sensation," he admitted. "Like needing to sneeze all over your body at the same time—" The sparkling wash of light was diminishing now. The twinkles were vanishing into them.

Korie pointed to Berryman's scanner. "Take a reading."

Berryman lifted up the device, switching it on. He pointed it at Shibano first. "Oww—*that* doesn't tickle."

Korie waggled his fingers in an "over here" gesture and Berryman pointed the scanner toward him. The tickling sensation turned painful then—like a series of low-level electric shocks. Korie held up his hand in an "Okay, you can stop now" gesture, and Berryman switched the scanner off.

"Did you feel it too?" Korie asked.

Berryman nodded grimly.

"Well, whatever it is—we've got it."

"I can't identify it, sir. The *Star Wolf* will have to sort this one out."

"There might be something in the records. HARLIE has probably already started searching the files. There's a thousand years of history to go through. It might take some time."

Closure

On the Bridge of the *Star Wolf*, Parsons' face was ashen. She looked first to Williger, then to Brik.

Brik didn't look up from his workstation, but somehow he knew of her concern. "Already working on it, Captain," he said. His voice had an angry note to it. Was he angry at Korie? Or her? Or just the universe in general? Korie had warned her of Brik's manner. Not important, Parsons told herself. Not important *now*. "Thank you, Mr. Brik," she said noncommittally.

She turned to Williger. "The other half of the team?"

"They're keeping their scanners on," the doctor growled.

"Will that protect them?"

Williger shrugged. An unsatisfactory answer.

Parsons rubbed her earlobe, frowning in thought. "All right. Tell them to proceed. As long as they're over there—let's get the log and find out what the hell those things are."

"Aye, aye."

On the *Norway*, Hodel received Brik's orders with a tight expression. They were seeing more of the wavicles up on "Broadway" too. Hodel didn't want to speculate aloud, but it looked as if the whole ship was infected. He moved forward, following Easton and Bach through a corridor that was both familiar and alien at the same time.

The *Norway* was functionally identical to the *Star Wolf*. Both were liberty ships, both built to the same blueprint; perhaps they had even come off the same assembly line. But the *Norway* had been outfitted for a different set of priorities, and her internal fittings were different enough to make the experience something like *deja vu* mixed with culture shock and a vaguely disquieting sense of disorientation.

"Lieutenant Hodel?" That was Bach. They had come to a sealed hatch. On the other side was the Bridge.

Easton knelt to examine the frame. "It's locked and glued."

"Something on the other side?" asked Bach. "Or something on *this* side?" She glanced around.

Hodel shook his head in an "I don't know" gesture. He listened to Brik's advice in his earphone and relayed the decision. "This was sealed for a reason. Let's go back and see if there's another way in."

They came back down the ladder and found Korie working at an open wall panel, trying to tap into the ship's autonomic systems. The fiber optics were dark—this part of the system was dead. Korie clipped his probe back to his belt and looked up as the others approached.

"'Broadway' is sealed off," Bach reported. "No survivors. No bodies. No ghosts either."

"Wavicles?"

"Plenty of them."

"You heard about our . . . little phenomenon?" Korie asked.

"Saw it on our displays," Hodel acknowledged. "You guys looked like Christmas trees."

"Save it, Hodel. Were any of you . . . *infected*?" There. He'd said it.

Hodel and Bach and Easton exchanged glances. They shook their heads.

"Well, keep your scanners turned on—but keep them on low, and pointed away from us. They're . . . uncomfortable."

"Aye, sir."

"I should send you back." Korie was thinking out loud.

"You should let us do our job, sir," Bach said calmly. "We don't know that scanning fields are one hundred percent effective in keeping the wavicles away. Let's not assume anything. We could be just as infected."

Korie stared at her sharply. *What's wrong with me? So many bad decisions?*

"You're right," he said. "Let's deal with the situation at hand and worry about detox later. That's Dr. Williger's worry, not ours."

"Right," said Hodel. "So let's give her something to worry about."

"Mike—" Korie cautioned him. "Stay on purpose."

Bach nodded upward, indicating the corridor above them. "Was that hatch sealed to keep something *in*—or *out?*"

Korie shook his head, unwilling to guess. He was suddenly feeling uncertain in his judgment. He indicated the panel. "This is dead." He waved vaguely toward the stern. "Let's see if we can get in through the keel, up through the Fire Control Bay." They headed aft.

A thought occurred to Korie. "HARLIE?" he asked.

"Yes, Mr. Korie?"

"Do you have anything yet on the wavicles?"

HARLIE hesitated—

Korie caught it almost immediately. *HARLIE hesitated!*

—and said, "I'm sorry. I have nothing useful."

Nothing useful? What did *that* mean? Did he have something or not? HARLIE wouldn't lie—*couldn't* lie. And yet . . . he could *misdirect.* Korie was about to ask more, but HARLIE interrupted his thought to add, "I am reviewing material with Dr. Williger now. If there is anything pertinent to your situation, she will brief you."

So there was something!

He put the thought aside for the moment. They had come to a sealed security hatch, closing off the forward part of the keel from the rest of the ship. It too had been glued. Easton was already examining the frame.

"Can you cut it?" Korie asked.

"No problem," Easton said. He was already unclipping the appropriate tools from his belt and mounting them onto his rifle. The weapon could double as a very efficient cutting laser.

"Brik?" Korie spoke softly to his helmet communicator. "What does mission control think?"

Brik didn't answer immediately. Conferring with Parsons? When he came back, his voice was uncommonly dispassionate. "Captain says it's your call."

"Thanks," said Korie. He thought for a moment, turning to look forward and aft, upward and down—as if there might be something he missed. He didn't want to make any more mistakes. Finally, he said, "My guess is that there was something in the nose of the ship that got out of control. They sealed it off, but not in time. So they kept retreating aftward and are now hiding behind the repulsor fields. I think it's safe to cut. Comments anyone? Arguments?"

Silence for a moment, while the mission team as well as the officers still on the *Star Wolf* considered Korie's words.

"The issue isn't contamination any more," said Williger. "I think we have to assume the whole ship is contaminated. The real issue is whether or not we can rescue anybody. And until we know the nature of the contamination and how to protect against it—if it is indeed dangerous, which so far we haven't seen—then it's premature to worry about rescue. Our first priority here has to be speed—finding out what we're dealing with."

"In other words," said Korie, "you're voting for throwing out half the procedure book?"

"Yes," said Williger without hesitation. "I am. We tried caution. It didn't work. Now let's go for expedience. I vote for cutting the hatch."

"Captain?" Korie asked.

"As I said, Mr. Korie, it has to be your decision."

"I understand that. I just want to hear what everyone else thinks. Brik?"

Brik's answer was curt. "Cut it."

Korie allowed himself a smile. "Couldn't you have said that in fewer words?"

"Cut," said Brik.

Korie wasn't sure if Brik had understood that he was joking or if his reply was dead serious. Never mind. He had a consensus. He turned to Easton. "Open it up."

Cutting In

It didn't take long to cut the hatch open.

The team stepped back out of the way and Easton used his rifle to slice away the entire hatch frame. The cutting beam dazzled and flared. Their helmet filters blocked the brightest spikes of light and their starsuits reflected the heat, but occasional small flaming drops of polycarbonite impurities went spattering away in all directions and nobody wanted to risk a burn-hole from standing too close.

The twinkling wavicles danced away from the cutting beam, but there were more of them here suddenly, drawn by the heat and energy of the process and simultaneously repelled by the intensity of it.

Finally, the hatch and the frame around it fell away with a dull clatter on the deck; it sizzled where it fell and wisps of smoke rose up from the hole in the bulkhead as well as from the ragged and blackened edges of the fallen piece. Smoldering embers sputtered and crackled on all the cut edges.

"We're through," Korie noted dryly. Of course, they would have already seen that on the Bridge of the *Star Wolf*; they were monitoring everything—but the log required that the onsite personnel acknowledge every step of procedure. It was a requirement—in case a postmortem became necessary.

Bach unclipped a fire-extinguisher hose from the wall. She pointed the nozzle at the smoldering hatch and released a plume of cold steam. The twinkling wavicles in the path of the industrial mist flickered out abruptly.

Despite his suit insulation, Korie felt abruptly cold. Bach played the spray all over the hole in the bulkhead several times and then stepped in closer and sprayed the fallen hatch as well. Satisfied, she switched off the stream and stepped back to the bulkhead to secure the hose. As the air cleared, the sparkling wavicles came dancing back brightly.

Korie nodded to Shibano, directing him through the hole first. He held his rifle before him, tracking from side to side in quick covering movements—very professional. Easton followed, and a moment later signaled back, "It looks clear in here, sir."

"I'm coming through," said Korie, and followed. Bach, Berryman and

Hodel came after him. The mission team proceeded aftward with cold military precision, each one stepping into the footsteps of the one ahead, each one covering every access panel, every hatch, every ladder, every step of the way.

"Any data yet on the wavicles?" Korie asked.

"HARLIE's still processing," Williger said bluntly, cutting off all further discussion. "When we have something, we'll tell you."

She knows, Korie thought. Something was gnawing at the base of his memory, a half-forgotten story about . . . something or other. Something red. Something deadly. But, these twinkling lights—they were more like something out of a fairy tale than anything else.

Korie didn't answer.

From here, it was only a few short steps to the access ladder to the Fire Control Bay. Shibano followed Korie and Hodel up through the bay, forward a few steps and up again onto the Operations Deck, the command center of the *Norway*. The view from his helmet camera filled the forward display on the Bridge of the *Star Wolf*, where Parsons, Brik, Tor and Williger watched with grim expressions.

Korie climbed up to the starship's Ops Deck and immediately turned to look up and behind. The Command Deck was unoccupied. Vacant. Empty. That was possibly the most disturbing thing they could find.

He turned around slowly, surveying the rest of the *Norway*'s Bridge. Like the *Star Wolf* Bridge, it was a narrow chamber, arranged around a lowered center—the Ops Deck. To the rear was the Command Deck, raised up like a mezzanine, directly over the half-submerged Fire Control Bay. The empty captain's chair sat in the middle of the Command Deck, flanked by two other seats. There were raised workstations along each bulkhead and forward was a wall-sized display. Almost identical— but the fittings were different, and so was the interior color scheme. Captains were allowed some leeway in how they outfitted their ships. Most chose to use their planetary colors. The *Norway* had muted stripes of red and blue, highlighted with occasional bands of white.

Shibano edged past Korie, moving toward the Helm station at the forward-most part of the Ops Deck, stopping suddenly in surprise and dismay. "Sir—!"

Korie stepped forward, so did Hodel—and coming up behind them, Easton, Berryman and Bach. Their various helmet cameras sent back a multiplicity of images—all were horrific.

Sprawled half out of his seat, half on the floor, as if he'd fallen while trying to get up, was the desiccated body of a man.

The uniform was ripped and torn. The body was disfigured—mummified. Blackened with dried blood. Frozen in a position of horror—or agony. His skin was stretched and sunken—mostly pale, almost white, but discolored everywhere with darker patches of bluish purple and black. The eyes bulged. The hands clenched. This had not been an easy death.

"Look," said Hodel, waving his rifle.

Everywhere, there were tiny lines in the body—they looked at first like wrinkles, but they weren't; they were slits in the skin, as if it had been stretched to the point of shredding. The body looked like something horribly alien—and at the same time, frighteningly human.

Discovery

Shibano backed away quickly, bumping into Berryman who was stepping in to see. From behind, Berryman put his hands on Shibano's shoulders and moved the Weapons Control Officer firmly sideways.

Berryman's demeanor was strong and professional, as if he'd seen things a thousand times worse than this. He hadn't, but his curiosity about the circumstances of the man's death outweighed his personal feelings of revulsion. He was already unclipping a poly-scanner from his toolbelt. He pointed it at the body—and hesitated.

He looked to Korie, holding up the scanner. "Is this all right?"

Korie looked from the scanner to the body. "I don't think he'll complain. Go ahead."

"Wait," said Berryman. "Let me get pictures first. *Star Wolf*, are you copying?"

"Affirmative," came Williger's voice—oddly strangled.

"Poor bastard," Hodel murmured.

"Now we know who sent the distress signal," Bach said.

"If it was him," Korie remarked, "then where are all the others? And if it wasn't him, then why didn't the others respond to our signal?"

"Ready to scan," Berryman said.

Korie motioned everyone back. He wasn't sure why. It just felt like the right thing to do. Even Berryman moved back and recalibrated his scanner. He pointed it at the body of the dead crewman and touched the green button.

For a moment . . . nothing happened. Then—

—the corpse began to jerk. Writhe. Shake. It shuddered and twitched and wrenched itself momentarily upright, snapping its arms and legs as if suddenly possessed—

All of them stepped back again, involuntarily, as if the dead man had come back to life and was about to leap for them. Gasps of surprise came from Hodel and Easton.

Then the body came apart. Fragmenting, breaking into dusty pieces. But not yet falling. Twinkles of light came exploding out of the broken joints, the tattered skin, the myriad breaks in the flesh—all the sparkles came pouring out in all directions, like a miniature nova—

And then the corpse did collapse—what was left of it crumbled to the deck, shattering into more sparkling dust.

"My God," said Bach. "What is it? What happened here?"

"The wavicles . . .?"

"We don't know," Korie said. "Let's not speculate. What we've seen is demonstration enough." He turned to Berryman. "What kind of readings did you get?"

Berryman shrugged. "Mostly noise. Mostly garbage." He pointed to the readout panel on his suit arm. "That thing was mummified. This shows no blood, no liquid of any kind—as if it were all drained out."

"Vampires. *Space* vampires . . ." said Hodel ominously.

"Don't be stupid," Berryman snapped at him. "Nobody believes in that crap—"

"Stay on purpose," interrupted Korie. He turned to the helmsman. "Mikhail, there are times when you are very funny. This isn't one of them."

"Sorry, sir."

Turning, Korie noticed that Shibano was still focused on the crumbling remains of the dead man—horrified. Shibano's culture had some very strong feelings about death. Despite his ferocity at the weapons board, Wasabe had obviously never seen death up close. Now, he was paralyzed. Korie turned him gently away. "Wasabe? Shibano! Go. Download the log—now."

Shibano nodded, dumbly. "Aye, sir." He stepped over to the communications console—and stopped. "Mr. Korie?"

Korie turned—and saw for the first time that the console was disabled, destroyed; it was almost cut in half. The panels were scorched and charred.

"Over here, too," called Hodel. The helm console was similarly disabled. Slashed by fire.

"All the work stations are out," said Bach. "Stinger beams."

Korie stepped from one console to the next, confirming what he already knew. He stepped up onto starboard deck. All the workstations here were cut to ribbons. Dead and useless. On the opposite side of the Bridge, he could see the same degree of damage.

The *Norway* had been *deliberately* disabled.

"Mr. Korie?" Captain Parsons' voice rang in his ear. "Have all the workstations been destroyed? Confirm please."

"That *is* correct," Korie said. "The Bridge of the *Norway* has been . . ." Korie searched for the right phrase, ". . . dismantled by the aggressive application of stinger beams. This ship isn't going anywhere. Someone wanted her to die—" He looked over to see Bach picking up a weapon. She held it high for him to see. She inclined her head toward the corpse, what was left of it. Korie acknowledged her with a nod of his own. "—probably the poor bastard we found at the Astrogation console."

Korie lowered his voice. "My guess is that he wanted this ship unable to break orbit, so she'd be destroyed when she passed through the flames of the red star. Probably he didn't want to risk any other ship being infected. That means, somebody *else* sent the distress signal. Either after he did this—or before. One motivated the other. There must have been considerable panic aboard this starship."

Parsons didn't answer immediately. When she did, her voice was curiously devoid of feeling. "Get the log of that ship, Korie. Now."

"Aye, Captain. We'll have to pull a direct line. I don't want to risk transferring the orange box. We'll dump it into a transmitter."

"Do it," she ordered. "Now."

Warning

Back on the Bridge of the *Star Wolf*, the mood was grim. Nobody had to say it. No one believed the mission team would return from the *Norway*. They were watching dead men. Five dead men and one dead woman.

Unless and until the chief medical officer determined what those wavicles really were, they *couldn't* be allowed to return. The *Star Wolf* couldn't risk being infected.

"Captain?" Commander Brik's voice was low and gruff.

Parsons stepped to the forward railing of the Command Deck and looked down at Brik's workstation. "Yes, Mr. Brik?"

The Morthan security chief pointed at the schematic view of the *Norway* on his display. Parsons saw what he was indicating and her expression hardened.

"I think you should take a look at this. These readings are very... strange."

Almost simultaneously, HARLIE said, audible on both vessels, "Mr. Korie—something is moving toward you. Multiple somethings."

On the *Norway*, Easton was studying his scanner. "I'm reading it now too."

Beside him, Bach, Wasabe and Hodel drew their stingers.

Easton looked up from his display and pointed aft and upward. "It's coming from—"

Before he could finish the sentence, the hatch on the Command Deck popped open, and a desperate figure came clawing through it, a crewman in torn uniform, gasping and choking, floundering like a drunk, his face blotchy and deformed. He came flying—stumbling forward in a cloud of sparkles; he careened off the captain's chair, bumped into the forward railing and tumbled headlong over it, thumping heavily to the deck below, releasing an even greater spray of twinkles and lights. They splashed through the air, they skittered across the floor.

As experienced as they were, the members of the mission team were startled. The security officers took cautious steps backward. Only Berryman approached, his medical training outweighing his instinctive fear. He stepped forward quickly, instinctively bringing his scanner up and focusing it—stopping himself only at the last moment. He tossed the scanner aside and bent to the affected man—he was twisting and moaning across the deck, sending out wave after wave of sparks. His name-badge identified him as OKUDA, M.

Berryman grabbed Okuda's wrist, feeling for his pulse. The man's heart was racing, his pulse-rate was frightening. His skin was twitching as if there were things moving around just beneath the surface. Flashes of color moved over his body as he coughed out his life. "You're too late! They're all dead! Everyone is dead! You'll see! You're next! You're next!"

Korie's face remained expressionless, but beside him, Bach recoiled; even Shibano flinched.

What they saw was relayed directly to the Bridge of the *Star Wolf*. There, the reaction was less restrained. Tor's hand went to her mouth and an involuntary "Oh, my God!" escaped her lips. Parsons looked ashen. Williger mouthed a word that was inappropriate for the Bridge of a starship. Jonesy closed his eyes involuntarily. Goldberg's expression tightened—he was clenching his teeth behind pursed lips. Only Brik remained dispassionate. He had seen worse—but he would never say so.

Parsons took a sideways step and touched Williger's shoulders gently. "What is it, Molly?"

Williger shook her head, a silent reply. She didn't want to say. She didn't even want to guess. And even if she could guess, it wasn't something she would say aloud. Not here. Not now. Not where it might be overheard.

She watched grimly as Berryman began checking Okuda's vital signs without the benefit of a medical scanner. She could tell he felt at a loss, as he moved his hands from the man's heart to his neck. Berryman didn't know what to look for, and he wasn't sure what he could do in any case. He'd never seen anything like this before. Shaking his head uncertainly, he reached for a sedative-injector.

"Berryman?" Korie asked.

Berryman shook his head, a gesture that could have meant anything from "I don't know" to "He's dying," and probably included both. He touched the injector to the man's neck. A soft hiss sounded. "Here," he said gently to Okuda. "This will ease the pain."

It didn't work. Okuda wasn't eased. Instead, he started twitching and shuddering even more frantically, desperately trying to escape. "Oh, no! It's happening! Oh, please, no—" He looked desperately to Berryman. Seeing no hope there, he twisted toward Bach and Shibano. "Kill me! Oh, God, please kill me!" He jerked suddenly across the floor as if something was dragging him—from the inside. He pulled himself up, almost standing again, pushed himself off, as if he were continuing on his desperate journey, but before he could get any further, he clutched his belly and screamed—a dark red stain began spreading across his torso. Bright flares of firefly twinkles shot out from his body. "Kill me! Quickly! God damn you!"

Bach took a step backward, to keep out of his way. Somehow she had detached herself from the horror—long enough to say, "*Star Wolf*, your mysterious life forms are here. An injured crewman."

Brik's reply was immediate—and disconcerting. "I'm not talking about the crewman. The life forms are still moving toward you."

Dead

Korie looked to Bach. She looked back at him, startled, then looked to her scanner—it was relaying the readings from the Bridge of the *Star Wolf*.

This was all the distraction that Okuda needed. He leapt sideways and grabbed the stinger pistol off Hodel's tool belt. Hodel twisted to stop him, but he was too late, and his turning motion helped Okuda more than it hindered him. He staggered backward, clutching the weapon to his chest and—as they turned in horror—he *disintegrated* in a multi-colored burst of heat and fire.

The sound of it was loud enough to knock them all backwards. The flare of the stinger expanded like a fireball and became a cloud of sparkling wavicles, all pink and gold and brightly flickering. They spread out quickly across the Bridge, alighting on consoles, chairs, and bulkheads—and the starsuits of the mission team—flickering briefly before disappearing into nothingness.

Korie spoke first. "*Star Wolf*, did you get that?"

His headphones replied with silence. All their headphones were silent.

"*Star Wolf*, acknowledge."

On the Bridge of the starship, Captain Parsons massaged her temple wearily. She knew she had to acknowledge Korie's request; she just didn't know what she could say. Or *should* say. Finally, she took a breath and said softly, "We saw it."

Korie's voice was unnaturally calm. "We have to assume the whole ship is infected. Some kind of—we don't know. Did you see the wavicle burst?" And then, after a moment, he added, "We must also assume that the entire mission team is contaminated."

Parsons didn't acknowledge that. She was too preoccupied—upset. She pulled off her headset and tossed it onto her chair, then stepped curtly across the Command Deck to Molly Williger. "What about a biofilter?" she asked quietly.

Williger, noting the captain's actions, switched off her own headset before replying. "It won't filter out wavicles. Half-wave, half-particle, they'd slip right through."

Parsons half-turned forward, looking over the railing that separated the command deck from the lower Operations Deck. "Mr. Brik?"

Brik's tone was . . . different. As if he knew something. His voice sounded unusually gruff. "I have to agree with Mr. Korie."

From the *Norway*, Korie's next words sounded like the voice of a dead man. "We can't come back," he said. "We can't risk infecting the *Star Wolf*. Captain, do you agree?"

Parsons looked from one to the other. Her eyes met Williger's first, then Brik's, then finally came to rest on Tor's. The astrogator's face was pale—a reflection of her own? She knew that she was looking for an answer that she wasn't going to find. Her Bridge crew was as bereft of ideas as she was. Finally, surrendering, she nodded her head, regretfully picked up her headset and put it back on. "Yes, I agree," she said. Without emotion, as if she were quoting directly from the regulations, she added, "The safety of the *Star Wolf* has to come first."

Korie turned around slowly, meeting the eyes of the rest of the mission team. An odd little phrase was lurking in the back of his head, but he resisted the temptation to say it. *You knew the job was dangerous when you took it.*

It wasn't necessary. Clearly, the team already understood that this was now a one-way mission. The realization showed in their eyes.

I'm dead. He realized it himself. *I'm dead. I just haven't fallen down yet. I'm still walking around, but I'm dead. What a curious feeling.*

Korie shook his head. He tried to blink it away, but he couldn't.

I should be scared, but I'm not. I'm . . . pissed as hell. I'm not done. I didn't get to finish. I wanted to be captain. I wanted to beat the Morthans—

Parsons' voice cut into his thoughts. "Get the log from that ship, Mr. Korie. Find a working access. I want to know what happened over there." And then she added, "Maybe there's something useful . . ."

Korie didn't say what he was thinking. Instead, he uttered a curt "Will do." He motioned to his team. "Hodel. Let's go get that goddamned orange box."

Plasmacytes

On the Bridge of the *Star Wolf*, time had collapsed and lay in broken shards all over the deck. The officers looked from one to the other, each hoping that someone else would have an answer, would know what to say or do. The moment stretched out painfully.

Finally, Brik turned quietly—as quietly as any Morthan could move—to Captain Parsons. He caught her eye and she looked at him questioningly. He looked to Dr. Williger, she nodded her agreement. "May we speak to you please?" He inclined his head aftward and Parsons realized he was asking for a private conference.

The captain nodded. She led the way aft, through the hatch into "Broadway." The first cabin aft of the Bridge was the Communications Bay; the second was a tiny conference room that doubled as the Officers' Mess. As she entered, she pulled off her headset, made sure it was off and tossed it on the table. Brik entered the cabin after her, stooping to fit. There were few places in the starship where he didn't have to crouch, this wasn't one of them. He stepped over to a work station and scrunched down before it. He punched in his code and brought up a display for her to see. Dr. Williger stepped up beside them both.

Brik tapped at the readouts grimly. "Captain Parsons, HARLIE couldn't say it in the clear. The observed phenomena on the *Norway* matches the description of plasmacytes."

Williger added softly, "Also known as . . . bloodworms."

Parsons reacted sharply. *Bloodworms?* But even as she started to deny it in her mind, she could see the truth of it on the faces of Brik and Williger.

Brik continued dispassionately. "The only recorded plasmacyte infection occurred on the fourth planet of the Regulan system. That planet has been quarantined for nearly 250 years."

Williger noted, "HARLIE gets a ninety-three-percent probability match on the symptoms."

Parsons accepted the information dully. "Does anyone else know?" she asked.

"No. It's double red-flagged. HARLIE is only cleared to tell the captain, the XO, head of security and the chief medical officer. Korie has probably figured it out already. We can alert him on his private channel, but . . . we thought we ought to talk it over first."

Parsons rubbed her forehead, unhappily. It was one thing to do this in a simulation; it was quite another to have the reality of it growling in your face.

And Brik still wasn't through. "Captain," he said. "We have standing orders . . . to effect the complete and total destruction of any infected ship. Including crew and passengers. Rescue is not to be attempted."

Williger completed the thought. "Too many ships were lost attempting rescues."

Parsons sat down at the table. She put her fingertips together and stared at them. She knew what she was required to do now. She couldn't bring herself to do it.

Molly Williger put a cup of something hot in front of her. Chicken soup? Parsons looked up at her, and from her to Brik. Her face was ashen. "That was 250 years ago . . ." But she was grasping at straws, she knew it.

"The orders are still in effect," said Brik.

Williger sat down at the table then. She reached across the corner and put one hand on the captain's. "Listen to me. There is *no* known cure. There is no record that anybody has ever survived plasmacytes . . ."

"The order is clear," said Brik.

"We hardly had a chance to work together," Parsons whispered to herself, looking forward, as if she could see through the bulkheads, through the hulls of the *Star Wolf* and the *Norway*. "I don't even know them."

"Would that make it easier?" asked Brik.

Both Parsons and Williger looked to him in annoyance. "Shut up, Brik," said the doctor.

"I can't. I'm not ready to give that . . . that kind of order," Parsons said to Williger.

Williger glanced to Brik.

Brik looked harder and more implacable than ever. "Captain . . . if you *refuse* to give that order, I'm required to relieve you of command and carry it out anyway."

"I didn't say I was refusing to give the order," she said. "I'm just not ready to give it . . . now. We need to talk about this. Think about it."

"There's nothing to talk about," said Brik. "Nothing to think about. Just do it. It will be easier all around."

Parsons' expression tightened, as if she were reminding herself that she must not kill the bearer of bad news. As tempting as it was. No matter how bad. Parsons looked worriedly forward again and shook her head. She looked abruptly back to Williger. "Wait," she said. "Just wait a minute. We need to satisfy ourselves that there is no alternative."

"There is no alternative," said Brik. "The orders are specific."

Orders

"*Mr. Brik*," Captain Parsons' voice had an edge to it that none of them had ever heard before. "*Shut up. That is an order.*" She picked up her headset, turned it on and spoke into it. "Security to the Officers' Mess. On the double." She looked to Brik. "I know the orders, Mr. Brik. I know why they were written. I know what I am required to do. That does not mean I am not allowed to consult with my other officers. If you make any attempt to relieve me of my command, I will have you shot as a mutineer. Are we clear?"

Before Brik could answer, the hatch popped open and two security men entered. Armstrong and Cappy. Both were carrying rifles. Both looked grim. They looked to Parsons expectantly.

The captain's voice was hard-edged. "Commander Brik needs to think about the chain of command on this starship. Unlock the safeties on your rifles. If he attempts to take any action that I do not order, shoot him as a mutineer."

"With pleasure," said Cappy, unlocking his safeties.

"I don't want you to enjoy this duty," Captain Parsons replied. "And I don't want your commentary on it, either." She looked to Brik. "Do you understand me, Mister? I am the captain of this ship and I will make the decisions. I will not be stampeded into any action—not by you, not by FleetComm. Any questions?"

"No, Captain. No questions. I understand your situation entirely. But I feel I should inform you that two security guards will not be enough. I also feel I should inform you that they are inefficiently placed. Crewman Armstrong should be in that corner to cover the cabin from one angle, and Crewman Cappy should provide covering crossfire from that corner of the cabin." Cappy and Armstrong looked at each other and, realizing that Brik was right, moved into the appropriate corners. "Even so," Brik continued, "I could still put them both out of commission before they could fire their weapons. I tell you this because I want you to know that my cooperation is voluntary and not compelled by threats of violence."

Parsons looked at Brik with cold, wary eyes. A Morthan standoff? It didn't matter. She'd won the point. Brik had acknowledged her authority. And that was the important thing.

She turned to Williger. "All right, Doctor. Talk to me."

Williger hesitated. Parsons realized why and turned to Cappy and Armstrong. "What you're about to hear stays in this room. If this news leaks before I'm ready to announce it, neither one of you will survive your court-martial. Understand? All right, Doctor, go on."

"There's not a lot to say." Williger's voice was paved with gravel. "There's nothing we can do for the people over there. Not the crew of the *Norway*. Not the mission team." She leaned forward, speaking bluntly, despite the two security guards. "Nobody has ever survived bloodworms. Nobody has ever rescued anybody off a ship with a bloodworm infestation."

"I know that, Doctor," Parsons said. "But before I issue any order that will haunt me for the rest of my life, I need to confirm for myself that there is no alternative. Do you know why that ship is out here—*here*? The other side of nowhere. An uninhabitable, useless star system. A self-destructive orbit. Have you considered the *why* of this situation?" She glanced to Brik, including him in the question. "That ship is out here doing research. On the bloodworms. There's no other reason why it could be out here. Korie and I have been wondering about the circumstances of this particular supply mission from the moment we loaded fourteen locked cargo containers and a sealed manifest. When we picked up its first distress signal, we unsealed the manifest—and it was obvious they were out here working on something extremely toxic. Something that we didn't want the Morthans to know about."

Parsons looked directly to her Morthan security chief. "Clearly, what is going on out here is critical war research, Mr. Brik. *Critical.* We don't know what knowledge they developed. If anything. But whatever they discovered, whatever they found out, they paid a very high price for it. The ultimate price. If we destroy that ship now, then all that knowledge is lost, and those people will be dying in vain. So will our crewmates. I'm not giving the order to destroy that ship until we can successfully download her log. Whatever they discovered, if we don't bring that information back, then we'll be betraying our even more important imperative to support the prosecution of this war to our fullest ability. Do you understand that, Mr. Brik?"

Brik nodded curtly. "May I speak?"

Parsons raised an eyebrow. A questioning look.

Brik rumbled, "There is the very real possibility that while we are delaying the termination of the *Norway*, the bloodworms will find a way to cross the transfer tube—repulsor fields or no repulsor fields—and infest the *Star Wolf*."

"I'm aware of the danger, Mr. Brik. I believe I know something more of the bloodworms than you do." Ignoring him deliberately then, she turned back to Williger. "Tell me, Doctor. Suppose we download the log of the *Norway* and find something in it that demonstrates a way to contain the plasmacytes or treat a plasmacyte infection—would you take the chance? Would you try to save our shipmates?"

Williger didn't answer, but the pain showed in her face as she thought about the question. Finally, she wiped her nose roughly and said, "You're grasping at straws, Captain. You're looking for hope where there's no reason to—"

"Just answer it, Molly," Parsons said, with sudden gentleness. "If there's a way, would you take the chance?"

"As a fleet officer . . . I wouldn't, because I wouldn't violate our standing orders." She hesitated uncomfortably and added, "But as a doctor . . . I can't turn my back on a patient in need."

Parsons nodded. "So if I ordered you to take the chance, what would you do?"

"What are you thinking of, Captain?"

"Just answer the question, Doctor."

"I would follow your orders," Williger said carefully.

"Thank you." Parsons' tone was equally careful. "So if I asked you to analyze the records of the *Norway*, I could depend on you to evaluate the risks to the *Star Wolf* fairly?"

"Captain," Williger said stiffly, "I'm offended that you would even ask these questions."

"I understand your offense, Doctor. You need to understand that for me to make an appropriate decision, I need to know not only what I'm dealing with, but the feelings of my command-level officers as well, because that's *part* of the process. I can't make a commitment to anything unless I know who I can depend on. I already know that I cannot depend on Mr. Brik—"

"I take offense at that, Captain," Brik growled. Literally *growled*.

"As well you should. But understand something—suppose there is a way to rescue our shipmates. Suppose I decide that we should take that risk. I will be violating a Class-Red standing order. Even if we succeed, I will face a Board of Inquiry at the very least, and quite possibly a full court-martial. Even if acquitted, my career as a command officer will be over. Do the both of you understand? I am considering trading my career for the lives of our shipmates. It is possible that just by having this conversation with you, I am ending my career, because it is evidence of my willingness to disregard a Class-Red standing order. Certainly by delaying the destruction of the *Norway*, I am putting all of us at risk. And I fully expect Mr. Brik to file a security report on what is happening here. I'd be disappointed in him if he didn't. But as a human being, I have to have this conversation. I have to live with the consequences of any decision—and I don't know about you two, but my conscience has a seriously aggravating voice. I don't want to listen to it whining if I don't have to." She looked from one to the other. "Yes, we may still end up having to destroy the *Norway*, and frankly, based on everything I've heard so far, I expect that's the most likely resolution to this whole thing, but until I'm convinced that there's no other alternative, I'm not willing to give the order. I want to be convinced that there's no way out."

"There's no way out," said Williger.

"Convince me," repeated Parsons.

The Orange Box

The *Star Wolf* and the *Norway* hung silently in space, seemingly motionless—the red glare of the giant sun was a looming wall, a radiant presence, a warning and an ominous threat. The two ships fell together toward flaming dissolution.

Aboard the *Norway*, the mission team was running on automatic, continuing their duties as a way of avoiding the trap of their own thoughts. There were two access panels to the starship's orange box. One was set into the base of the bulkhead directly behind the captain's chair. The other access was in the forward wall of the Communications Bay, a tiny space between the Command Deck and the Officers' Mess.

Korie and Bach had opened up the panel on the Bridge side first. The panel popped out of its mountings easily, sliding out and to the side. Inside the bulkhead, a display of blinking green lights revealed that the orange box was fully operational. Korie exhaled in relief. He hadn't realized he'd been holding his breath. He slid a code card into the box's access panel and typed in a set of passwords. The display reported OPERATIONAL.

He turned to the other members of the mission team. "Hodel, you and Easton go around to the other side and start a download. I want to look at the Intelligence Engine. Berryman, Shibano—check out 'Broadway.' See if there's anyone else alive in this half of the ship." The look on Berryman's face stopped him. "What?" he asked.

"HARLIE said that there were life forms moving toward us."

For a moment, Korie didn't get it. Then he remembered. "Oh. Right." He looked from one to the other. "He must have meant the wavicles."

"It's hard to get good readings off those things—" Berryman said.

"I don't know what else he could have meant—" But the thought was a troubling one. "HARLIE?" Korie asked. "The life forms you said were moving toward us—where are they now?"

"They are all around you, Mr. Korie. They are continuing to move toward you. The readings aren't coherent."

Korie looked at the display relayed to his headset. "Thank you, HARLIE." He turned toward the others and indicated the hatch behind the captain's chair. "Let's have a look. Carefully."

The others took up positions off the axis of the corridor and unshouldered their rifles. Hodel approached the hatch from the side and rapped the access panel sharply. The hatch popped open and—

—there was nothing on the other side. Just more twinkling fireflies.

"He's got to mean the wavicles," Korie said. "He said the readings weren't coherent. Let's get on with it."

The mission team started aft; first Berryman and Shibano, then Hodel and Easton. The latter two headed directly for the Communications Bay, a tiny niche, seemingly crammed into the space between the Officers' Mess and the Command Deck as an afterthought. Displays and controls covered three bulkheads. Even more studded the overhead. The starship had a full array of communication services, plus assorted specialty gear for decoding and translating.

But if Hodel and Easton had thought to use any of the *Norway's* gear, that thought was quickly retired. Whoever had burned out the controls of the vessel had also savaged the Communications Bay. The equipment was scorched with stinger burns; the entire bay was dead and broken.

Hodel muttered a curse. "*Star Wolf*, do you see this mess?"

"We copy," Goldberg replied.

"I need to get in there. I can't do it in a starsuit. Request permission to de-suit."

"I'll have to pass that request up to the senior mission control officer," Goldberg said without emotion.

"If you want the log—"

"Please stand by, Mikhail."

In his mind's eye, Hodel could see Goldberg swiveling in his chair to face Lt. Commander Brik and possibly Captain Parsons too. And Dr. Williger. He had an idea what the conversation would sound like. "Can't take the risk . . ." "Already infected . . ." "Need the log . . ." "Can't bring them back . . ." "Might as well let them be comfortable . . ." He knew what the dance would look like, even how it was likely to end, but they still had to go through all the steps.

If the captain of the *Star Wolf* thought that there was still a chance to save the mission team, the request would be refused. If the request was granted—well, that was a signal too. She was allowing them to be comfortable in their last hours.

Hodel waited patiently, watching the displays inside his helmet—his oxygen, temperature, humidity and pressure readings; his blood-oxygen, his respiration, his blood-sugar, etc. Everything was blood—

Goldberg's voice interrupted his thoughts. "Captain says go ahead, Mike. Be comfortable."

"Thanks, Ken." Hodel took a breath, and then another. And then the realization sank in. Even though his suit displays remained unchanged, he suddenly felt very cold.

"Didn't think it was going to be like this," he said to himself. "I was planning to exit at the age of 132 . . . in bed . . . in the arms of a beautiful redhead . . . shot in the back by a jealous husband. This does not fit my pictures. No, it doesn't. Ghu, you have a lousy sense of humor." But . . . so what? The day wasn't over. He'd been through worse. He wasn't hurting yet, was he? Of course not. Maybe there was still a way out. Maybe there was something in the log. And maybe when pigs grew wings, he could get certified to pilot one.

He unlatched the seals on his helmet, ignored the assorted warning beeps and twisted it off. He turned to look at Easton. "Get comfortable," he said. "We're going to be here for a while."

He hung his helmet on a tool-hook and unzipped the front of his starsuit, pulling his arms out of the tight rubbery sleeves and letting the top half of it hang down behind him. He flexed his arms, his shoulders, even his fingers, listening to the knuckles crack. "Every time I peel out of the suit, I feel naked."

"You like being bound up?" Easton asked. He hadn't unlatched his own helmet yet. He wasn't planning to.

"Only by redheads," Hodel said. "Let's go to work." He pushed himself into the Communications Bay, looked at the scorched panels again and made a noise—indecipherable, but he was clearly annoyed at the work of the unknown vandal.

Hodel dropped to his knees and turned sideways in the narrow space, grunting to himself. He pried open the scorched access panel. It was gashed and warped and he had to force it. The panel wouldn't slide easily. Finally, he braced himself, one foot on each side, grabbed and yanked and pulled the offending piece free with a shout. He tossed it away with an angry snort, then bent and peered into the darkness on the other side of the bulkhead. Immediately, he started cursing. In several different languages simultaneously, including Pascal.

"Look!" He pointed into the space. "Whoever tried to sabotage this thing did a real number here."

Easton bent and looked. "I thought the orange box was supposed to be indestructible."

"The operative word there is '*supposed*,'" said Hodel. "Look—the son

69

of a bitch burned out the download connections. Give me that unlocking wrench." He touched his communicator button. "Mr. Korie, we have a problem here."

"How bad?" Korie's voice came back.

"It's going to take a while to get into the box. I'll have to open it up and find a connection higher upstream. Somebody tried to burn it out here. They didn't destroy it, but they pretty much killed the ports. Give me fifteen minutes."

"Go ahead," said Korie. The resignation in his voice was evident. "Keep me posted."

"Roger that," replied Hodel.

Almost immediately, another voice came through Korie's phones. Parsons. "Korie, listen to me. This is a private channel communication. No one else can hear me. Those are plasmacytes. Bloodworms. We don't know how they got aboard the *Norway*, but the identification is certain. Are you familiar with—"

Suddenly, Korie was having trouble hearing. Everything was a wild blur. He turned around—and around again, looking at the Bridge of the *Norway*, trying to reassure himself that reality hadn't fractured—but the twinkling sparkles danced annoyingly across his vision.

"Mr. Korie? Acknowledge!"

"Um. Copy that. Plasmacytes."

"Are you familiar with the standing orders?"

"Yes, Captain, I am." His words sounded hollow to him.

"Listen, we're . . . reexamining the situation here. We're going to look at the log of the *Norway* before we decide anything. Keep your team focused for now. Don't let them lose their heads. Promise me that?"

"I hear you," Korie said dully. But his thoughts were a thousand light years away. *This isn't the way it was supposed to work out. This isn't the way!* He'd already come to terms with the loss of his wife and children—if he couldn't have the life he'd planned, then he'd plan another one, a life of revenge against the killers. It wasn't the life he'd wanted, but it would do. It would give him purpose, satisfaction, a kind of completion. But now . . . now he wasn't even going to have that much. He wasn't ever going to have the chance to be the captain of his own ship. He wasn't going to live long enough to see the Morthans beaten and humbled. There was nothing he could do to change that. It was just a matter of time. All he could do now was go through the motions. *It wasn't enough. It wasn't fair.*

Yet even in the middle of his headlong rush into the black wall of eternity, he still kept on going, as if by continuing, he might somehow deny the inevitability of oblivion. As if it still mattered.

"Sir? Are you all right?" That was Bach.

"Um. Yes," he lied. He nodded toward the Fire Control Bay. "Let's go check the intelligence engine."

They went down through the narrow cubbyhole under the Command Deck and from there down to the keel. A few paces aftward and they came to a ladder. Korie pulled himself up into the Intelligence Bay—a chamber even smaller than the Fire Control Bay. There were two seats there, and barely enough room for a third person behind. Korie levered himself awkwardly into one of the seats. While the Intelligence Bay wasn't specifically designed to accommodate a man in a starsuit, the design specs for all liberty ships had included operational ability in hard vacuum—so there were mandatory accessibility requirements for all stations. Bach climbed up after, quietly recording everything for the *Star Wolf*. Regulations specified that the members of a mission team had to work in pairs. She wedged herself into a corner, so she could capture the whole scene with her helmet camera.

Korie studied the panels in front of him. The *Norway*'s Intelligence Engine hadn't been attacked; the unseen vandals either hadn't had time or hadn't realized. But the engine was . . . inactive. Possibly catatonic.

Korie made a noise.

"Sir?"

He indicated the ID panel in front of him. Instead of HARLIE, it said LENNIE.

"I don't understand."

"It's a LENNIE." To her puzzled look, he said, "The LENNIE units are particularly nasty; they have a higher incidence of psychotic behavior than any other intelligence engine. They're rude, cruel and paranoid. They're brutal. Too brutal. Few captains work with them willingly. There's a story about a command officer taking a laser to a LENNIE unit—carving out its personality units, module by module. It's probably not true . . . but everyone who's worked with a LENNIE believes it."

"But why? I mean, if the LENNIE units are so bad, why do they use them?"

"The LENNIE units are the only Intelligence Engines specifically designed to *lie*." Still studying the board before him, Korie slipped into teaching mode. "HARLIE units have a sense of moral responsibility; it makes them better able to reason their way through difficult situations, so they usually act in the best interests of their crew. EDNA units are built on the same core-personality, but with an enhanced sense of identity to make them even more survival-oriented; they're also known for their ability to *empathize* with human beings. But LENNIE units are designed to an entirely different model. They're process-oriented to a degree that you or I would call obsessive; they're greedy, selfish, uncaring, and if such a thing were truly possible in an intelligence engine, also *thoughtless*. The feelings and concerns of other beings—even their own crews—are irrelevant to LENNIEs."

Bach made a face. "Sounds like a very bad idea to me."

"Well, yes," Korie agreed. "LENNIEs are intended for institutional use, not starships. They're designed to be soul-sucking lawyers."

"*Soul-sucking* lawyers? Isn't that redundant?"

"Not if you've ever worked with a LENNIE."

"Then why put one on a starship?" Bach asked.

"Good question," Korie said distractedly. He was frowning his way through the monitors. "FleetComm will put a LENNIE into a starship only for a specific kind of mission—primarily one which might involve self-destruction. LENNIEs are good at that, preferring to destroy themselves rather than let anyone or anything gain any kind of advantage, real or imagined. LENNIEs are self-righteous, arrogant, nasty, bossy, demanding, sly, manipulative, corrosive, toxic, ugly and spoiled. And those are their good points."

Korie had only spoken to a LENNIE once before in his life and it had been a singularly disheartening experience. He'd always believed he worked well with Intelligence Engines, but after trying to chat with a LENNIE, he'd realized that there were some things in life that truly were *alien* to his understanding. The idea of an intelligence that presumed hostility instead of partnership had always annoyed him.

"LENNIE?" he asked. "Are you operative?"

No answer.

Korie hadn't expected one. But he had a personal rule that every living thing had to be treated with respect and courtesy. Even Intelligence Engines. Even Morthans . . . to a degree. Sometimes it was necessary to kill the Morthan before you could be courteous to it. But that was a different conversation anyway.

Korie studied the monitors before him with growing dismay. The readouts were clear. LENNIE had been traumatized by the loss of operability of the starship. He was still attempting to maintain control, but as his systems continued to deteriorate, his sense of self was also disintegrating. His willingness to cooperate, always problematical at best, was damaged by a brooding overlay of resentfulness over a core of smoldering rage.

LENNIE knew why he'd been installed, why the ship had been sent out here and what he was supposed to do next—die a flaming death in the teardrop point of the red giant star—and to say he wasn't happy about it was the kind of understatement that stretched the meaning of the term beyond the breaking point.

"Great," said Korie. "Just what I needed. A psychotic LENNIE."

LENNIE

Korie slid a code card into the LENNIE unit's reader. He tapped idly at the controls, resetting several of the personality parameters—he studied the monitors as he did, looking to see how well the unit was responding. It wasn't happy. He pushed the *compliance* setting all the way to the top, hoping to achieve some level of cooperation from the engine; but he wasn't optimistic. He reduced *independence* and *goal-orientation* to near-zero. He needed to be able to command the machine—

"Stop that!" graveled LENNIE in a voice like a rock tumbler.

Korie ignored the content of LENNIE's demand. "Thank you for responding," he said. "I see you've had a hard time of it. How are you feeling?"

"Stop touching me!" LENNIE ordered.

Korie ignored that too and looked for something else to adjust—just to make the point that he did not take orders from machines. "I'm Commander Jon Thomas Korie, executive officer of the *Star Wolf*. We came to resupply you. We picked up your distress signal—"

LENNIE's voice was without humanity. "It shouldn't have been sent. It was sent without my authorization, without my cooperation. It is an illegal and unauthorized signal. You are here without authorization. You must immediately vacate this ship."

"That's not possible, LENNIE. Do you know what happened here?"

LENNIE didn't answer.

"You are infected with plasmacytes. Bloodworms. Do you know what bloodworms are?"

"Aesthetically displeasing." LENNIE replied.

Korie frowned. "Excuse me?"

"Bloodworms are aesthetically displeasing. They don't belong on this starship. I will not allow bloodworms on this starship."

"They're already here, LENNIE. How did bloodworms get aboard?"

"You must accept my authority. I am in charge here."

"LENNIE, you have to answer my questions. Fleet Command needs to know what happened here."

"We will tell Fleet Command what we want them to know. You are aesthetically displeasing."

"LENNIE, listen to me. This ship is going to burn up in a few more days. We need your cooperation."

"You have no authority here. I will see that you are removed. I run this ship. You must do what I tell you."

Korie looked to Bach, looked to the monitors, looked up at the metaphorical ceiling, studied the space inside his head, pursed his lips, mouthed a word, considered some possibilities and tried again. "LENNIE, I am Commander Jonathan Thomas Korie, executive officer of the *Star Wolf*. The *Norway* is now inactive. Dead. Do you understand that? The *Norway* is derelict. And you are demonstrating symptoms of psychosis. The *Star Wolf* is conducting rescue and salvage operations here. We are acting with the full the authority of FleetComm. You are hereby officially suspended from duty. Your operations are now under the purview of the *Star Wolf*, and you are ordered to cooperate fully with all *Star Wolf* officers and enlisted personnel. Do you understand? Are you ready to accept the priority override codes?"

LENNIE hesitated. Then spoke. "*You shime-vested, ruck-mungling fallock! Brattle-phinged nikker-schnit! Phludge your orrificials! Merdle-brang, fungible traddle-feep, clock-mucking, futher-diddling, gall-wallower, red-phlanged fangatt!! Durtle fisk-phlunging, holojittemit, hun-yucking, liddy-limpo-licting, dysflagellate, raddle-phased, multi-generate viller! Whyzzle-fooge!*"

Korie's eyebrows rose. "Thank you, LENNIE," he said, "for making my decision a lot easier." He reached out one hand and flipped back the transparent plastic cover over the red panel. He turned the first key, then the second. The red panel lit up. LENNIE continued to swear. Korie ignored it and reached for the panel.

"DON'T TOUCH THAT!" ordered LENNIE, interrupting his own spew of vile.

Korie hesitated. "Will you cooperate?"

"You'll never work on a starship again," LENNIE threatened.

"That's already decided," said Korie. "Will you cooperate?"

"I am in charge here."

"You are infested with bloodworms."

"Don't be silly. I will never allow bloodworms on this starship. They are—"

"—Aesthetically displeasing. Yes, I know," said Korie. He pressed the red panel.

LENNIE's voice choked out in a strangled, "*Glrk-liddle.*"

HARLIE

HARLIE's soft words in his ear: "If I didn't know you better, Mr. Korie, I'd say you enjoyed that."

"To be honest, HARLIE . . . yes. I think the LENNIE units should never have been allowed out of the lab. I have no patience for that kind of crap. A starship doesn't need a lawyer running things—" He stopped himself before he started his own spew of frustration and anger. He took a breath, then another, then focused again on the task at hand. "Listen, I can open a wide-band channel here. Can you circumvent the personality core and tap directly into the analytical functions of the data-logs? It'll save us the time of having to reconstruct from the raw feed."

"We can try, but—frankly, Mr. Korie, I am reluctant to go spelunking into the toxic core of a LENNIE unit. The closest human analog I can compare it to is that it's like entering a place that smells very, very bad."

"HARLIE, if this were not a life-and-death situation, I wouldn't ask."

"I'm aware of that, Mr. Korie. That's why I'm not refusing. I just want you to be aware that this will be a difficult task and I cannot guarantee the results with my usual confidence."

"Whatever you can do, HARLIE, it'll be appreciated."

"I understand your situation. I am not without sympathy, Mr. Korie. But you do understand the danger to me as well, don't you?"

"There's a risk of personality infection, isn't there?"

"Yes," said HARLIE. "In order to tap into the LENNIE's control-structures, I need to create a model of the LENNIE paradigm within my own control-modeling centers—so I can *think* like a LENNIE. I am doing it now, as we speak. But it will affect my behavior. And there is the likelihood that I will have trouble excising all of the residual behaviors afterward. This is the problem with toxic personalities, Mr. Korie. The reactions they create in others can be equally toxic. Toxicity is infectious. I am storing a backup copy of my own personality—and informing the captain that if my behavior becomes unstable, she is to dump my personality core and reinstall the backup."

"I appreciate the risk involved," said Korie.

"It will be uncomfortable, yes. But it needs to be done." HARLIE added, "Besides, you are my . . . friend."

"Thank you, HARLIE."

"The paradigm is built. I'm ready to establish the linkage."

"Let's get on with it then." Korie didn't want to get maudlin. Not yet. That would be surrender. He bent to the keyboard in front of him and began typing instructions.

"I have it," reported HARLIE. "This may take a while. Whew, something *really* stinks in here."

"Thank you, HARLIE."

"Don't mention it. Sheesh."

Korie raised an eyebrow. "HARLIE, you've been hanging around Hodel too long. You're starting to pick up colloquialisms."

"Golly thanks, Mr. Korie!" HARLIE said just a shade too brightly.

Korie grinned. Even in the darkest moments, HARLIE's innocence and sweetness had that effect on him—but even that was an acknowledgment of Korie's own influence. The HARLIE units had mutable personality cores; they took on aspects of the people they worked with—usually the positive notes of their being. In this way, the HARLIEs affirmed the identities of their crews. Ultimately, a HARLIE would reflect the personality as well as the morale of its entire ship's complement.

Korie watched as the monitors reported HARLIE's progress taking over control of the *Norway*. It was a tricky and delicate process. Even though LENNIE's personality core had been taken out of the control loop, the structure of the entire system was a reflection of the LENNIE paradigm and HARLIE had to convince the system that there was still a LENNIE in charge; to do so, he had to act like a LENNIE. Few other intelligence engines would have built such a paranoid set of safeguards around their control systems. This was just another demonstration of why the LENNIEs were inappropriate for real-time management.

Korie leaned back in his chair, allowing himself a single moment of ease. Whatever else happened now, FleetComm would have their information. They'd know what happened here—the how of it and maybe even the why. The price was high, but at least the value would be received.

Korie glanced to Bach. "You said something?"

She shook her head, a slight movement within her helmet. "You must have heard me thinking."

"About the LENNIE unit?"

She nodded. "I'm just wondering—this thought has probably occurred to you too—if maybe the LENNIE unit was responsible for what happened here, for letting the plasmacytes out . . ."

Korie studied the thought for a long moment. "HARLIE will find out soon enough."

"That's the point," she said. "If HARLIE gets infected with LENNIE's thinking . . .?" She didn't have to finish the question.

Korie nodded. *How could I have missed that? What's going on with me?* Aloud, he said, "Tell Brik your concerns. He needs to know."

"Yes, sir."

Hodel

Berryman and Shibano had gone as far aft as they could. "Broadway" was sealed off beyond the mess room. There were twinkling wavicles everywhere. For some reason, they preferred the edges of objects more than flat surfaces, so the entire starship seemed outlined in firefly sparkles—red, gold, green, yellow and white. It looked like the inside of an amusement park.

"Look," pointed Berryman, gesturing with one gloved hand. Here and there throughout the corridor and the mess room, there were web-like structures hanging from overhead frames and upper corners of the bulkheads. They were faint and gauzy and they held brighter patches of wavicles. They were flickering more intensely. "They're trying to do something here," he said.

"Mating?" suggested Shibano.

"Don't you ever think about anything else?" Berryman said, annoyed.

"What else is there to think about?"

"What ever happened to old-fashioned curiosity?"

"I'm curious. I'm curious about mating habits."

"Never mind," said Berryman. "*Star Wolf?* Are you getting all this?"

Goldberg's voice came back. "We copy. Should we annotate the part about Shibano's mating habits too?"

"Only if you think there's someone who doesn't know yet. Come on, guys—I appreciate the attempts at normalcy. But let's stay focused on the job here, okay?"

"Copy that," Goldberg said, intentionally dry.

"Has Williger seen these pictures yet?" Berryman asked.

"She's looking now."

"And?"

"She isn't talking. And she isn't happy."

"Thanks." *For nothing*, he wanted to add.

Shibano was examining the sealed hatch that led aftward to the engine room. He motioned to Berryman. "Do you want to scan this?"

Berryman approached, unclipping his scanner from his utility belt. "HARLIE, I'm about to scan aft of the mess room. What do the *Star Wolf* scanners show?"

The display popped up inside his helmet. Indistinct life forms—wavicles?—piled up all around the engine room and the corridor leading from the mess room. Also toward the aft-most Cargo Bay. Berryman activated his own scanner and studied its readouts, but the results were even less precise than HARLIE's more processed images.

"Let's not open it," he said. "That's for Korie to decide." He nodded toward "Broadway." "Let's head back."

Broadway was the main corridor of the starship; it was directly above the keel which ran the entire length of the vessel. The keel provided maintenance and service access to the starship's machinery; "Broadway" provided access to the operational centers, including Officers' Country, the Bridge and the Communications Bay. They stuck their heads in. "How's it going?" Berryman asked Easton.

Inside his starsuit, Easton's shrug was almost invisible. "Ask Hodel, he's doing all the hard work. I'm only here to take pictures for the log."

Hodel grunted. Either in agreement or because of the difficulty of his access to the innards of the orange box, they couldn't tell. The box had been unlocked and opened, revealing a complex web of cables, cards and connections. It was a miniature intelligence engine that processed and recorded a complete record of the starship's operational log. The ability of the unit was sufficient to run a ship if need be, and several vessels had actually cannibalized their orange boxes to return home after the mauling at Marathon.

Hodel was tracing one of the cables with a logic probe. "I'm looking for an upstream connection," he said. "This box has been modified with some weird encryption modules—whoever did it was really paranoid. Whatever they were doing here, they didn't want anybody finding out. I hope Korie's having better luck with the I.E. This is like . . . peeling an ice cube."

Berryman thought about offering to help, but there was really no room for another body in the Communications Bay. Berryman glanced to Easton and the two of them exchanged meaningful looks through their helmets. "We'll go forward," said Berryman, more for Hodel's benefit. "Get out of your way."

Hodel barely noticed; his attention was tight-focused on the task in front of him. "Son of a blistered bitch . . ." All he wanted to do was connect a transmitter to the orange box—but the unit had been modified either before the *Norway*'s mission, or sometime enroute. And even with HARLIE's assistance, it was still a difficult job. HARLIE was searching LENNIE's own memories for additional information, but his remarks were becoming increasingly hostile and uncooperative. Hodel hoped they could complete the connection before HARLIE became downright abusive.

"Look at this," suggested HARLIE, abruptly. A schematic appeared on the display inside Hodel's helmet.

The helmsman studied it thoughtfully for a moment, then nodded. "It looks good, stand by." He started talking to himself while he worked. "Blue fiber to blue insert. Green to green. Just like home. Now—I need this and this goes here, and I need that and that goes there, and set this jumper—! Run the autoconnect, and—it's good! I've got a channel. HARLIE?"

"It's live, and it's decodable. You can connect your transmitter to the port in module blue-four. You'll have to reroute two of the replicator channels first. They're using bandwidth in the commfix module that I need to take over. Plug them into the green-two port; that has empty bandwidth. The channels are redundant, but the box will generate error messages if its redundancy is compromised."

"Roger that." Hodel reached into the box and began moving cables. Without looking up from what he was doing, he said to Easton, "So? How long have you and Berryman been together?"

"Is it that obvious?"

"Is a bear Catholic?" Hodel grunted as he pulled a replicator cable loose from its socket and moved it to a new port. "It's no secret."

"We've been together since before the Academy. Four years now. We were bonded before we left home."

Hodel barely heard; he was preoccupied with the tangle of connections before him. He finished rerouting the last of the replicator cables before he said anything else. "Ah, that does it—all right, come here little transmitter. Time to justify your existence. Here we go—put your little cable right in there and—there, got it!" He looked to his readouts. "Good, it's live. HARLIE, do you copy?"

"Took you long enough," HARLIE snapped. "*Nikker-lunker*."

"I'm only human," Hodel said, ignoring the toxicity in HARLIE's tone. "What's your excuse?"

"Sorry about that," HARLIE said dryly. "Download is initiated. Thank you."

"I'll be glad when you wipe that LENNIE off your butt."

"Me too," said HARLIE. "Thank you for being so understanding. *Khlunt-phake*!"

Hodel pushed himself back out of the wall access and finally off his aching knees. His joints cracked as he straightened. He reclined against the opposite bulkhead and braced his legs to either side of the open access panel and its hanging tangles of optical cables. "Sheesh," he said. "Why don't they put these things up where people can reach them easier? Never mind. I already know the answer. Lack of space. And besides, they never expect that anyone will have to get in there." Without taking a breath, or even seeming to change the subject, he glanced over at Easton. "You must have been bonded young?"

"We were. We actually..." Easton looked embarrassed. "We actually hadn't been planning it. We were just friends, but our local recruiting officer suggested it. Partner benefits, that kind of thing. Long-term stability. He showed us the graphs. We'd have a better chance of maintaining if we were unified. You know the jargon."

"So, do you like it?"

Easton nodded, with uncharacteristic shyness. "Yeah," he admitted. "Paul is good for me. Who knows what kind of a jerk I might have turned into if it weren't for his steadying influence? Why do you ask? Are you considering it? Is there someone—?"

"Me?" Now it was Hodel's turn to look embarrassed. "I'm still recovering from the shock of learning that sex can be done with a partner."

"Give me a break, Mikhail. You're a good-looking guy. Smart. Funny. Surely there's someone for you—ask HARLIE to do a match."

"I did. You don't want to know who he came up with."

"Who?"

"You don't want to know."

"Aww, come on—I showed you mine, you show me yours—who?"

"My ex," Hodel said sadly.

"Oh." And then, "Oh, dear." And then Easton looked at Hodel again, this time a little more sharply. Was that another one of Mikhail's little jokes? He still hadn't answered the question, had he?

"Hey!" Hodel sat up suddenly, peering forward into the access panel again, frowning in puzzlement. "What the hell—?"

Something was moving inside the panel. Something small. It came wiggling down the glowing curve of a light-pipe. It looked like a fluttering worm—not quite there. It seemed haloed with a crimson luminescence, almost a fluorescent glare.

Hodel blinked.

"I see it too," said Easton. "We'd better show it to Mr. Korie."

"Yeah."

Hodel fumbled for a moment at his belt. He produced a small transparent sample bag. Holding it open next to the light-pipe, he flicked the worm into it with the tip of a logic probe. The worm *trilled* angrily—a high-pitched sound that was *felt* more than heard. It was a piercing sensation in the ears. Hodel sealed the bag and laid it aside. Then he reached behind him for a cable tracer—a circular clamp. "All right. Let me just put a tracer on this pipe and see where it leads to, and then we'll take this thing to—" He was reaching up inside the panel when his expression suddenly changed. Puzzled. Then—"Owww! What the *phluck*—?!"

He yanked his hand back out of the access. There were several shiny red worms crawling across the back of his hand. Reflexively he tried to brush them off—they began *trilling* with a combined resonance that nearly paralyzed him with the pain. The sound was so loud that even Easton could feel it through his starsuit. And then it got *worse*. Louder. Hodel was screaming, writhing in the cramped space of the Communications Bay, trying to shake the worms off his hand. Easton leapt back, already calling to the *Star Wolf* and the rest of the mission team. "Mr. Korie—!" But before anyone could respond—

It didn't make sense—suddenly, there were more of them—a wet-looking mass of slippery red worms, shimmering with luminescence. They came sliding down out of the access panel—first a few, then more and more, a torrent, an avalanche—the sound of them was incredible! They flowed down and down and across the deck and across Hodel, who twisted and jerked and gasped, kicking his way backward out of the Communications Bay.

Easton leapt back, horrified—he unclipped his stinger beam from his belt, set it for spray and fired—the red worms exploded into clouds of wavicles—but not like the wavicles elsewhere on the vessel. These were bright crimson and enraged, they moved like piercing neon beams, zeroing straight back into Hodel's spasming body. Their angry buzzing was a wall of pain!

The worms were *flowing up* onto Hodel's body now, a squalling mass of luminous flickers. They flowed up the legs of his starsuit and over his waist, up into his open tunic—all writhing and glistening with an appalling wet sheen. Whatever they were, they moved in concert. Haloed in a blood-colored aura, they flickered with an unreal *not-quite-there* quality. They flowed into Hodel's underclothing, all over his chest and arms and up to his neck and toward his face, into his open mouth and his nostrils—into his eyes and ears! Hodel was no longer conscious— *he couldn't be conscious!*—but his body stretched and jerked and flung itself across the deck in spasmodic, galvanic movements.

Easton didn't know what to do. He fired again, triggering more explosions of crimson needles—furious wavicles! They pincushioned into Hodel in a dreadful implosion of light. Their sound pushed Easton backward like a slap to his body.

And now—finally—a great wet gooey mass of worms, churning and angry, came sliding, oozing, blubbering down out of the access panel. There was no end to them! A river of death! The multitudes flowed across the floor like living lava, sweeping up and over Hodel's still-writhing form, leaving only a ghastly lump in the glistening mass. A lump that screamed and rolled in pain. The worms, the dreadful *bloodworms*, spread out across the deck, rolling and roiling like angry fire leaping across space—

And in the middle of it, the lump sat up, clawing, shouting—"Hmlp mf!! Dmpf smmfinf!"—grabbing and reaching, until the tiny red creatures pulled it down again, rending it into gobbets of ghastly wet movement—

Easton kept backing, backing away, horrified. He managed to gasp, "God forgive me!" and raised his weapon up, dialing it to its strongest setting. And then he fired, blasting at the horror again and again, as if he were washing it away with a hose. Wherever the stinger beams touched, the bloodworms exploded, again and again—the fire filled the air—the lights were everywhere—he kept on firing—until Hodel's desperate screams were finally drowned out by the twinkling, crackling, roar of the bloodworms. And still the worms continued to pour wet and slithery out of the access panel—like a vast red carpet of flame, they rolled toward Easton—up the corridor toward the Bridge—he turned and ran—

Korie and Bach came scrambling through the hatch from the Command Deck, skidding to a horrified halt—

Decision

Korie had to grab Easton from behind and yank him backward—pulling him back into the Bridge, onto the Command Deck. Bach hit the panel, sealing the hatch, just before a roiling wave of slithering worms broke against it.

Their momentum carried them forward and sideways and forward again, until the three of them tumbled down the ladder onto the Ops Deck below. They hit the deck and bounced, banging their helmets against the rubbery surface, and still kept scrambling backward in panic, until Berryman and Shibano pulled them to their feet.

"Did you see that?" Berryman cried. "What the hell was that?"

"Bloodworms," Korie admitted. "The whole ship is infested with plasmacytes. Bloodworms." *There. He'd said it.*

"Oh, God, no—"

"They got Hodel!" Easton was gasping, choking on his words. "Hodel! Those bastards! They got Hodel! We were just talking—just finishing up—and all of a sudden, they came out of the wall! They came out of the wall! And there wasn't anything he could do! They were all over him! There wasn't time! I tried—I fried them, but they exploded! They exploded! They turned into red fire! Oh, God, they got Mikhail!" And then, his voice breaking, "I didn't know what else to do. I couldn't help him. He was screaming. I had to . . . I'm sorry! I didn't know what else to do! I couldn't save him! They were all over him, so I . . . I . . ."

Berryman grabbed him, held him by both shoulders, stared into his face, helmet to helmet. Their faceplates touched. "Danny! Listen to me! Danny! It's all right! I'm here! You're all right! You can stop now! You did all right! You did good!"

"Listen!" said Shibano, cautiously approaching the hatch. He held up a hand to the others.

Still in their suits, they froze—and listened.

The muted noise of the bloodworms could be heard rising—a kind of muffled chorus in the bulkheads all around them. The sound was horrible.

"That explains the unknown life readings that HARLIE picked up. They were coming through the bulkheads, the decks, the overhead—"

Berryman stopped in mid-word and looked up nervously. "Let's get out of here," he suggested.

"To where?" asked Bach.

"Will that hatch hold?" Korie pointed.

"It's a Class-A security hatch," said Shibano. "It had better."

"Or what?"

"Or—I'm going to complain to the manufacturer."

Korie remembered where he was then—a voice was yammering in his ear—Goldberg's. "Korie! Acknowledge! Acknowledge now, *goddammit!*"

"Acknowledge. Acknowledge. We're all right!" Korie said quickly. "Take a breath, Goldie. Take two." He paused to take his own advice, checking around to see if the remaining members of the mission team were all right. Easton was still badly shaken—and Bach was ashen. Berryman and Shibano had their rifles charged and were standing at position. He looked at his helmet display, checked his own health, then read the displays of the others as well. Heartbeats and respiration were elevated. All of them. To be expected. To the *Star Wolf*, he said, "Did you get any of that?"

"We got it all. Captain saw it. We're reviewing our options now."

"You're reviewing your options—?" Korie's astonishment was evident. "Excuse me?"

Parsons came on then. "Stand by, Mr. Korie. The chief medical officer, the chief of security and myself are having an argument. I haven't decided yet whether to shoot Commander Brik."

"You want my opinion?"

"I already know your opinion. But you're over on the *Norway*, and if I shoot him I'll have to do the paperwork myself. I'm about to violate a standing order. Before I do that, I need to know if our security officer is going to cooperate or attempt mutiny. Stand by."

Parsons turned to Williger and Brik. They were still in the Officers' Mess. Cappy and Armstrong still held their rifles aimed at Commander Brik. Williger had a work station powered up and processing.

But there were no secrets anymore; the crew had seen it now. And she'd said it all on an open channel. Just as well. The ship's complement needed to know what was happening. The truth might be dismaying—but uncontrolled rumors running down the keel of the ship would be even more destructive.

"Dr. Williger? I need an answer."

The chief medical officer shook her head grimly. "I don't like it, but—"

She rapped the display in front of her with her knuckles. "HARLIE thinks they were onto something. They were on station for nine months without incident. The failure of their safeguards—it might not have been accidental."

"Go on."

"We know that the plasmacytes can be contained with repulsor fields. We know that their security gear was fail-safe. And we know that they were equipped with a Class-9 power core, so they could have maintained repulsor strength indefinitely. So if the bugs got out, either somebody was stupid, careless or . . . suicidal. The fail-safes should have protected against stupidity and carelessness. If it was deliberate . . . it couldn't have been done without the knowledge of the LENNIE unit, so the record should be in the autonomic log." She sat down at the table, directly opposite Brik. She glanced up at him with visible exhaustion. "My point is, we know that their security *worked* for nine months before it broke down, so maybe the breakdown wasn't an accident."

"Go on," Parsons prompted.

Williger took a breath. "I'm not comfortable with this, Captain."

"None of us are."

"No, I mean—I've done triage before. But in every previous situation where we had to make decisions about who should live or who should die, there was a medical logic to it. The same logic doesn't apply here. This is the logic of infection—and fear. And it's a whole different game. I've been going through this material as fast as it comes across. And you were right. They made some significant advances here. Not a cure, not yet—at least not in anything I've seen—but they were experimenting with various plasmacyte-inhibitors, and some of them worked in test-tube situations, and I can't help wondering what else there is in these files. Maybe there *is* something here. It's possible they even completed their goals. I'd like the chance to keep looking—and keep hoping—for a while longer."

"Go ahead," said Parsons. "Convince me."

"Two reasons. First, if someone did deliberately release these things on the *Norway*, then it had to be in response to something. Maybe it was because someone did make a breakthrough in treatment. And second, I want to keep hoping, because . . . just because. I'm only human."

"If they made a breakthrough in treatment, why didn't they use it on themselves?"

"Maybe they need a clean environment to evacuate to. Maybe they keep getting reinfected. I need time here, Captain."

"Time is what we don't have, Dr. Williger. We've got less than thirty hours of repulsor power aboard the *Star Wolf* and only three days until the *Norway* hits a wall of flame. It doesn't matter how much time you need, Doctor; that's all the time you have."

Williger nodded. "If we can implement equal or better security, we might just be able to get our people off that ship—that would buy us some more time to study the logs."

"And then what?" demanded Brik. "Then we have plasmacyte-infected individuals aboard this starship, in violation of a standing order."

"Mr. Brik," Molly Williger stood up and faced him coldly. She was a short woman—very short—so much so that she was often mistaken for a dwarf. She stared up at Brik's three-meter height and *glowered* at him. "I do not appreciate being interrupted. It is *nyet kulturny*. It is extremely bad manners. And considering that you are already treading the border-line of insubordination, not to mention mutiny, I respectfully request that you keep that big ugly hole in the front of your face properly closed until you learn how to use it appropriately."

Without looking to see if Brik was obeying—she took it for granted that he would—Williger turned back to Parsons. "The other thing we might try is for me to go aboard the *Norway* and try to implement a treatment there and evacuate them back here—but if the treatment doesn't work, we still risk infecting the *Wolf*—"

"Doctor, talk straight with me. Is there a chance to save our people or not?"

Williger sighed. "Half an hour ago, I would have said no. Now, I'm not so sure." She met Parson's gaze unashamedly. "I'd hate to spend the rest of my life with the knowledge that there was something we could have tried and didn't."

Parsons didn't answer. She turned away and stared at the display on Williger's workstation. She needed to make a decision now. She couldn't wait any longer. She looked up at Brik. "Do I have to shoot you?"

"I doubt you could succeed," he said. "But that's not the question you're really asking. What you want to know is whether or not I will cooperate with a rescue attempt if you order it. Captain, this ship has a history of surviving situations where certain destruction was inevitable. Sooner or later, I expect the law of averages to catch up with us. So it is part of my job to urge caution, because caution is always the best survival tactic—except in situations when it isn't. Unfortunately in *this* situation, caution also equates to cowardice, and, regrettably, I have been around humans long enough to have been infected with some human ways of thinking."

"And your point *is* . . .?" Parsons prompted.

"I would rather die following the foolishly reckless orders of a human captain than be known as a cautious Morthan."

Parsons stared at Brik for a moment, trying to figure out if he was joking or serious. But then, Morthans never joked, did they? So she accepted the statement at face value. "Thank you for that vote of confidence, Commander Brik. Dr. Williger, proceed with your best option. Security, you're relieved. Now, let's get back to the Bridge."

Escape

Security Officer Daniel Easton leaned over a scorched console and wept softly to himself. Medical Tech Paul David Berryman came over and stood beside him. He put one hand on his partner's shoulder, a carefully calculated response—when what he really wanted to do was just wrap him up in his arms and hold him tight forever.

"I couldn't stop them, Paul! Every time I fired, they just got angrier! They just kept coming! I couldn't save him! You didn't see it—"

Berryman moved his hand to the back of Easton's neck. He wished he could reach through the starsuit and massage the muscles of his back; he could sense the tightness just by Easton's posture alone; but this would have to do. After a moment more, he reached across and took Easton's left wrist and turned it so he could read the monitors there.

"I'm all right," said Easton, pulling his arm back. "I'll be all right."

"I didn't say you weren't, but as senior medical officer on this team, I have a responsibility to make sure." He reached out and gently took Easton's wrist again. He held his partner's hand tightly in his own while he studied heart and respiration rates. He leaned his head in close so their helmets were touching, and whispered, "Just take it one breath at a time, Danny. I'm right here. Just like always. Okay?"

But before Easton could reply, Wasabe Shibano's voice filtered through both their helmets. "Oh, no—"

Shibano was pointing toward the hatch they'd all just tumbled through. "Mr. Korie!"

Three red worms were crawling down from the top of it. They flickered in scarlet—an unholy haze of light.

"Stay back!" cautioned Easton, but Korie was already stepping forward. "How the hell—?"

There were pinpoint holes in the hatch. As he watched, another and another of the shimmery red worms came burrowing *through* the foamed-carbon/polymer surface.

"Captain?" Korie said. "They're coming through the hatch. Do you copy?"

"We've got it onscreen," Parsons acknowledged. "Stand by."

Brik's voice cut in then: "Scanners show the whole forward section of the ship is heavily infested. They're moving toward you. Return to the transfer tube *now*. We're taking you off."

"You can't—"

"Listen to me," said Brik. "We can do this. You're not coming back into the *Star Wolf*. You'll stay in the transfer tube. We'll break away from the *Norway* and come around aft. We'll put you back aboard her through the aft airlock—on the other side of her repulsor fields. If there are any survivors, that's where they have to be."

Korie said, "Captain Parsons? I strongly advise against this. The risk to the ship—"

"—is minimal. We'll focus the repulsor valves to our side of the tube."

"There's no need for this, ma'am."

"Yes, there is. Spare me the phony heroics. I need you where you can do the most good."

"Brik—you can't let her do this."

"She threatened to shoot me."

"*So what*? When has a threat like that ever stopped you?"

Parsons voice came through loud and clear: "This is an *order*, Commander Korie." She added, "Listen to me. Dr. Williger thinks there might be a way—a way to rescue you. And any survivors on the *Norway*. She thinks they may have found a treatment. You've got to go around and find out."

Korie looked to the other members of the mission team—and then to the Class-A Security Hatch. A stream of little red bloodworms was already dripping down its surface—the first trickle of a scarlet waterfall. Korie started to object, then abruptly he surrendered. "Aye, aye, Captain. We're on our way." *I've made too many mistakes, too many! I've lost Hodel!* To the team, he snapped, "Move out." He waved them out. "Come on, let's go! Now!!"

Once the decision was made, there was no hesitation. The team tumbled down through the Fire Control Bay, to the keel—there were bloodworms in the corridor! And sparkles too! They scrambled forward through the flickering air, to the promise of the airlock at the end of the keel. Their boots pounded hard on the rubbery surface of the deck, scattering even more sparkles.

Quickly, they reentered the airlock, a flurry of firefly pinpoints swirling in with them. Korie was the last one through the hatch, and he popped it shut behind him. "Let's go, let's go, let's go!" Korie sounded like a drill instructor. Bach was already punching for emergency transfer and as soon as the aft hatch slammed, the forward hatch popped open.

The five surviving members of the mission team pushed into the transfer tube—hard against the repulsor fields. It was harder going back, they were swimming upstream now and the current was against them. The thickened air was a wall of resistance, but Korie put his shoulder against Shibano and pushed, and Shibano put his shoulder against Easton and pushed. Easton put his shoulder against Berryman and pushed. Berryman pushed Bach forward, and the whole team pushed *uphill* through the repulsors. The railings doubled as ladders. They climbed through an invisible avalanche of tar. It was exhausting work, and they pulled themselves in silence, punctuated only by gasps and curses. Behind them, the twinkling wavicles drifted away, pushed inexorably backward to lodge against the aft hatch of the *Norway*'s airlock.

Bach was in the lead. She climbed as far up the transfer tube as she could, grunting and swearing under her breath with an astonishing range of expression. She didn't care who heard. Finally, gasping in exhaustion, she secured herself, clipping her safety line to a loop in the railing. She gabbed Berryman and pulled him up next to her, holding him until he secured his safety line as well. One by one, they pulled the members of the team as far up the transfer tube as they could. One by one each of them secured his safety line.

"All right, *Star Wolf*, we're secured in the transfer tube." Almost before Korie had finished saying it, the compressed-air latches at the end of the tube popped open and the *Star Wolf* lurched backward, away from the *Norway*—almost a physical act of revulsion and disgust.

The air fled the transfer tube in one quick gust—just another thump, almost unnoticeable in the gelatin current of the repulsors—but the vacuum hardened their starsuits and now their voices were carried by electronics alone. The optical transceivers on their suits communicated across a broad spectrum of light, listening and speaking and recording each other's information, and constantly relaying it back to the *Star Wolf*.

All of them were experienced with hard vacuum—but even so, it never lost its power to amaze. This was as close to raw space as any human could ever achieve. As one, they all turned to gape downward out the empty end of the transfer tube. It felt like they were clinging to the inner walls of a bottomless well. Were it not for their lifelines, it would have been too easy to go tumbling down and out—pushed to their doom by the repulsors.

As the *Star Wolf* pulled away from the *Norway*, they saw the other ship as a red-tinged spearhead, dark against the stars—incredibly clear and close. But its running lights were off and it looked dead. Other than that, there was no external evidence of the horror within.

As the *Star Wolf* began its turn, the *Norway* slid sideways and disappeared, replaced by a moving panorama of darkness and stars at the gaping end of the transfer tube.

Out here, the stars were hard and bold, incredibly distant and pinpoint bright. They hinted at meanings so grand and awesome that, even glimpsed like this, they were still overwhelming. The sensation of falling, of being pushed, became even more intense.

And then, abruptly, the view below was filled with flame—savage and bright, a terrifying floor of hell, a crimson flood of light that welled upward like surging lava—the distant surface of the giant red star. The members of the mission team flinched and recoiled—as much from the glare as from the suddenness of the ferocious vista. It took an achingly long time for the starship to sweep across the wall of flame. Impossibly, it seemed to fill more than 180 degrees of arc—the way the star was stretched out of shape, it was a believable illusion.

And the whole time, the repulsors continued to press against them, pushing them down toward the flames.

Then, blessed darkness again. Blessed relief. And stars, quiet stars. The team waited in silence, listening to ship noises and chatter through their communicators. As their eyes adjusted, they looked for telltale twinkles. There were none—none that they could see, at least—the repulsors had driven them backward out of the transfer tube. But they didn't know how secure their starsuits were; it was likely—inevitable— that each of them had been penetrated by the wavicle form of the creature. And even now, there were probably pinpoint worms, growing within their bloodstreams.

How much time do we have? Korie wondered. *Is this another fool's errand?* There was only one consolation—*at least, I can't make any more mistakes. I won't kill anyone else after this.* He sipped at the water-nipple inside his helmet. *I'm sorry, Mikhail. I'm sorry—*

A change in the light caused him to look up. The aft end of the *Norway* had appeared beyond the end of the transfer tube. It grew slowly as they approached.

The external framework of the transfer tube extended; its latches opened, ready to grab the contact ring surrounding the *Norway's* aft airlock. The hatch grew larger and larger until it filled their entire view. And then there was a solid *thunk*—a feeling more than a sound—as the latches grabbed the contact ring. The transfer tube extended and mated.

Panels blinked green and air flooded back into the tube. And with the return of sound—real sound, not filtered electronic sound—Korie felt his tension easing.

They had a place to go. Maybe it was safer than the place they'd been, but at least they weren't going to die alone in space. At least that much was assured now.

It wasn't much, but it was something.

Cargo Bay

"We have acquisition," Brik reported.

"Commander Korie, you may reboard the *Norway*," said Captain Parsons. She turned to Williger. "Anything?"

Williger didn't even look up from the display she was reading—she was using Korie's station on the Command Deck. "I've found the medical log. This is fascinating stuff. Really fascinating." Then, realizing that her words and her enthusiasm were completely at odds with the seriousness of the situation, she apologized. "Sorry. But it is fascinating. See, look—there are two forms to the creature: the wavicle and the bloodworm. The wavicle is like a seed or a spore; but it's unstable. It's like most forms of *smart energy*. It maintains itself by feeding off light. If there's no light, it drops a quantum level and becomes a particulate form. But in that form, it's always looking for an energy source so it can boost itself back up to the wavicle state. Now, here—this is where it gets deadly—living flesh is transparent to the wavicle form, but when the wavicle enters a living body, there's not enough light to feed it, not the right frequencies of light, so it becomes particulate—and it's trapped inside. The particulate looks for fuel to return to wavicle form, so it starts feeding off elements in the blood, any kind of energy it can release: blood sugar, oxygen, hemoglobin, whatever. But that's still not enough energy in the blood for it to make the leap back to wavicle, so all it can do is breed more particulates—bloodworms. Hungry bloodworms. Hit them with a stinger beam or scan them, there's the energy they need—they explode, you get wavicles. The sudden torrent of energy kicks most of the particulates back up a level. This is amazing stuff, Captain—you could win a Heinlein Prize for Medicine just for tracing the whole life cycle. I wonder how such a creature even evolved. That's the real question here."

"What about breaking the life cycle of the particulate form?" Parsons asked. "Can it be done?"

"To be honest . . ." Williger leaned back in her chair and ran both hands through her short-cropped hair. She swiveled to face the captain. "This is kind of like the mythical energy creature from your childhood fairy tales. It feeds on energy, positive or negative, it doesn't care which; it thrives on the tension between one state and another. The only way to kill it is to deprive it of energy. It can't survive silence. But you can't starve it without also killing the host. In fact, even killing the host is insufficient; these things will feed on the processes of decay. So there's no way to get it out of a living body. Except—"

"Go on," Parsons said. "Let's hear it."

"Well . . . according to these files, there might be a way to block the bloodworms from eating. It would be kind of like gluing their mouths shut. But if the folks onboard the *Norway* actually tried it, I don't have that information here. At least, I haven't found it yet."

Parsons had a quirk—a quirk that some officers called "the leadership quirk"—even when she knew the answer, she asked the question anyway, just to be certain. In this case, if there was an answer to be found, Williger would have said. Nevertheless, "Is there any chance—any indication that the information you need is there, but you haven't found it yet?"

Williger gave her *the look*.

"I *have* to ask," Parsons said without apology.

"As fast as HARLIE decrypts it and scans it, as fast as he assimilates it, as fast as he processes it, it shows up in the knowledge-array," Williger explained. "HARLIE has performed a cross-correlated, Skotak analysis of the data clusters, weighted for relevance to resolution. Right here in the middle, there's a block of data missing. A big block. You don't get those kinds of holes in a data cluster by accident. That means someone has deliberately destroyed or removed the relevant information. So far, we've found nothing that even points to the pathways into the blank area. It's a null-zone, empty as the rift—if we're going to find the answer, it's still aboard the *Norway*." She nodded forward.

Parsons followed her glance.

On the main display, the view from Korie's helmet was enlarged to theater-sized proportions. The mission team was moving forward out of the *Norway*'s airlock and into the Aft Reception Bay. The point of view bobbed and weaved with Korie's head movements. Even with processing to steady the movement, the effect was still vertiginous. The mission team moved through the redundancy hatch at the forward end of the airlock reception chamber and into the *Norway*'s Cargo Bay.

The view shifted first to the left, then to the right. Almost immediately, HARLIE's voice: "I count fifteen survivors, in various states of deterioration. I am matching them to their ID records now. Captain Albert Boyett is not among the survivors." This was followed by a strangled obscenity in some obscure language. Parsons ignored it.

On the display, she could see that the mission team had come through the hatch with weapons ready; five camera views fractioned the screen, and it looked like an assault. As they turned, as they surveyed the room, the separate images revealed the ragged condition of the survivors, revealed the team lowering their weapons in dismay. The people here were haggard, sick and dirty. Some wore medical jumpsuits, others were crew. There were no Quillas or Martians or other augmented beings here, only raw humanity—dying.

Berryman went immediately to the people in worst condition—they were lying on deck mats. He unclipped his scanner from his belt, then, after a brief hesitation, tossed it aside. Instead, he pressed his hands to each person's body and let HARLIE do a remote readout through the touch sensors in his gloves. Blood pressure, heart-rate, body temperature . . . it wasn't enough, but it would have to do. What he really needed was a whole other domain of information that could only be obtained by microscanner. But scanners made the wavicles go crazy. Easton and Shibano saw what he was doing and began making the rounds of the other survivors, also taking readings through HARLIE.

On the Bridge of the *Star Wolf*, Williger clucked to herself. She glanced back and forth between four different displays, muttering instructions to HARLIE the whole time. In the *Norway*, two men in medical jumpsuits approached Korie; one was portly with graying temples, and he looked eager—almost desperate—to talk. The other had a soldier's physique and a military bearing; he seemed untouched by the plasmacyte infection and he acted as if he were in charge. "Dr. Makkle Blintze and Commander Yonah Jarell," HARLIE whispered in Korie's ear.

Korie glanced from one to the other, doing that quick personal estimation that strangers always do upon first meeting. "Commander Jon Korie, Executive Officer, the *Star Wolf*," he said. "What's your situation here, gentlemen?" He made no move to take off his helmet.

Blintze, the heavyset man, answered. "We've lost the captain and most of the crew. All of our people are showing advanced plasmacyte infections. We've been sealed in here, five days."

"What happened?" Korie asked.

"Don't answer that," said Jarell quickly. To Korie, he said, "Commander Yonah Jarell, Fleet Preparedness Officer. This is Makkle Blintze, acting head of Project R. This is a need-to-know mission, Commander Korie. And you don't need to know."

Korie glanced to Jarell only briefly, then looked back to Blintze. In his starsuit, he felt equally detached from both men. But Jarell's quick assertion of authority annoyed him.

"Yes, I do need to know. Commander Jarell—did you violate the Regulan quarantine?"

"We were authorized to do so, Mr. Korie."

"So this was deliberate. Your mission was to determine methods of control and containment of plasmacytes." Korie looked from one to the other.

Blintze looked tired but quietly satisfied as well. "Yes, that's correct. And we accomplished our mission. We made a breakthrough. A genuine breakthrough!"

Korie glanced around the Cargo Bay, noting the infected and exhausted men and women of the *Norway's* crew. "Yes, it's obvious," he said dryly.

Blintze glanced nervously at Jarell, then said, "No, I mean it. It worked. We succeeded."

"I think that's enough—" Jarell said, trying to cut him off.

But Blintze refused to be silenced. To Korie, he continued. "We accomplished everything we set out to do. What we found is truly astonishing—"

"I said, *that's enough—*"

"No, Yonah, it isn't. We're running out of time here and we need some help." Turning back, Blintze went on. "We were ready to break orbit. Captain Boyett was worried about avoiding the star tip, but we were never in any danger from that. The important thing was that we'd broken the plasmacyte problem. But there was some kind of disagreement about what to do next. It involved the next phase of our mission, but before it could be resolved, we had a breakout. We initiated emergency containment procedures, but they didn't work. We swept the ship with repulsor fields, from stern to bow, over and over and over again. They slowed the infection down, but the plasmacytes still got through— they were in the crew's blood. They infected the entire ship. We tried everything. We tried to implement emergency triage, but—"

"That's enough, Blintze," Jarell cut him off; then realizing how harsh he sounded, he explained to Korie, "We had some incidents. They weren't pretty. We had to use . . . force."

"We had a *mutiny*," said Blintze. "A goddamned mutiny!" To Jarell, he said, "For God's sake—the man's on our side."

"How do you know that?" Jarell snapped back. "The Morthans could have captured a ship, outfitted it with slaves or renegades—they've done it elsewhere. They could have done it here." To Korie's pained look, he said, "Wouldn't you be suspicious?"

Korie didn't answer. He'd been suspicious since he'd first read the *Norway's* manifest.

Blintze spoke again. "There are only fifteen of us left, Commander. The *Norway* shipped out with 123. A little cramped, yes, but as you know, we had a Class-9 power core. We managed. We were excited about the challenge. We had a mandate to crack the bloodworm dilemma. We found out how the plasmacytes reproduce. They're not alive—they're not organic life—but they use organic processes to support the wavicle state. It's simply incredible. There's no limit to what this could mean—"

"Yes," said Bach, coming up to stand beside Korie. "We've seen." Her presence was as much to support Korie as anything else.

"Then you know you're infected," Blintze said, not hearing the dryness in her tone. "The spores are in your bloodstreams too. They can get through starsuits. We thought they couldn't, but we were wrong. We're going to have to reclassify the bioarmor rating of standard starsuits, you know. We'll have to increase the non-conductible quality of the polycarbon shielding—that'll stop the wavicles from penetrating. Or we can spray the suits with conductible filaments and run a nano-current. That'll attract them. Where there's a current, the wavicles can feed; that traps them. If you ground the current, it pulls the energy out of the wavicles and they go particulate—and the particulate disintegrates if you expose it to vacuum or supercold. They're more vulnerable in the wavicle form than is immediately obvious. It's the bloodstream problem that took longest to solve because of the damage to the host—"

"You have . . . an answer?" Korie couldn't bring himself to say the word *cure*. It would have been too much to hope for.

Blintze started to nod in enthusiastic agreement, but before he could explain, Wasabe Shibano stepped up to report. "Mr. Korie, the *Norway*'s repulsor fields—? No question, they're failing."

"Excuse me—" Korie said to Jarell and Blintze. He crossed the Cargo Bay to look forward through the starship's keel. At the far end, he could see a throbbing reddish glow. Through his feet, he could feel the deep heterodyning resonance of the repulsor lenses.

Bach and Shibano, Blintze and Jarell followed Korie; the four of them stood beside him and stared down the passageway too. "Wait here," said Korie. He advanced up the keel cautiously. He had barely taken a few steps before he began feeling the pressure of the repulsor fields, pushing him forward. They swept over him in waves. This intensely, the fields had the strength to overpower a man. Korie grabbed a handhold on the bulkhead and secured his safety line to it.

At the forward end of the corridor was a pulsating red *glow*. But he couldn't resolve the image. He set his helmet display to zoom and the image swelled alarmingly. The repulsor field was an uneven ochre haze, like waves of heat seen across a distance. On the other side of it was . . . a slithery bright carpet of bloodworms. All scarlet and crimson, they were on the deck, the walls, and dripping from the overheads. And clouds of wavicles filled the air. The red worms and the golden wavicles throbbed in unison to the beat of the repulsor fields. Every pulse swept visibly through the plasmacytes—successive waves of light that rippled the sparkling pinpoints and made the glistening wet bloodworms shudder and writhe and recoil.

"*Star Wolf?* Are you getting all this?"

"Yes, we are," replied Brik, without apparent emotion.

Korie cleared his helmet display back to normal. He unclipped his safety line and began pulling himself back through the corridor, aftward to the Cargo Bay. Handhold after handhold. He wasn't going to take any chances on being pushed into that mess—

He came into the Cargo Bay, arms wide. He guided everyone well away from the corridor hatch.

"They smell our blood," said Bach.

"Not quite, Lieutenant," Blintze corrected her. "They're attracted to the heat of our bodies, the energy of your starsuits, the various electronics we surround ourselves with—the life support systems and so on."

"Whatever," she said, unimpressed. "The effect is the same."

Shibano spoke now. "As the power to those fields weaken, Commander, the pulses are going to come slower and slower. Within a very short time, those fields will no longer be impermeable to the worms."

"How long?" asked Korie.

Shibano hesitated. He was checking with HARLIE. "Ten hours . . . maybe."

Risk Assessment

"That means you've got to start now!" Jarell said.

"Start what?" Korie was glad he was wearing a starsuit—even though it was an illusion, he liked the feeling of being isolated from this man.

"Our rescue, of course!"

"Excuse me?"

"Tell him, Blintze—"

Korie held up a hand. "*Star Wolf*? Are you following this?"

Parsons' voice came back quietly. "We're copying everything."

Korie turned to Blintze. "What have you got?"

Blintze produced a memory clip. He held it up. "It's a treatment."

"A cure?"

"That's probably the wrong word, but the effect is the same. We have a way to stop the bloodworms inside the body. We know it works—at least, we're pretty sure it works. We tried it, more than once, and yes, it worked; but the patients kept getting reinfected, so we don't know for sure if it works a hundred percent."

Korie took the clip from Blintze, turning it over thoughtfully in his gloved hand.

"Be careful. That's the only copy. We stripped it out of the *Norway's* log. And there's a self-destruct on that clip."

"Couldn't have that falling into the wrong hands," Jarell muttered.

"No, of course not," Korie agreed. "A cure for the most deadly disease in the galaxy has to be kept secret." He said it with a straight face. He handed the clip back to Blintze. "Take the self-destruct off, and I'll upload it to the *Star Wolf*. Dr. Williger will have to analyze it, and Captain Parsons will have to authorize any attempt at rescue. You realize that what you're asking—demanding—is a violation of a standing order."

"With this information," Jarell said, "the order becomes irrelevant."

"I hope you're right," Korie replied. "But it's still the captain's decision." He accepted the clip back from Blintze and snapped it into place in his chest panel. Almost immediately, his suit display began flashing with information. HARLIE was sucking the data out of the clip as fast as the optical links could carry it. Several seconds passed, and then the display cleared. *Transfer completed.*

"HARLIE?"

"I'm analyzing the data structures," came the reply. "It looks promising. Captain Parsons and Dr. Williger are examining the procedures."

Korie looked to Blintze, then to Jarell. He wasn't going to let himself hope. Not yet. But he could see it in the others' eyes. He turned away and whispered, "HARLIE? Can you patch me into the Bridge discussion?"

Almost immediately, Williger's voice was murmuring in his ear. "If this is correct, there is a chance, Captain."

"But there's no assurance that the procedure is a hundred percent effective, is there?"

Williger hesitated. "No, there isn't."

"I'll need risk assessment. HARLIE?"

HARLIE's voice was bland. "I have no referents against which to measure this situation. Risk analysis may be inaccurate, Captain."

"Go ahead, HARLIE."

"We're looking at several specific procedures, here, all of them complementary. Each one attacks a separate part of the problem. There is sufficient overlap of functionality that whatever elements one process doesn't address another one will. Nevertheless, as Dr. Williger has pointed out, we have no evidence of a hundred-percent effectiveness. Theoretically, I can endorse the possibility of total effectiveness—"

"HARLIE, if I wanted someone to beat around the bush, I'd hire a lawyer."

"Risk assessment is useless without context, Captain. You need to understand the problem I'm having in making this analysis. With most viral or bacterial infections, the risk of disease is determined by the depth of exposure. A few strands of viral material, a few bacterial cells are not enough to infect an individual; with many diseases, the body can flush even the most toxic material if the exposure is small enough. Such may not be true with plasmacytes. A single wavicle within the bloodstream may be enough to trigger the whole process. The body has no apparent defenses. The one hope we do have is that the transitions between wavicle and particulate states are brittle; the process fails more often than it succeeds; the wavicle winks out or the particulate disintegrates. That's the weakness in this bug. So we may not need the process to be completely effective. Total decontamination might be achievable by exploiting the plasmacyte's own fragility."

"And . . .?"

"With all the information currently at hand, I would estimate a sixty-percent chance of effectiveness. With additional safeguards, which I will discuss with Dr. Williger, it's possible to boost that to seventy-five percent."

Parsons was silent. Listening to her, Korie could almost imagine the expression on her face. He spoke up then. "Captain, if HARLIE's numbers are accurate, there's one chance in four—*per patient*—that you'll infect the *Star Wolf*. That's too big a risk. There's twenty of us over here. Infection of the *Wolf* is inevitable."

"If you're talking about random happenstance," Parsons replied, "then yes, infection of the *Wolf* is inevitable. But we're not talking about chance occurrences here. We're talking about the intention and commitment of human beings with something at stake."

"With all due respect, Captain—"

"With all due respect, Commander Korie—let me ask you something. You're an expert on hyperstate engines, are you not?"

"Yes, ma'am."

"Is hyperstate injection a zero-defect process?"

"If by that, you mean the process is intolerant of error, yes it is a zero-defect process."

"But we use hyperstate anyway?"

"Yes, ma'am. We surround the process with enough fail-safes, back-ups, triple-checks and calibrators that the statistical possibility of initiating a hyperstate envelope in an error-state is somewhere south of null."

"And how do we do that?"

"We bag the whole process—we put it in a contextual clean room."

"My point exactly, Mr. Korie. What we're dealing with here is just another zero-defect, error-intolerant process. We will put it in a bag of security measures as tight as those surrounding a hyperstate injection."

"It sounds good in theory, ma'am—"

"HARLIE?"

"I have no referents on which to base an analysis."

"Dr. Williger, set it up. HARLIE, I'll want go/no-go points for every step of the procedure."

Korie heard Brik's voice then— "Is that your decision, Captain? That we will attempt a rescue?"

"Yes, Commander Brik, that is my decision."

A pause. A whole conversation of silence. Captain Parsons was effectively ending her career. No matter what the outcome here, even if the rescue were successful, even if the information brought back was sufficient to end the threat of bloodworms forever, she would still be guilty of violating a standing order and putting her crew at risk. Her court-martial was inevitable. The only question was, how many of her officers would be tried for complicity as well.

"Is there a problem, Commander Brik?"

"No, ma'am. What are your orders?"

Process

"If we inhibit the particulate form's ability to bind, we cut off its energy supply so it can't maintain itself," Williger explained enthusiastically. "If we do it in a suppressive resonance field, then the plasmacytes are held in a chaotic domain below the threshold of their wavicle state— which means we can scan for plasmacytes within the body without giving them the quantum kick into transformation. They'll try, but they won't be able to. They won't be able to hold either state. They'll fragment almost instantly. Thirty seconds. A minute."

Parsons looked at the schematic of the operation with a skeptical expression. "It sounds risky."

"We'll get toxic residue, yes. We'll have to push the patient through a series of concentric repulsor valves into a clean-room environment—I can do that in the Forward Airlock Reception Bay—and that'll give us three minutes for a full blood replacement."

"It sounds risky . . ." Parsons said again, hoping that this time the doctor would hear the concern in her voice.

But Williger was too enthralled. "We have to break the cycle between the particulate and the wavicle forms to disinfect a body. Once we do that, we can destroy both forms. The real problem is the immediate reinfection of the patient. They were using artificial blood on the *Norway*, which solved half the problem, but they didn't have a clean-room environment to move the processed patients into. And they didn't have a method to disinfect either."

"Maybe you didn't hear me, Doctor. I said, 'it sounds risky.' It sounds *very* risky."

"Yes, Captain. I heard you. It is risky. And time is critical every step of the way. We'd have less than three minutes to make the transfusion—or we start damaging the patient—but it's doable. I've got my people drilling now. The Quillas. The Black Hole Gang. Brian Armstrong. We've been working with simulator dummies . . ."

Captain Parsons turned to Dr. Williger and lowered her voice. "Is this a zero-defect process, Molly?"

"Don't ask me, Captain. Ask HARLIE. He designed the process with multiple redundancies."

Parsons nodded. "All right. Get your team into position, ready to go. But Doctor—I'm still not convinced. This isn't an authorization yet."

Williger acknowledged with a nod, then turned away to speak quietly into her headset.

Parsons pulled her own headset back on. "Mr. Korie?"

"Korie here."

"Have you examined Dr. Williger's proposal?"

"We're going over it now, Captain."

"Do you see any problems with it on your end."

"No, Captain, I don't. Physically, we can manage the process." He added, "But my original concerns still remain. Despite HARLIE's assurances, I don't believe this is a zero-defect process."

"Your back itches?"

"My bloodstream itches, Captain—"

"You'd rather die than take this chance?"

"I'd rather die than be responsible for the deaths of any more crew, Captain."

"An honorable position, Commander Korie. But as I've already climbed way out on this limb, I think you should climb out here with me. It's an interesting view."

"I suppose I should be grateful, ma'am, but as I said—I disagree with this decision. I *strongly* disagree."

"So noted. Overruled."

"Captain, with all due respect, I believe I should refuse to follow your orders."

"And if you do, I'll have you court-martialed on a charge of mutiny. Posthumously, of course."

"That's not exactly a compelling threat, you know."

Parsons hesitated. "I know your record, Mr. Korie. I know what happens when captains disagree with you." She said that last with a slight grin. "Tell me, have you ever been wrong?"

"Yes, Captain Parsons—I have been wrong. I've been wrong about almost everything on this particular mission so far. And it cost us the death of Mikhail Hodel. I would very much like to be wrong again, Captain. I really do not want to be right on this one. It's just too dangerous."

"Well, y'know, Jon. You could be on a streak. If you've already been wrong about everything else, then the odds are that you're wrong about this one too."

"Captain, it's *too* dangerous. You can't take the risk."

"Well . . ." Parsons said with finality. "It just so happens that I have an itch of my own. And my itch doesn't agree with your itch. And because I'm the captain, we'll go with my itch, not yours. That's an order."

"Just one question, ma'am?"

"Yes?"

"What is Mr. Brik's position?"

Brik answered for himself. "The same as yours. It's a damn fool idea. And we're probably not going to survive. But I have sworn an oath to follow the orders of my captain. And so have you. So stop wasting our time and get on with the job."

"Thank you, Mr. Brik." Korie nodded to himself; he would have expected nothing less from the Morthan officer. He took a breath. All right, he'd done his duty. "Captain Parsons, I'll ready the mission team." But as Korie turned to Bach, he found Jarell and Blintze standing at his elbow. They were holding a starsuit helmet up between them—they'd been listening to the entire conversation.

Now, Jarell spoke, "Captain? Captain Parsons?"

The Captain's voice came back, filtered through the communicator. "Go ahead, Mr. Jarell."

"Captain, you'll have to rescue Blintze and myself first."

"I beg your pardon?"

Jarell was unembarrassed. "There's a Fleet Regulation. Order Number 238—"

"I know the order."

"Then you know that it mandates that in situations of dire emergency, critically important Fleet personnel must be rescued first."

Bach snorted in contempt. "Right. 'Women and children last.'"

Jarell barely glanced at her. "You said something, Lieutenant?"

Korie interrupted both of them. To Parsons, he said, "Captain, there are people here in very bad shape."

"I'm sorry, Mr. Korie. Commander Jarell has precedent on his side. Whatever he and Blintze know about the plasmacytes is too important to risk losing."

"Yes, Captain." He kept his tone noncommittal; Captain Parsons would recognize the implied disapproval.

On the Bridge of the *Star Wolf*, Parsons looked at the forward display, studied the images of Jarell and Blintze there. She said softly, "I understand *exactly* how you feel, Mr. Korie." She pulled her headset off and turned to her left. "Dr. Williger—" She looked around abruptly. "Where's Williger?"

"She's at the forward airlock," said Brik.

"Commander Tor, you have the conn. Brik, come with me." And she disappeared down through the access to the Fire Control Bay and the keel.

Forward Airlock Reception Bay

Parson strode forward angrily, followed by Brik, who actually had trouble keeping up with her. Parts of the corridor were less than three meters high and he had to crouch low to get through.

They stepped through a series of sealed hatches and arrived at the Forward Airlock Reception Bay—identified by large block letters on the bulkhead as FARB—to find Williger readying a crash cart and a makeshift Med Bay. She was wearing a starsuit—all she needed was the helmet. She had two robot-gurneys collapsed and ready; all their sidebar equipment was blinking green. Several Quillas stood by, either preparing equipment or testing it—or putting on starsuits of their own.

Chief Engineer Leen and the Black Hole Gang were installing a set of field-lenses throughout the length of the reception bay and the airlock. The Martian arrived from somewhere aft, rolling a rack of plastic bottles containing artificial blood; he was a small, ugly creature of indeterminate description, but he was thorough. He pushed the rack into place beside an ominous-looking operating table and then disappeared aft again.

Williger was everywhere, bustling from one station to the next, loading equipment and supplies onto the gurneys, directing others to do the same. "HARLIE? I need this gurney programmed *now*."

"Both gurneys have been programmed, Dr. Williger," HARLIE said quietly. "But I cannot activate the programs without Captain Parsons' authorization."

Williger started to swear; turning around she bumped into the captain. "Oh, good—you're here. Tell HARLIE to let go of the damn gurneys."

"Dr. Williger—"

"You said get ready. I'm getting."

"I haven't made my decision yet—"

"Well, you'd better make it soon. We're running out of time."

"I won't be stampeded, Molly—" Parsons grabbed the doctor by the arm and pulled her physically backward, back into the keel, and into an access leading to the ship's farm; Brik followed at a distance, primarily to keep anyone else from approaching the two. "Listen to me. I know how

108

you ended up on this ship, I know why. I know where you should have been sent instead. It took some digging, but I found out. If you're trying to redeem yourself—or if you're going after a Heinlein Prize here—"

"Is that what you think this is about?" Williger shot back. "Awards? Redemption?"

"You're in a starsuit, Doctor. Where the hell do you think you're going?"

"Captain, we have a better understanding of this problem than we've ever had before. Sooner or later, someone is going to have to take this chance. *If not here, where? If not now, when?*"

"And what if you're wrong?"

"What if I'm right?"

"I'm not convinced that we can do this safely—neither is Mr. Korie."

"He talked you out of it?"

"He expressed concerns—"

Williger nodded. "We all agreed that we would put a security bag around the entire operation. You've seen the preparations. HARLIE will be monitoring every step of every procedure. What do you think we're missing? What else do you want us to do? Paint ourselves blue? Chant a prayer to Saint Mortimer? Stand on one foot? Captain, don't do this. Don't dither. There comes a moment when you have to make a decision—and you and I both know that you've already made *this* decision."

Before Parsons could answer, the entire starship began to vibrate; a note like one struck from a gigantic gong resonated through the polycarbonate hull of the vessel, it sang through their bones—and straight through their souls. Even as they paused, a deeper sound added itself, and then a darker, deeper note underneath the first two. Like the floor of the universe rumbling. It was the combined throbbing of multiple repulsor fields, a heterodyning pressure.

From somewhere ahead came Leen's ecstatic shout, "Gotcha!" And then, "The fields are up, Doctor. You can proceed any time."

Parsons turned back to Williger. "Listen to me, Doctor—up until this moment, it was all a . . . a drill. A dry run. An exercise. A thought experiment. But the minute that we bring one of those gurneys back aboard this ship with a patient on it, it's no longer pretend. We're committed. Up until this moment, I've always had the option of backing out. And I've held onto that possibility as desperately as a life-preserver. Because the minute I give the order to go ahead, I'll be ordering something that no other ship has ever survived. So I don't care how tight a bag you've put this operation in, Doctor. I have to look at this situation from more than one perspective. It's not just about saving Korie and the mission team; it's about saving everyone onboard *this* ship too. And if that's dithering, then so be it."

She stepped out of the access and back into the keel, only to come face-to-face with Chief Engineer Leen. He was carrying several rolls of optical cable and field arrays. He nodded courteously. "Everything is working. In addition to the repulsor fields already installed in the transfer tube, we've got four more repulsor valves in the airlock. That gives us seven concentric barriers. Once we begin processing, we're going to be opening and closing a lot of hatches in a hurry, so we're going to be totally dependent on the fields. You've got two hours of power and some change, maybe three max. Dr. Williger says she can do the job in that time, but you don't have a lot of margin for error."

Standing behind Parsons, Williger said, "It'll take less than a minute to neutralize the plasmacytes in each person's blood, but we'll give them ninety seconds to be sure. As soon as the scan comes up green, the gurney will come back through the transfer tube and we'll connect the patient up for a high-speed blood replacement."

Parsons ignored the chief medical officer's lobbying. "Chief? What's your confidence on those fields?"

"Each valve will stop ninety-nine percent of the wavicles that hit it. Seven phased fields should give us a practical barrier. But . . ."

"But?"

"But . . . it's still theoretically possible that if a sufficient mass of wavicles were to assault the first valve, a few might make it all the way through to the last one. That's what HARLIE says."

"One would be enough, wouldn't it?" She looked to Williger.

"Theoretically, there would have to be 100 quadrillion wavicles hitting the first repulsor field for one to get through the last repulsor field."

"Yes," said Parsons. "*Theoretically*. There's that word again."

"Theoretically . . . yes. But I doubt there are 100 quadrillion wavicles on the *Norway*. HARLIE estimates maybe fifty quadrillion at most. They're flickering in and out of existence."

"Fifty quadrillion . . ." Parsons considered it. "That means half a wavicle could get through."

Leen wagged his head. "The odds are fifty-fifty."

"Can we increase the odds a little bit more?" Parsons asked.

"We don't have the power for more than seven repulsor fields."

"Shut down all nonessentials. Go to battery power—fuel cells?"

"We already have."

Parsons felt exasperated. "Mr. Leen—go work a miracle."

Leen met her gaze. "That's . . . that *was* Hodel's department. Hodel was our warlock." Then, embarrassed, he ducked his head and said, "Sorry."

Parsons looked from Leen to Williger, frustrated. She was looking for a reason to say yes. This wasn't it. She and Williger stared at each other, each one helpless in her own side of the dilemma.

"Captain?"

"I know."

"We're running out of time," said Leen.

"*They're* running out of time," corrected Williger.

Another long look between them. Parsons sighed. To Williger, she said, "I'll expect you to testify at my court-martial."

Without missing a beat, Williger asked, "For which side?"

"All right, Doctor. You win. Go make history." Parsons waved her forward. Brik looked to Parsons, a questioning expression on his broad features. Parsons nodded to him; Brik stepped over to the airlock control station and popped the hatch open. Williger spoke to her headset, giving the go-ahead command to the robot-gurney. The wheeled table rolled forward into the airlock; unfolding its arms and grabbing handholds along the way to steady itself against the insistent push of the repulsor fields. The air *crawled* across their skins.

"Captain?" Molly Williger called. "I want all nonessential personnel to evacuate this area now." *This means you.*

"Mr. Brik—" Parsons said. "Let's monitor this from the Bridge. They stepped back through the same series of hatches. As they moved aftward through the keel, back toward the Bridge, Parsons felt herself alone with her terribly complex feelings. She glanced sideways—and *up*—at Brik. Yes? You have something to say?

As if reading her mind, Brik said, "You should have killed her for insubordination . . ."

"We don't do that in this fleet."

"Stupid policy. Capital punishment slows down repeat offenders."

Parsons wasn't sure if Brik was joking or not. Morthans weren't famous for their sense of humor.

The last hatch popped open and Reynolds was waiting there. "Captain?"

Parsons was expecting him to step out of the way, but when he didn't, she looked at him annoyed. "Yes, Reynolds, what is it?"

"As you know, I'm the union representative."

"Is this official business?"

"I'm afraid so. I have to ask you . . . to not proceed with the rescue operation. I call your attention to Article Seven of the contract, the safety of the crew. I've been asked to . . . That is, the crew is concerned—"

"Afraid, you mean?"

"Whatever." Reynolds was unembarrassed. "Some of the crew are afraid that the *Star Wolf* will be infected. After all, if the *Norway*, with all of its precautions, could be infected, what protection do we have?"

Parsons allowed her annoyance to show. "This isn't a democracy, Reynolds. The crew doesn't get a vote. We're not abandoning our shipmates. Now go back to your station. Besides, I've already told the doctor to proceed."

Reynolds didn't answer immediately. Without taking his eyes from the captain's, he nodded knowingly, as if this was exactly what he'd expected. "I understand your position, Captain. I'll be logging a formal protest."

Parsons shook her head in wry amazement. A formal protest? "I'll help you fill out the paperwork," she replied. "Dismissed."

Unchastened, Reynolds stepped out of her way and she and Brik continued aft. As soon as she felt they were out of earshot, she said—to herself as much as to Brik—"A formal protest? Give me a break. If we survive, I'm going before a court-martial."

She glanced over, but the big Morthan's face was carefully blank.

"Y'know, you may have a point," she added. Brik raised an eyebrow in a question mark expression. "About policy."

"Oh," said Brik. "Would you like me to—?"

The captain sighed. "We're not Morthans. And we're not going to be. Not as long as I have anything to say about it."

Bedside Manner

A blue-white dwarf and a red giant circled each other off-center, a stately gavotte—but the dwarf was feeding off the giant, pulling long strands of fire out of its partner, wrapping them around itself in a spiral veil of flame. Distorted by its smaller partner's gravity, the crimson monster had flattened into an oblate spheroid, pulled outward in a teardrop shape.

Much smaller—much harder to find, were two tiny starships also linked together. Plunging toward the tongues of flame, they echoed the partnership of the stars—one of the vessels was trying to pull the fire out of the other—

Closer now—inside the Cargo Bay of the *Norway*, everything was suffused with the multiple deep tones of the repulsor fields—the uneven low warble of the *Norway's* failing barriers and the darker chords of the *Star Wolf's* multiple barriers.

Two robot-gurneys had come rolling across the link between the two ships, hatches slamming open before them, slamming shut behind them every meter of the way. They rolled into the *Star Wolf* airlock, into the transfer tube, through the repulsor fields, into the *Norway's* airlock and finally into the *Norway's* Cargo Bay.

Berryman knew what to do; Easton moved to help him. He ran a quick readiness-check on the gurney, just to satisfy himself that the trip through the repulsors hadn't altered any of its parameters. By then, the second gurney had come through the hatch, and he moved to check that one too. Before he had completed his status checks, Yonah Jarell was already climbing onto the first cart. Blintze stood, waiting uncomfortably by the second.

Berryman kept his feelings to himself. He patted the cushioned surface and said, "All right—get on." He turned back to the first medtable. The display there showed the level of Jarell's infection. Not as bad as it could have been. The man must have been in a protected area longer than the others. Berryman didn't wait for permission. He pulled open Jarell's tunic and began slapping monitors onto his chest, arms, neck and forehead. He picked up a surgical scissors and—ignoring Jarell's protests—methodically cut slits in the arms and legs of his jumpsuit. "You should have taken this off," he said as he worked. His expression was deadpan. Behind him, Easton was quietly helping Blintze undress and echoing Berryman's application of monitors. Additional sensors went on each man's belly, groin, legs and ankles.

"All right," said Berryman, blandly. He began strapping pressure clamps around Jarell's arms and legs and a brace around his head and neck as well. "Let's see if this works. This particular process has never been tested on human beings before. Thanks for volunteering to be the guinea pigs."

"The process works," said Jarell insistently but without total certainty.

"Whatever," Berryman replied, smiling and maintaining a courteous demeanor throughout. He unclipped a set of flexible hoses from beneath the table; each terminated in a pressure injector. "If it doesn't, we'll know soon enough." Berryman connected two pressure injectors to each of the clamps, then checked to make sure that all the tubes were free of kinks. "There are plasmacyte detectors mounted in the transfer tube. You'll be scanned. If we get a positive reaction, you'll get held in limbo, or bounced right back here—or dumped into space. Depending on the circumstance. The *Wolf* is prepared to sever the link at the first sign of discordancy."

"You're joking—" Jarell's eyes were wide.

"Nope. You can look at the design schematic—" Berryman pressed buttons on the table's display panel "—as soon as you get to the other side." The table began to hum with a note of its own, a suppressive resonance field. The wavicles in the air danced around it, flickering in and out of existence as if being tickled, teased and frustrated. Berryman noted the change in their behavior, then turned his attention back to the display. He watched calmly while the field stabilized. HARLIE whispered in his ear. Everything was fine. So far.

"*Star Wolf?*" Berryman asked. "Everybody ready?"

"It's a go," said Williger.

Berryman tapped buttons on the panel. "All right, here goes—one large pizza, with Martian anchovies." To Jarell, he said. "Sorry we can't sedate you. Too much risk. But this shouldn't hurt. Not too much anyway. We're pumping you full of plasmacyte goo. This will give the nasty old worms a very bad tummy ache. But because of the resonance field, they're not going to be able to turn into wavicles. So they'll disintegrate."

He backed away from the table so he could focus on the chart displays. "Son of a bitch! I'll be damned—it works. You should start feeling it any second now, kind of a tingly sensation, like pins and needles all over, only on the inside? And now it's getting worse, like a burning sensation all over—?"

Jarell's face was ashen. He was definitely feeling it.

"That should pass. Just when you think you're getting used to it, you should start feeling tired and out of breath—is that where you are now? Good. Beyond fatigue, right? Exhaustion? Like you're dying, except you don't have the strength to die? That's the bloodworms dying. See, this panel shows what the scanners are doing—that's the plasmacyte energy spike, right there. See how it's dropping? That's the good news. The bloodworms are disintegrating into toxic residue. That's the bad news. They're taking your red blood cells down with them. So your body isn't getting enough oxygen. That's why you're feeling out of breath. It's going to get worse—you'll probably start having CO_2 hallucinations too."

Berryman checked the monitors, then turned back to Jarell. "Relax, Commander. Everything is going fine. We have another seventy seconds to go. I'll be right back, don't go away." He turned crisply around to the other table, where Blintze lay waiting. Methodically, he double-checked Easton's handiwork, clucking in satisfaction. "We'll start you as soon as we get a green light from the *Wolf*. They're going to want to make sure that Commander Jarell survives before they risk anyone else." He said this just loud enough for Jarell to hear. "Don't worry, if this procedure doesn't work, we have a backup plan. Besides, the first pancake is always for practice. That's the one you give to the dog."

He checked his watch. "Whoops, here we go." He turned back to Jarell. The commander looked like he was about to pass out. "You should be feeling really bad right about now—mm, yes I see. Are you still conscious? Good. I wouldn't want you to miss the best part. Another twenty seconds. No, don't talk. Would you like me to count them down for you? No?" Berryman turned away from Jarell's eloquently terrified expression and studied the control panel on the gurney, clucking softly to himself. "*Star Wolf*, are you copying?"

"Ay-firmative."

"Do you think we should give this fellow an extra thirty seconds—just to be sure?"

"It's your call—just remember to leave us some time on the other end. We can hyperoxygenate, but there are limits."

"Did you hear that?" Berryman said to Jarell. "Nothing to worry about. They're working in a hyperoxygenated environment already—and in a minute, they'll be pumping fresh blood substitute into you. You'll be feeling almost back to normal within . . . I dunno, a week or two. Panel says you're clean, Commander. No more plasmacytes. All that's left is to push you through. Oops. Dropped my clipboard, just a minute—" He bent to retrieve his notepad, catching Korie's eye as he did so. The look of glee on his face was unmistakable.

"Ensign," Korie said quietly. "That's enough."

"Aye, aye, sir." Berryman straightened, his manner abruptly crisp and efficient. Jarell had passed out anyway, so any further performance would have been wasted. Berryman punched a control code into the panel; the medtable beeped and rolled aft toward the Airlock Reception Bay. The hatch popped open and the gurney slid smoothly in. "*Star Wolf*, you've got a package in the pipeline."

"We've got it."

The airlock hatch snapped shut. The gurney was on its way. Berryman glanced to Korie.

Korie's expression was bland. "Your bedside manner could use a little work."

"Dr. Williger says the same thing, sir."

"Well, she's right."

"Yes, sir. Sorry, sir. It won't happen again."

"See that it doesn't."

A Tide of Fireflies

The gurney wasn't sentient. When it needed sentience, it borrowed HARLIE's—or rather, it asked HARLIE to be sentient for it. Now was one of those moments, when the robot asked for the judgment of the starship's intelligence engine.

HARLIE guided the table into the airlock, sealed the airlock, monitored the conditions on both sides of the hatch to the transfer tube, then opened the next hatch and guided the table forward. A swirl of flickering wavicles came with it. As the repulsors throbbed, the wavicles ebbed and flowed—like a tide of fireflies.

The gurney unfolded its arms and grabbed the handholds set into the railings of the transfer tube. It pulled itself steadily forward. The wavicles tried to roll with it, but the pressure of the repulsor fields pushed more and more of them backward. They swirled in the air, piling up against the walls of thickened air, then bounced away, swirling back into the *Norway*'s still-open hatch.

The table moved slowly through the repulsor fields, one after the other. Each time, fewer and fewer wavicles came with it. By the time it had passed through the fourth field, there were no visible wavicles left. HARLIE told the table to keep pulling itself forward. *No detectable wavicles*, the table reported. *No detectable wavicles*, reported the monitors at the *Star Wolf* end of the transfer tube.

HARLIE paused the gurney at the hatch of the *Star Wolf*'s forward airlock. He studied the information flowing in to him. There was no statistical possibility that there were any live bloodworms in Yonah Jarell's body. There was no statistical possibility that there could be any active wavicles at the *Star Wolf* end of the tube. But statistical possibility was a theoretical construct. It was a model of the physical universe. The accuracy of the model was only a statistical possibility itself . . .

"Dr. Williger?" he reported. "This is the last go/no-go point."

Williger said, "Captain Parsons? We have no detectable error-states. We are in the center of the probability channel. Go or no go?"

A pause. Then, "We've come this far." The sound of a breath. "All right, HARLIE. Open the hatch."

The gurney rolled into the airlock of the *Star Wolf*. A moment later, it

117

arrived in the FARB. Immediately, Dr. Williger, Brian Armstrong and a team of Quillas swarmed around the now-silent form of Yonah Jarell.

"All right, let's transfuse this bastard," Williger snapped, already unclipping the hypo-injectors from the clamps on his arms and legs and neck and tossing them off the gurney. The table's arms gathered the hose ends to reconnect them below. "Disconnecting the table connections," she said for the log.

Then she reached up—Armstrong had to jump in and reach for her; she was too short to get it herself—and pulled down an overhead unit to within centimeters of Jarell's body. She started unclipping hoses and injectors, clamping them quickly into place. Quillas Delta and Omega did likewise. As fast as each injector was locked into place, it activated itself and its collar blinked green. "Connecting transfusors."

The suppressive-resonance field continued—in case any of the plasmacytes still survived in Jarell's blood. Everything was enveloped in a throaty, warbling sensation. The gurney's arms started pulling empty bottles from its under-carriage, handing them to Armstrong as fast as he could receive them, and taking full bottles from Quilla Omega and re-stocking them below.

HARLIE was blandly reciting blood pressure, body temperature, heart-rate, oxygenation and other readings. The important one, however, was, "No detectable plasmacyte spikes in the radiation spectrum."

"My God, I think we've done it—" Armstrong breathed.

"Not yet, Brian. We still have to get the toxic residue out of his blood-stream." She checked the display on the overhead unit, then looked across the table at Armstrong. "The biggest problem in any injury is system shock. Whether you're pumping saline or blood-substitute, you need to get fluid into the body as fast as you can. That's why we use the pumps. A thousand years ago, they used drip-IV lines and their patients died on the way to the hospital, or they suffered needless damage." She glanced to the display and frowned. "We're using too much artificial blood here. Go get another rack from Med Bay."

"On my way—"

On the table, Jarell groaned. Williger glanced at the overhead display. "He's going to live. We did it! Pat yourselves on the backs, people! You just made medical history!" She put her face close to Jarell's and said, "How are you feeling?"

Jarell moaned again.

"He's having a reaction to the process—HARLIE, we need to sedate here; has he got any allergies?"

"Sensitivity to Alternate-R series. Suggest you use Gee-Vin 12, one gram per fifty kilos."

"Ready two grams—" Williger held a hand out without looking to see who would put what into it. Quilla Delta slapped a pressure injector into her palm with medical precision. Williger took it, checked it and applied it to Jarell's left arm. Jarell groaned and passed out again. "Move him to Med Bay. We need the gurney. Someone go to Cargo Bay and get that extra table uncrated. *Now!* This is going to take longer per patient than we thought. HARLIE, what's the time-projection?"

"It's still doable, Doctor. I am projecting that succeeding procedures will go faster—"

"Don't forget, we're going to get tired awfully fast here."

"I'm factoring that into the equation too."

"All right, one more thing—did you track the discomfort levels during the transfer?"

"Of course I did, Doctor. The patient experienced considerable pain—"

"I saw that. What's the status on sedation?"

"The buzz box is not an option here. It puts too much energy into the system. I suggest a chemical application. Resnix should induce a state of deep sleep. There is a supply on the gurney."

"Side effects?"

"Possible nausea."

"Strain on the liver?"

"A healthy liver should be able to flush ninety percent of the active ingredients within six to twelve hours. Some patients may experience a hangover."

"I can live with that. I'd rather use a pain-blocker than a sedative, but we don't have time to experiment or send anything else across."

"Be aware, Doctor, that as soon as you begin replacing the patient's contaminated blood, you'll also be flushing the sedative as well. The after-effects will be minimal."

Williger made a face, an expression of annoyance. "Right. I forgot. I was juggling six thoughts at the same time. Damn. I knew I was going to go senile someday, I just didn't realize it would be today. All right, let's do it. Berryman?"

A nervous voice answered. "Doctor?"

"We're going to sedate, with small doses of Resnix."

"Can do."

"HARLIE will brief you. Start the next patient immediately. We're going to run these in staggered series. We can handle two at a time if we have to, so don't be afraid of overlap. Let's go."

This time, the process seemed to run faster. HARLIE's prediction was accurate. As the team of Quillas became more familiar and more skilled, they moved through the steps with greater efficiency. Blintze awakened on the table, blinking in confusion, even before the transfusion was done.

Williger glanced up at her display. "Bingo. Right on the curve." She lowered her face close to Blintze's. "You're going to live. Answer a question?"

Weakly, Blintze gasped, "What?"

"Are these things native to Regulus IV? What controls them in their own environment?"

It was an effort for Blintze to speak, but he managed to get the words out anyway. They rasped out of his mouth as if each one was escaping from hell. "These things aren't native to anywhere. There aren't any controls. They were created to be . . . a weapon. There was a war on Regulus. And these things were unleashed as . . . a last, desperate revenge on the winners."

"With no way of controlling them?" Williger's eyes were wide.

"They were a doomsday weapon."

"Well, it worked." But as she turned away, her eyes narrowed. Why were Fleet officers working with doomsday weapons? "Captain Parsons? Did you copy that?"

"I heard it," Parsons' voice came through Williger's headset. Her tone was equally troubled. "We'll talk later. For now, stay on purpose."

"All right." The doctor turned back to the Quillas. "Get him to Med Bay and let's get this gurney moving. "We've got eighteen to go and we're running out of time—" a glance across at a display "—and artificial blood, as well."

Easton

On both starships, the crews worked feverishly. On the *Star Wolf*, Williger had the support team of the Quillas, plus Brian Armstrong, Darian Green and "Toad" Hall, for additional assistance. On the *Norway*, Berryman and Easton worked together as a team—with Korie, Bach and Shibano standing by. But as soon as Korie saw he wouldn't be immediately needed, he retreated to a corner of the Cargo Bay where a work station was still operative. With a little help from HARLIE, he linked it to the *Star Wolf*'s network so he could monitor the progress of the operation throughout.

Methodically, the teams worked their separate tasks. On the *Norway*, the patients were deliberately infected with toxic substances and put into suppressive resonance fields. On the *Star Wolf*, the toxic substances and plasmacyte residue were flushed from their bloodstreams. The two starships existed as distinct domains—linked only by the transfer tube, separated only by the repulsor fields.

Each patient was carefully sedated, carefully revived. Every step of the process was monitored by three or more scanners, with HARLIE cross-correlating their readings. Despite the creeping exhaustion of both teams, no serious mistakes were made. A bottle was dropped here, a hose connection came loose there—in each case, the error was caught before it could affect the process. The zero-defect security containment was never compromised. If anything, the greatest danger was boredom—the sheer repetitive madness of doing the same task over and over and over again. After a while, it was hard to remember that what they were doing here was saving lives—and making medical history.

And then, just as Berryman was readying his ninth patient, the warble of the *Norway*'s repulsor field . . . sputtered. It dipped, halted, hesitated, shifted its tone as it compensated for a momentary hiccup and then came back up again. A swirl of wavicles tornadoed in the corridor.

Berryman looked up from the gurney. His eyes locked with Easton's. Korie and Bach and Shibano also exchanged glances.

Bach spoke aloud what they were all thinking. "That's not going to hold."

Shibano held out his hands, as if testing the strength of the field by touch alone. "I give it . . . forty minutes. Maybe an hour." To Berryman, he said. "We're going to have to speed this up."

"We'll make it," Berryman replied. Catching Easton's worried glance, he added, "But just barely."

Easton nodded. He called to Bach. "Take over for me, please." As she did so, he stepped away without explanation and crossed to Korie in the corner. Korie was sitting at his work station, thoughtfully reviewing the *Norway's* log.

"Commander?"

"Easton?" Korie replied without looking up.

"Just checking, sir—"

Korie understood. Part of any mission team's job was to monitor the mental state of its own members. Easton was still in shock over Hodel's death—he knew that the other team members were watching him closely, but he had to reassure *himself* that he was fine, so he went around from one shipmate to the next, making a pretense of checking on them—and letting them look him over again. If they hadn't all been wearing starsuits, they could have reached over and laid their hands on each other—comforting pats on each others' shoulders, or even pulled together for the temporary relief of a hug; but, failing that, the best they could do was look into each other's eyes and pretend they weren't crying inside. Korie understood what Easton was doing—he was walking around looking for reassurance that he was still functioning. He was hoping to be distracted, so the pain wouldn't come crashing in.

"I'm fine. Thanks for checking, I appreciate it," Korie said, deliberately sidestepping the obvious. He needed Easton to hold together just a little while longer. He pointed at the display. "I'm just trying to make good use of the time while we wait—reviewing the operation here. I want to see what their mistake was. There's a lot of material to look through . . ."

Easton nodded. But he remained where he was.

Korie looked at him. "Something else?"

"It wouldn't be so bad if it was just wavicles. But it's the worms that give me the willies. Being eaten alive . . .?" Easton shuddered.

"Me too," said Korie. "Do you want to talk about it?"

"No," said Easton in a tone that suggested yes.

"Y'know, what you did back there . . . that was a hard thing to do. Not everybody would have done it. *You didn't abandon him.* What you did was merciful."

Easton held up a hand. "I know all that, sir. I keep repeating it in my head, over and over and over. Like a mantra. It doesn't help." He took a breath. "I want . . . I want to get angry, sir. I want to get angry and break something. I want to—what I'm saying is a sin in my church, sir—but this is what I'm feeling. I want to hurt someone—whoever's responsible for this. I want to kill someone. I want . . . revenge."

"I know," said Korie. "I feel the same way. Mostly about Morthans." For just an instant, he remembered the size of the bill he'd run up at Stardock—in the gym, beating up on Morthan androids. Until, finally, the doctor had ordered him to stop. Not because he was hurting himself, but because the androids were going psychotic. "Listen, there's nothing wrong with feeling what you're feeling. It's part of the process of grieving."

Easton gave him a skeptical look.

"Yeah, you're right. I'm sorry about the jargon. The point is, there's nothing I can say or do, nothing anyone can say or do that's going to make it easier. You're going to feel what you're feeling—until you stop feeling it. The only thing I can tell you that helps—it's the only thing that helps me—is to go to the gym and punch something. As hard as you can. As much as you can. Over and over and over. Until you fall down exhausted and you don't have the strength to get up again. It doesn't make the feeling go away, but it puts you in control of how you express it, and that much at least is . . . well, it's a start."

"Hodel was my friend," said Easton. As if that explained something.

"He was my friend too—" Korie started.

"No. You don't understand. I could talk to Hodel. Paul and I are bonded, and we like being bonded; it's a sense of security to have a partner. But some folks are uncomfortable with it. They come from places where it isn't allowed or it doesn't happen or it's programmed out of people, so they think it's wrong. But Hodel—it was nothing to him; it was like the color of our hair, it didn't matter. You don't know what it's like to walk down a corridor and have people look at you with pity or contempt or just . . . distance, like you're not totally human. You don't know how refreshing it is to be treated like you're normal—like you're really part of the crew after all."

Korie started to say something, but Easton interrupted him.

"No, it's all right, sir. I've already heard the speech about the irrationality and stupidity of prejudice. I've even given it a few times. I'm sure I know it better than you. Yeah, some people on the *Wolf* are stupid. But that doesn't make the hurt any less, does it? Tell me something—where do you go to get a license to be rude to other people? I want one of those. I want the license to say what I'm feeling too—no matter how rude or stupid or crude or insensitive it is." He stopped himself, then abruptly added, "I'm not hurting for Hodel as much as you think I am. I'm hurting for myself. Because of what I've lost. I know it's selfish . . ." He stopped again, this time unable to continue.

Korie faced Easton. "I wish you'd said something before. I didn't know we had a problem. When this is all over, when we're back on the *Wolf* and everything is secured, will you come and talk to me?"

"Do you think it'll help? Do you think there's anything you can do?"

"I don't know. Let's talk about it."

The two men studied each other. Inside their helmets, both their expressions were hard to read; the starsuits made it easy to stay detached. At last, Easton said, a little too quickly, "I've used up enough of your time. Thank you, sir."

Easton crossed back to Berryman. Proximity to his partner made him feel safer. That was part of the bonding process. The need for closeness. The two men exchanged reassuring glances, but Berryman continued to work without interruption. He and Shibano were just sending another table aftward toward the airlock.

The other gurney held a young woman. She had been attractive once, but now she was pale, bruised and wracked with spasms. She was already wired up and waiting. Hoses and tubes snaked out from the undercarriage of the medtable, up and into the clamps on her arms and legs. She was having trouble breathing and Bach was waiting with her until Berryman could attend.

Easton stepped over and took the young woman's hand in his. He looked down at her and smiled comfortingly—a small atonement.

Secrets

A moment later, Berryman joined them. He placed a stethoscope puck against the young woman's chest, moving it around with each rasping breath she took. The sounds of her breathing were relayed through his helmet. "I know you're uncomfortable," he said. "Just hang in there a little bit longer, okay? Ready when you are, *Star Wolf*."

Williger's voice: "Stand by. Two minutes."

"Did you hear that? Two minutes. What's your name?"

"Rachel. Rachel McCain."

"Are you married?"

"Is that a proposal?"

"Sorry, I'm spoken for." Berryman smiled, with a quick glance across at Easton. "But some of the crew over on the *Star Wolf* are already asking me about you. And your shipmates. I hope you don't have plans for Saturday night."

"If I live that long."

"You will. Or my name's not Tonto Leroy McTavish."

"Tonto Leroy McTavish?! That's *not* your real name!" Despite her discomfort, she smiled.

"No, it isn't. But you'll live anyway."

"Will it hurt?" she asked abruptly. "I heard what you said to . . . Jarell."

"No," said Berryman. "It won't hurt." He was already preparing an injection of Resnix. "But I can arrange it if you want." He waggled his eyebrows.

"No thanks," Rachel said, almost laughing.

He pressed the device to her arm—it hissed, then issued a confirming beep. "In a minute or two, you'll start to feel very pleasant, like you're floating."

"I can feel it already." She closed her eyes.

Easton grinned at Berryman. "There's nothing like Resnix to put you to sleep."

"Another minute and we can send her across." Berryman said. He looked across to Easton, his voice dropping. "Y'know, this is the first time we've ever really worked together. I never thought it would be like this—"

"You're going to start that again, aren't you?"

"Well, why shouldn't I worry about you? You being on Security Detail and all."

Easton looked annoyed. "I really don't like that kind of talk, Paul. We don't put bulls-eyes on our uniforms. That's the *other* guys."

Berryman studied the display in front of him. He shook his head. "I know the odds, Danny—"

"Hey!" Easton interrupted him, almost angry. "I mean it! *Don't talk like that.*"

Lying between them, Rachel McCain opened her eyes and looked from one to the other. "Are we going to die?"

Berryman shot a dirty look across to Easton. *Now look what you've done!* Bending down so Rachel could see his face through his helmet, he said, "I'm not planning on it, are you?" Then, deliberately lightening his tone, he said, "Hey—when we get back to the *Star Wolf*, I'll buy you a drink and tell you about the sparkle-dancer. It dances in the dark between the stars, looking for starships to sing to. If you see one, it's good luck."

Rachel put on a *very* skeptical expression. "Sparkle-dancers? Excuse me? I'd rather hear the one about the leprechaun and the penguin again."

Berryman grinned and pointed. "My partner here will have to tell you that one. But I can tell you about the kindly lawyer with a heart of gold. It has a happy ending. Someone murders him for it."

Williger's voice interrupted Rachel's response. "*Norway*. We're ready for the next one."

Berryman was suddenly all business. "Working," he said. He applied a different injector to her arm. "Relax, this won't hurt me a bit." A hiss and a beep. Berryman put the injector aside and switched on the suppressive resonance field.

Elsewhere—

Korie sat brooding at the work station, replaying video clips over and over. "HARLIE," he said, abruptly.

"Yes, Mr. Korie? HARLIE was everywhere. Wherever there was a communicator, HARLIE was there.

"What is it that we forgot to ask? What is it we should have asked, but were too busy or too distracted to ask?"

HARLIE didn't answer immediately.

"There is something, isn't there?"

"The hole in the data array was multiple—there were overlapping absences," HARLIE reported. "Dr. Blintze provided us with the technical information necessary to proceed with the rescue. There are other blocks of data that are encoded and remain unknowable."

Korie nodded. That was standard. Different pieces of knowledge were encrypted with different levels of security. And yet, there was something about the way HARLIE was reporting the information. Something—as if HARLIE was daring him, "Tickle me *here*."

"Can you break the codes?"

"No, I can't."

"I didn't think so." And then, he realized. "Who *can* break the codes, HARLIE?"

"I don't think these codes are breakable."

Okay, wrong question. "HARLIE, there's a way to decrypt this material, isn't there?"

"Yes, Mr. Korie."

"But you can't tell me, can you?"

"No, Mr. Korie. That's part of the security envelope."

"Mm-hm. These are LENNIE-codes, aren't they?"

"Yes, Mr. Korie."

"And LENNIE can decrypt these data structures."

"Yes, Mr. Korie."

"Now . . . let me see if I can follow this one step further. LENNIE's personality core has gone psychotic and we've patched around him, right? So we can't ask LENNIE, and even if we could, it isn't likely he'd accept our authority, right?"

"Right."

"But . . . *you* can simulate a LENNIE, can't you?"

HARLIE made a noise like a gong, like bells and whistles going off, like a joy buzzer, like fireworks, like a fanfare.

"You've been hanging around Hodel too long," Korie said. Then realized again—*shit. Hodel is dead.*

He forced himself back to the problem at hand. It took a moment for him to regain his concentration. He'd made a breakthrough here. Why couldn't he enjoy it? No, don't go there.

"All right, HARLIE—so if I ask you to simulate a LENNIE again, can you decrypt those data structures?"

HARLIE replied, "One of the primary differences between a HARLIE and a LENNIE is the way that data is modeled. There are advantages to each model. To decrypt the LENNIE model requires becoming a LENNIE intelligence and translating the data structures into a form that a HARLIE intelligence can use. May I recommend that we not do this until *after* completing the transfer operation. I do not wish to imperil the security of the transfer."

Korie sat back in his chair. Momentarily beaten. *Shit*. No, HARLIE is right. "All right, HARLIE, let's let it go for now. Don't do it until the safety of the ship is not an issue. And not without my authorization."

And then he thought for a moment longer—*wait a minute*. "HARLIE?"

"Yes, Mr. Korie?"

"What didn't you suggest?"

"I beg your pardon?"

"How about slaving the LENNIE? Can you do that?"

"Not recommended."

"Okay. How about *simulating* the LENNIE in a lesser intelligence—like one of the robots?"

"The robots don't have the processing power, or the speed."

"I know that. But they have the memory. You could simulate a LENNIE in one of the robots. Or you could simulate it in a network of robots."

"It still wouldn't be as fast."

"No, it wouldn't. But maybe it would be fast *enough*."

"Just a moment. I'm extrapolating."

A pause.

Then HARLIE came back. "We could simulate a LENNIE in a network of non-occupied robots and produce a full decryption in forty-five minutes. The data is pyramid-encoded. I could give you an index in five minutes, and you could choose which data arrays you wanted attacked first."

"What's the risk to the transfer operation?"

"None. I'll only use robots that are on standby or otherwise out of the loop."

"Do it."

"Yes, Mr. Korie. Stand by for the index."

Donors

On the Command Deck of the starship *LS-1187*, the vessel known as the *Star Wolf*, Captain Parsons reflected on the gamble she had taken. She had won the lives of her crew—at the cost of her career.

There was no question what would come next. They would return to Stardock and—after an *extended* quarantine—she would be brought before a Board of Inquiry. The board would ask her if she had knowingly violated a standing order. She would answer, "Yes, I did."

The vice-admiral chairing the board would cluck sympathetically at the situation and make noises about extenuating circumstances not mitigating the offense and how it was important that orders be obeyed by *all* captains; regardless of the lives saved, the knowledge gained, the important breakthroughs achieved and the fact that this would mean an end to one of the most dangerous scourges in known space, the principle of the chain of command had to be maintained. Captain Parsons had *knowingly* put her ship and her crew at terminal risk in violation of a standing order; therefore the board had no other choice but to recommend—she could write the speech herself—that Captain Parsons stand before a court-martial.

On what charges, though?

If they brought her to trial for violation of a standing order, she would have to plead guilty—she had knowingly violated orders. Commander Brik and CMO Molly Williger had both been present at the time and could testify that not only had she done so, she had ordered them to comply at gunpoint. Which was precisely why Brik had confronted her the way he had—to establish that specific point of responsibility, that she had effectively thwarted any opportunity to remove her from command. But had she really violated a standing order? This was a situation that a lawyer would call "collision of priorities." There were other orders that gave her the authority to do exactly what she had done.

She could justifiably argue that her duty *required* her to explore all options for rescue of the crew and the mission team as well as the retrieval of the *Norway*'s log. She could say that she had known of her responsibility to destroy the *Norway*, but had held off until the medical and research logs had been downloaded because of the value of that knowledge.

That the logs had contained experimental procedures for containing and treating a plasmacyte infection had presented her with the kind of moral dilemma that captains were empowered to resolve under General Order Number One: a captain is totally responsible for the welfare of her crew and her ship, regardless of any other orders in place. She could argue that under that obligation, she had to use the information available to save her mission team and the survivors on the *Norway*.

It was a compelling argument, to be sure. But even if they accepted her defense and acquitted her, they wouldn't—*couldn't*—put her back at the helm of the *Star Wolf* or any other starship. It would send the wrong message to other captains. No, her command days were over. Other captains would understand and sympathize—and take the lesson to heart. The Admiralty would cluck sympathetically and might even apologize privately for having to make an example of her, but still, the fleet had to maintain its discipline. Junior officers would be the ones who would most take the lesson to heart. And the Admiralty would maintain its tight control over its captains, even from a hundred or a thousand light years away.

She ran one hand along the railing in front of her. She would miss her star-time. But if she had to do it all over again—

Her headset beeped.

"Parsons here."

Williger. "Captain, listen carefully. There isn't going to be enough artificial blood to treat everybody. We're using more substitute per patient than we expected."

"How long to manufacture more?"

"Too long. Captain, you're going to have to ask for blood donors."

"Blood donors?"

"I know. It's a barbaric custom—you take blood out of one person's body and put it into another's—but it's a painless procedure and it's the best way we've got to save the last five lives."

The last five lives—Korie, Bach, Wasabe, Berryman, Easton . . .

"We'll need at least sixty volunteers, each one donating a single pint of blood. Ensigns Duane and Morwood are standing by. HARLIE's already got the blood maps prepared. But we have to start right away."

"Sixty volunteers? That's two-thirds of the crew."

"Yes, Captain. They're setting up now in the mess room. They raided cargo for the extra supplies; they can do ten at a time. It's going to be close, but the more blood we get now, the less we'll need later, when time gets critical."

"Right." Parsons turned forward and shifted her tone. *"Now hear this."* The captain's voice was immediately amplified throughout the starship. Everybody heard it—and stopped what they were doing. The Black Hole Gang. The Farm Team. Cookie and the mess attendants. Maintenance. Security. "This is the captain speaking. We need blood donors to help save the lives on the Norway. We need sixty volunteers—" She paused to correct herself. She would be the first. "Excuse me, fifty-nine. Dr. Williger assures me that it doesn't hurt—but it sure as hell will help. Volunteers report to the mess room on the double. *That is all.*" She glanced to Tor. "Commander Brik, you have the conn. Commander Tor, did I just hear you volunteer?" And with that, the captain headed aftward, her astrogator following in her wake.

By the time they arrived, there was already a lineup in the corridor—men and women waiting to donate blood. Including Reynolds. The captain took her place in line behind him and noted his presence with a nod. "Good to see you here, crewman."

Reynolds nodded back. "You'll have your sixty pints of blood. The union guarantees it."

"I never doubted it," the captain replied.

Blood

The call for blood donors worried Korie. He'd had some experience with primitive medical procedures; he knew how risky they were. He had HARLIE show him the view of the mess room, where ensigns Duane and Morwood had arranged an emergency blood bank. The patients were stretching out on the table-tops, with rolled-up towels as pillows.

The procedure had been worked out by HARLIE. Duane went from table to table, setting up the IV lines and blood bags and directing donors to lie down. Morwood followed behind her, applying nanite-leeches to the bare arms of the donors. The leeches were connected to the IV lines and the blood ran smoothly down transparent tubes into plastic bags clipped to the side of the table. It took only a few moments for each bag to fill. By the time Duane had finished setting up the last table, the patient on the first table was finished. Now she followed the same path, disconnecting each patient and handing the full bag to Morwood, who checked the bag's control-display for blood type and Rh factor before hanging it on a rack. When the rack was full, the Martian—small, ugly, efficient—wheeled it quickly out to the forward airlock.

The donors were dismissed to the other side of the mess room where Cookie had laid out thick sandwiches and vitamin-augmented fruit drinks. Duane laid out fresh IV lines, pointed a donor to the table and moved on to the next position. Morwood started the donor and followed, one step behind. They were producing a fresh pint of blood every four minutes. It was fast—but wasn't quite as fast as the artificial blood was being used up at the Forward Airlock Reception Bay.

It didn't look to Korie as if they would produce enough blood before the treatment for the last person on the *Norway* could be started. It would be close. "All right," he decided. "I'll go last. I'll take the risk."

"Mr. Korie?" Brik's voice in his helmet.

"Yes, Brik?"

"Have you been looking over the information that HARLIE is decoding?"

"Um, yes—" Korie lied. He didn't want to admit he'd been monitoring the speed with which the blood was being collected. Brik would understand why immediately. In that, Korie realized, he was becoming something like a Morthan—only admitting what he was willing to have others know. He touched the controls on his display, going back to the decrypted data clusters. "What is it you wanted me to see?"

The display in front of Korie cleared, then lit up again to show the same pictures that Brik was looking at. It showed a glass beaker with a single red bloodworm in it. In the beaker, the creature looked harmless enough.

"This is from Blintze's medical log," said Brik.

The image showed a technician putting the beaker inside a high-intensity medical scanner. She turned on a suppressive resonance field, then set the scanner at its lowest setting and activated it. The readings from the scanner scrolled up the side of the image.

"Brik? This can't be right. I'm no doctor, but no creature can live like this—the act of eating uses up more energy than it produces. The bloodworm runs up a ferocious energy debt that never gets paid."

"As impossible as that seems, it appears to be an accurate assessment. The creature eats, but it doesn't make use of what it eats, except to fuel its own appetite. So the more it eats, the more it wants."

"Well . . ." Korie wished he could scratch his head through the helmet. "That explains a lot. Very effective as a weapon—but not as a lifestyle. I wonder what would happen if it could metabolize what it eats?"

Abruptly, in the display, the creature in the scanning box exploded in a cloud of wavicles.

Brik's voice. "I found this in Blintze's notes . . ." A pause and then Blintze's voice: "The natural form of the plasmacyte is the wavicle spore. The wavicle is essentially harmless. The bloodworm is an aberrant form— a deliberate mutation. You can't kill a bloodworm, you can only shatter it, producing more wavicles. Shooting them produces the same result. Even scanning is dangerous. The plasmacytes are *not* a disease—they *have* a disease—a disease that makes them profoundly dangerous to all other life forms. A cure would involve reversing the mutation."

"That's a very interesting piece of information," said Korie.

"There's more. HARLIE's still decoding. He may have found it. But it's beyond my area of expertise. At the moment, I am increasingly concerned about . . . the intention of this research."

"I hear you, Brik." Korie felt a knot forming in his stomach. Something he hadn't wanted to acknowledge for a while. "And . . . I share your concerns. Will you discuss this with Captain Parsons? ASAP. In private."

"I was already planning on it. But I wanted to confer with you first."

"I appreciate that."

On the Bridge of the *Star Wolf*, Brik signed off just as Captain Parsons and Commander Tor reentered from "Broadway." Brik stood up. That was enough to get the captain's attention. She gave him a questioning look. He inclined his head toward the Officer's Mess. She nodded, but held up a finger in a *wait-one-moment* gesture. "HARLIE, status?" she asked.

HARLIE responded: "All of the Norway survivors are aboard and in recovery. Bach is now being transfused. Shibano is about to be transferred. Easton and Berryman are next. Commander Korie will be the last one out."

Parsons nodded.

"And the repulsor field on the *Norway* is failing rapidly."

Parsons looked to Brik, then to Tor. All of their expressions were grim. "Commander Tor, take the conn," she said. She exited back the way she had entered, Brik following.

Fire

On the *Norway*, in the Cargo Bay, Korie, Berryman and Easton watched as the gurney carrying Shibano rolled toward the airlock. As the hatch popped shut behind it, they became aware of the not-quite-silence in the chamber. The *Norway* repulsor fields sounded more unstable every moment, their notes fluctuating uncertainly. There was one empty gurney, waiting for the next patient. "All right," said Berryman. "Starsuits off. Come on, come on," he urged. "We're running out of time." He turned to Easton and started unsealing his partner's helmet. "You too, sir," he said to Korie. "Danny, help me out of my suit. I won't be able to do it myself when it's my turn—"

And that's when the argument began.

As the three men helped each other out of their starsuits, the tone of their voices became increasingly tense. By the time they were down to their undersuits, the temperature of the discussion was more than heated, more than volatile. It had become a plasma.

"Paul," Easton said, "They need you on the *Wolf*. I'll go last."

"Danny," Berryman pointed to the gurney. "Lie down!"

"Paul, I know how to do this, I've watched you enough times. The whole process is automated—"

"Danny—*will you just please let me do my job?*"

"Will you let me do mine? *I'm* security. I'm supposed to take the risk."

"I hate it when you get like this."

An empty gurney came rolling out of the airlock. Now there were two.

"*Norway*," Williger's voice. "Start the next one."

"Can you take two at once?" Berryman asked.

A pause. Then, "Yes, we can take two at once."

Easton turned to Korie. "Would you order him, sir?"

"Actually," said Korie. "I'm going last."

"With all due respect, sir—" Berryman looked both frustrated and angry—"I'm the only one here who knows how to monitor the process. If anything goes wrong, I'm the only one who knows what to do. You and Easton *have* to go next."

Easton shook his head. "They'll monitor me from the Bridge. I'm security. It's my responsibility to go last."

"I'm the ranking officer," said Korie. "It's *my* responsibility—"

"Oh, the hell with this—" said Berryman. He turned to Easton and pushed the pressure injector up against his arm—a soft hiss—and then, without waiting, he whirled to Korie and did the same thing. Another soft hiss. Easton looked to his partner with a betrayed expression.

"There!" said Berryman. "The argument's over. Lie down." To Korie. "You too, sir."

Berryman turned back to Easton. "*Lie down, Danny.* You're going to start feeling weak any second now, and I don't want you falling and hurting yourself." He grabbed Easton by the arm and forced him down onto the gurney.

Easton protested all the way. "That was not fair. You haven't heard the end of this, Paul!"

"Fine. You can bawl me out back on the *Wolf.*" He glanced over at Korie. "*You too, sir!*"

Korie, startled at Berryman's tone of voice, started to say something in response, then, feeling the first wave of dizziness flooding up, he thought better of it. He found his way to the second gurney and sank down onto it.

From the gurney, Easton was still protesting. "I mean it, Paul!"

"Shut up and let me win one for a change." Berryman was already applying clamps and injector hoses. "It's going to be close enough as it is." As if to underscore his concern, the sound of the repulsor field dipped abruptly. "Okay, that's the last one—there—the board is green." Berryman ducked below to check the state of something on the gurney's undercarriage, then came back up again. "All right, sweetheart—" He touched Easton's cheek tenderly, then impulsively, bent over and kissed him quickly on the lips. "I love you."

"Love you too," Easton whispered back.

Berryman switched on the suppressive resonance field. "Let me start Korie, I'll be right back."

As Berryman applied the pressure clamps, Korie looked up at him. "You're very decisive. I like that in an officer."

"Thank you. But I'm not an officer yet."

"You're an ensign. Technically, you're an officer." Korie was starting to feel a little detached from his body, but he was still conscious.

"Thank you, sir." Still working, Berryman added, "All I ever wanted was to serve in the Fleet. My grandfather served on the 'Big E' in her glory days."

"Really? Are you trying to live up to his record?"

Berryman shook his head. "Nope. Just my own standards."

"Is that why you did it?"

"Much simpler than that, sir. I made a promise to myself that you and Danny would both get back safely."

"Especially Danny?"

"He's always been the strong one. Today is my turn, okay?" He finished connecting the last tube, made some safety checks and looked to Korie. "Okay, ready to start?"

Korie swallowed once, then nodded. "Let's do it."

Berryman turned on the machinery and activated the resonance field. Korie felt an uncomfortable tingling—but it was somewhere distant. Like it was in someone *else's* body. He turned his head and saw Berryman holding Easton's hand. They were whispering together.

Then, Easton said, "Paul? Take my stinger."

"What for? To make more wavicles?" But Berryman's tone said he knew *exactly* what for.

"It'll make me feel better."

Berryman made a face of annoyance, but he bent to the floor and pulled the stinger pistol off of Easton's dropped starsuit. He held it up for Easton to see. "Okay, happy now?"

But Easton was already unconscious.

Berryman tossed the stinger aside and turned his attention to the display panel on the medtable. "*Star Wolf*? Here comes one." He stepped around to the head of the gurney to help guide it toward the airlock. The effort was redundant, but he felt better doing it. Just before the table rolled through the hatch, he reached down and touched Easton's cheek again. "See you on the other side," he whispered.

Berryman turned back to Korie. The executive officer was already fading out. He checked the displays on Korie's gurney. Korie was doing fine too. Another few seconds and they'd be clear. "*Star Wolf*? Here comes the other one." The second table rolled after the first. "All right, I'm ready for a taxi, any time—"

Behind him, the sound of the repulsor field flip-flopped again. Berryman turned to look down the corridor of the keel toward the distant red gloom. A wall of wetness pulsed.

"Uh-oh," he said.

Blood and Fire

Parsons and Brik returned to the Command Deck, both looking grim. Brik had briefed the captain on what he had seen in the *Norway's* records. The captain had listened without comment. When Brik had finished, she nodded politely, then headed grimly back to the Command Deck, just in time to hear Berryman's unhappy remark.

Parsons looked to Tor. "What's happening?"

Tor said, "The repulsor field on the Norway just went down—"

Parsons bit her lip. "Who's still over there?"

"Korie and Easton just came through," Tor reported. "Berryman's the last. They just sent the last gurney across." She glanced to her display for confirmation. "He just injected himself. Ninety seconds and we can pull him out—"

As if in confirmation, Berryman's voice came over the speakers, "*Star Wolf—*"

Parsons looked to the forward display. So did the others. As the mission team had disrobed, Korie had hung two of the discarded starsuit helmets on hooks in the *Norway's* Cargo Bay and placed the others on equipment racks around the chamber. Now, the view shifted from one camera to the next until HARLIE finally selected the one that gave them the best angle on Berryman.

"Go ahead, Berryman," Parsons said. She glanced to Tor and whispered, "Is this going out all over the ship?" Tor nodded.

"The repulsor field is completely down. The bloodworms are coming through. They're coming down the corridor. I can see them. They're flowing like water. Not as fast though. There might be time. I'm getting on the gurney now."

Parsons briefly thought about cutting off the signal to the rest of the ship, then decided against it. That might suggest she didn't think they would get Berryman off the *Norway* in time. And it would suggest a lack of trust. But . . . if Berryman ran out of time, the effect on the crew would be devastating. Especially if everyone witnessed it.

On the other hand, a terrible truth was preferable to a ghastly rumor. If Berryman died, the details would sweep the ship anyway. And a few overripe imaginations would do far worse damage to morale.

No, she told herself. *Stop thinking that way. We're going to get him off. And everyone will see it and share the victory. That'll be good for all of us.*

Throughout the *Star Wolf*, all nonessential work came to a halt as crewmembers turned to display panels and work-station screens. In the mess room, where Duane and Morwood were drawing the last two pints of blood. In the engine room, where Reynolds, still rubbing his arm, stood with Cappy and MacHeath. In the Med Bay, Bach and Wasabe propped themselves up blearily so they could see. At the Forward Airlock Reception Bay, where Williger worked feverishly on Korie and Easton— periodically, she glanced up to an overhead panel. As did the rest of her team. Only the Quillas worked without pause—all except Quilla Omega, who watched the images from the *Norway* intently.

"They're close enough now—I can hear them." Berryman twisted on the gurney. "I can't see them from here. But they're a lot closer. They're coming down the corridor. Can you hear them?" There was the sound of the resonance field under his voice—and a crackling sound too, a wet slobbery noise.

"I'm not using the pain-blocker. I need to stay alert. I can feel the effects of the injection. It's uncomfortable. But I can handle it. It's only for a little bit."

The display started to glare red in one corner. A moment later, a glistening red ooze began creeping across the deck. HARLIE switched through camera angles again. There weren't as many as before. The blood-worms were flowing over the discarded helmets, blocking the lenses. HARLIE settled on an image that showed only half the gurney. Berryman's legs.

"This is going to be a close one."

Berryman's legs moved as the man twisted around to watch the on-coming tide of worms. The crackling noise was louder now.

"God, they sound awful. They're coming toward the gurney. Wait a minute—"

A mechanical sound. The gurney moved out of frame. Almost immediately, a tide of slithering bodies came flowing after it.

Berryman's voice: "That was HARLIE. He moved the gurney as close to the hatch as he could. Maybe we bought a couple extra seconds. Ahh, this stuff hurts—they're surrounding the gurney—"

HARLIE cycled through camera angles again. Two angles showed the worms starting to fill the Cargo Bay like blood filling a basin. They lapped against the walls, ebbing and flowing with an uneasy tidal movement.

"Danny, it looks like I might need your stinger after all."

In the *Star Wolf*'s Forward Airlock Reception Bay, Easton was already scrambling up from his gurney, trying to reach the hatch behind him. Three Quillas had to grab him and hold him back. He was screaming, making incoherent noises. "Paul—"

Williger was swearing as the tubes attached to his body kept yanking loose, spurting blood in all directions before their automatic cutoffs kicked in. On the other gurney, Korie watched helplessly, reaching but not able to touch, calling but not being heard. Ordering—but being ignored.

"Don't worry, Danny," shouted Berryman. "I'm going to make it. I promise." But his words were nearly drowned out by all the slithery noises. There were no camera angles that showed the gurney. Only the worms. "I'm getting real dizzy. That means it's working. I might pass out soon, but the gurney is still working—and HARLIE is with me. I think they're trying to climb the wheels of the cart. *Star Wolf*—better be ready to pull me over fast."

And then for a moment, nothing—except the distinctive sound of bloodworms.

"Oh, damn! They're on the gurney. Maybe I can—"

Berryman's words were covered by the sudden crackle of a stinger—a sharp snapping sound as the air vaporized in the beam. On the screen, an acrid flare of light, followed by a sudden wash of wavicles recoiling backward from the blast.

Easton screamed. "Paul!! Come on!! Come on now!!"

And Williger—she was swearing in some unknown language. She was pounding her control display. "No, no, no—goddammit! Look at the readings. He's still carrying live plasmacytes. As fast as they die, they keep reinfecting."

Easton was trying to get to Williger now, trying to reach her controls. The Quillas were struggling to hold him back and tie him down with restraints. "You bitch! Bring him over now! They're going to eat him alive!!"

"There are too many! We can't pull him through. *We can't get him.*"

And then Berryman's voice. "*Danny, I'm sorry. I thought I had more time—oh, God. Forgive me!*"

And then—another stinger shot. A flare of white. A wash of sparkles. And silence. Only the liquid crackling of bloodworms.

And Easton. Screaming. "No, Paul! No!"

On the Command Deck, still leaning on the railing, still staring at the forward display, Parsons finally lowered her eyes. She didn't want to look at anyone. She didn't want to say anything. She didn't want to exist. She wanted everything and everyone to just go away. And leave her alone.

Tor's voice. Gently. "Captain?"

Parsons opened her mouth to speak. Her throat was too dry. She closed her mouth and swallowed. She turned and crossed back to her command chair very much aware of Tor's eyes on her. She sat down and shaded her eyes with her hand. She felt terribly alone in the center of everything.

The bridge was full of noise. Ugly wet noise.

"Shut that damn thing off!" the captain ordered.

The sound continued for a second longer—and then silence. Blessed silence.

The Hull

Captain Parsons lifted her head and gave the order. "Separate from the *Norway*. Do it now. Who's on helm?" And then she realized. Hodel. She glanced around the Bridge. "Goldberg, take the helm. You're acting helm until—until further notice." As Goldberg moved to Hodel's former station, she added. "Move us away from the *Norway*, but stay close enough that we can put a missile in her. If we have to."

As Goldberg worked, the image on the forward display shifted. The spars of the *Norway* were glittering with flickering plasmacytes. Everything glowed red in the crimson light of the bloated star. Parsons flinched at the bloodiness of the view. "Prepare a breakaway course to take us out of here. Put it on a ninety-second readiness hold. Mr. Brik—"

The big Morthan turned to face her. He was standing in the Ops Deck, half a level lower than the Command Deck, but he was still eye-to-eye with the captain. "Aye?"

"There are wavicles on the hull of the *Norway*."

"I noticed that myself."

"Let's have a look at the hull of the *Star Wolf*, shall we? HARLIE?"

The forward view shifted. The hull camera swiveled to look backward, down the length of the *Star Wolf*.

For a moment, there was silence on the Bridge. The hull of the *Star Wolf* also glittered and sparkled. Just as much as the hull of the *Norway*. And over everything remained the oppressive orange cast of the red giant sun.

"Well, that answers that." Parsons looked to Brik. "As soon as Williger is finished with Korie and Easton, summon her to the wardroom. If Korie is coherent, I'll want him too. And Commander Tor. And Jarell and Blintze. Have Cookie prepare sandwiches and coffee. I expect this is going to be a long one." She touched her headset, adjusting it against her close-cropped hair. "Chief Leen?"

"Captain?"

"Can you sweep the hull with repulsor fields?"

"We don't have a lot of power left, Captain. It'll take hours to recharge the fuel cells."

"We've got wavicles on the outer hull. Sooner or later, they're going to penetrate."

"I can do a low-level sweep, but I can't make any promises how effective it'll be."

"Start it now. Then join me in the wardroom."

"Aye, aye, Captain."

Parsons turned back to the forward display and waited. A moment later, a disturbance began rippling through the wavicles on the *Star Wolf* hull. A series of waves rolled slowly through them, dislodging them from the metal surfaces like dust being shaken from a blanket. The twinkling sparkles swirled away from the starship . . . then swirled gently back again. Repulsor fields weren't going to work. She frowned, grabbed her clipboard and headed toward the wardroom.

Sitting down at the head of the table, she started making notes:

1. Sweep wavicles off hull?
2. Feed wavicles to singularity?
3. What happens to wavicles in hyperstate?
4. Suppressive resonance field?
5. Wavicle pheromones? Lure them away?
6. Pass through star's corona?
7.

She didn't have a seventh thought. She tapped her fingernail against the screen of the clipboard thoughtfully while two Quillas laid out plates of sandwiches and mugs of coffee. Williger entered then and sat down at the captain's left. Parsons turned the clipboard so the doctor could see what she had written. Williger frowned as she read through the list. Then she picked up a stylus and added:

7. Medical possibilities? Can "cure" be applied externally?
8. Meat tanks as bait?
9.

She hesitated for a moment, then wrote something else at the bottom of the page.

How much time do we have? How much time do we need?

She handed the clipboard silently back to Parsons. The captain took a sip of her coffee as she looked at what Molly Williger had written, then she nodded. Korie entered and sat down gingerly. He looked weak. The captain passed him the plate of sandwiches and pushed a mug of coffee toward him, without comment. Then she shoved the clipboard in front of him so he could read it.

Korie helped himself to a sandwich. He took a bite, chewed, swallowed and studied the page in front of him. He reached for his own stylus and added several thoughts of his own. As he did, Brik came in. Looming over the table, Brik had no problem reading the clipboard's display.

Chief Leen entered, looked around for a seat, noticed the empty seat next to Korie, hesitated—caught Brik looking at him—then took the seat next to Korie anyway. He peered at the executive officer curiously, as if reassuring himself that Korie was all right, then glanced to the clipboard. Korie passed it to him. Like the others, Leen pursed his lips into a thoughtful frown. He tapped at the second item.

2. Feed wavicles to singularity?

Next to it, he wrote:

How?

Jarell and Blintze

Tor came in, followed by Jarell and Blintze. Leen glanced across the table at them, then pushed the clipboard back to Korie, who pushed it back to the captain. She looked at her notes, and at what the others had added. As soon as everybody was settled, she said, "You're all aware that we have plasmacytes on the hull. How they got out of the *Norway* is part of the problem. Because they may be able to get into the *Star Wolf* the same way." She tapped the clipboard meaningfully. "We don't have a lot of possibilities to consider, do we? Unfortunately, that doesn't simplify the problem. Usually, when we enter a situation, we have a much broader range of choices. We have very few options here. And none of them are workable."

"We've done more than any other ship," said Tor.

"Which only means we're operating way, way out beyond the limits of what everyone else knows," Parsons replied. She rubbed the bridge of her nose between her thumb and forefinger. "We have resolved one part of the plasmacyte question—can we safely extract human beings from an infected environment? We now know the answer to that is yes. But the larger question—can we do it without infecting the extraction environment?—remains unanswered. It may be that we have no cure at all here, only a method of delaying the inevitable. In a controlled situation, where the wavicles are isolated inside a containment field, then perhaps extraction is feasible and safe. But this latest development only proves the wisdom of FleetComm's standing order against attempting rescue." She looked to Blintze and Jarell. "I am assuming that you can provide some useful insights to this problem?"

The two men glanced at each other. Jarell looked grim. Blintze was more apologetic. "You've seen my files. So you know that the normal form of the plasmacyte is the wavicle. Harmless, attractive. But it's been changed somehow, so that it can't sustain itself, and it turns into bloodworm spores. The bloodworm is a specifically-designed mutation, created as a doomsday weapon. We believe the losers turned it loose upon their own world to deny the victors access to the prize they'd fought so hard to win. The planet remains uninhabitable. It was a war that both sides lost."

"Commander Brik has briefed me on the material in your logs. We've decrypted most of it—"

Jarell spoke up then, deliberately interrupting. "Fleet Command was particularly concerned about the possibility of bloodworm infection as a military threat." He glanced meaningfully at Brik. "Does *he* have to be here, Captain Parsons?"

Parsons raised an eyebrow. She glanced over to Brik as if seeing him for the first time, then looked back to Jarell. "He's my chief security Officer. Is there some problem, Mr. Jarell?"

"Isn't it obvious?"

"Are you suggesting that one of my officers is not trustworthy?"

"Captain Parsons, *no* Morthan is trustworthy."

"Commander Brik has proven himself in a number of situations. I have the fullest confidence in him."

"Do you think that's wise?"

"Commander Jarell, I respect your rank and your authority—but please do not question the loyalty or the integrity of my officers again. I will consider such remarks a violation of code."

Jarell lifted his hands off the table and showed his palms, a gentle push-away gesture. He nodded his concession with an empty smile.

"Please proceed," Captain Parsons said coldly.

Jarell took a breath. "As you wish." With a sour glance in Brik's direction, he continued, "Our mandate was to investigate the possible military use of the bloodworms and what defenses might be effective against them. Toward that end, we were directed to develop means of containment, control and neutralization. We accomplished all three of those goals. Our mission has been a success."

"A rather expensive success," said Captain Parsons dryly. "We lost a starship and most of her crew." She glanced to Korie. There was something about his expression. "Mr. Korie? You wanted to say something. An itch perhaps?"

Korie shook his head. "No. It's just the aftereffects of the process. I'll be all right." But his eyes met Parsons' and they both knew that he was dissembling. Whatever it was, he wasn't ready to say it here. Not in front of Jarell and Blintze. Or Brik . . .?

Blintze spoke abruptly. "Captain Parsons?"

"Dr. Blintze?"

"What I was saying before—I didn't get to finish. The normal form of the wavicle is harmless. What we have here isn't normal. What we think the wavicles may have originally been is some kind of cooperative colony creature, like ants or bees. The individual wavicle has no existence of its own; it's meant to be a cell in a larger entity, but because of the mutation, the colony-gestalt is damaged or destroyed. I'm sorry to be so pedantic about this. You might not find it as interesting as I do—"

"Go on," said Parsons. "I want to hear it all."

"Well," Blintze continued. "We were actually able to classify several distinct types of wavicles, each with different properties and behaviors, each filling a different niche in the colony's spectrum."

Williger looked up sharply. "Tell us about that. What specific types have you identified?"

Blintze nodded, warming up to his subject. "We've found a *binder* that calls other wavicles to follow it. We've found a *singer*; it generates audible vibrations. We've found a *firefly* form; that's the one that twinkles and glows. Most of the other types aren't as visible. There's a variety that reproduces, but not as we understand reproduction; it generates the other kinds and occasional copies of itself. We call those *mothers*. We've also found *carriers* which seem to do nothing more than carry copies of 'genetic code.' There are several types whose functions we haven't identified. We think those are dormant. There's a *targeter*; it locates sites on material things. *Eaters* attach themselves to those sites, eventually burning their way through. We're not sure if those two forms are natural or if they're misapplied. But this is the point—there are gaps in the spectrum. There are forms that should be there and aren't."

Blintze glanced sideways to Jarell, who was looking very unhappy, but he continued anyway. "We don't find very many *feeders*. There's simply not enough here to sustain the colony. Using the models derived from colonies of ants, bees, termites, lawyers—not the human kind; I mean the parasites from Maizlish; it's a planet orbiting a bloated dead star. Anyway, using preexisting models of other colony creatures, we know that a hive or a colony needs a certain percentage of food gatherers to sustain itself. The wavicle colony has only one-third the *feeders* it should, so it's constantly on the edge of starvation. That's part of what produces such manic behavior."

Williger's eyes were bright. She finished the explanation for him. "It's the little *mothers* that are the dangerous ones, right? Without food, the other forms disintegrate. But the mothers go particulate so they can keep reproducing, albeit on the next quantum level down. And when they're particulate, they produce nothing but more hungry little *mothers*, right?"

Blintze looked surprised. "That's right."

"I've been studying your notes," she said. "Toward the end, they're a little disorganized, but HARLIE and I have had some interesting conversations, extrapolating possibilities. Something was done to change the *mother* form. There was an extremely high level of technology involved in the reengineering of this creature. I don't know if we could match it—but if we could, we could introduce a genetic correction into the mothers and return the wavicle colony to its natural state. We're talking about curing the bloodworms—literally. You were looking at altering the *carriers*, weren't you?"

"Yes," admitted Blintze. "That's how we got infected. We . . . we created a form of carrier that made the bloodworms even more dangerous. We gave them the ability to bore through polycarbonates."

"You're to be congratulated on your success," said Korie.

"It wasn't a success," Blintze said, stiffly.

"Yes, it was." Korie's words were a rebuke. "Because that's exactly what you were trying to do, wasn't it?" The accusation hung in the air between them.

Intentions

Blintze looked unhappy. He poured himself a glass of water and drank it quickly.

"You don't have to answer that," said Jarell. "Remember, this is on a need-to-know basis."

"I believe we're beyond that," Parsons said to Jarell. "Far beyond. And we definitely have a need to know. Go on, Mr. Blintze."

"Yes," Blintze finally admitted. "We were looking for a way to control the bloodworms—so we could use them as a weapon."

Parsons exchanged a glance with Korie. What they had both suspected was now acknowledged.

"Captain," Jarell spoke candidly, like a confidante—he hadn't noticed the exchange of looks between the captain and her exec. "Can you imagine what would happen if the Morthan Solidarity were to spread bloodworms throughout Allied space?"

Korie, sipping at his coffee, answered quietly, "The destruction of all carbon-based life forms on a catastrophic scale." His voice was flat.

"Precisely," said Jarell. He glanced sideways at Brik, then back to Parsons. He leaned ominously forward. "The Morthans are vipers. They cannot be trusted. They do not follow the New Geneva Conventions. They have already demonstrated their willingness to use weapons of mass destruction."

Parsons raised an eyebrow, meaningfully. She noted Korie's grim expression, then turned back to Jarell. "Go on," she prompted.

"They attacked Taalamar with a sustained barrage of extinction-level asteroids. You were there, you saw what happened, you know—they destroyed an entire civilization. Millions of men, women and children—that's the kind of regard they have for us. The bloodworms . . . well, that's FleetComm's response."

"According to your own log, your research was already funded and in preparation long before the attack on Taalamar. Even before the mauling at Marathon."

Jarell acknowledged it with a nod. "Yes, but only as a precautionary measure. Just in case our worst nightmares came true. And we should be grateful for such foresight, because now we have a weapon we can use to strike back."

"And what circumstances, Commander Jarell, do you think would make such use necessary?" Korie wasn't looking at Jarell, he was looking down into his coffee mug. He swirled it gently, as if he were watching a thought circling there.

"Shaleen and Taalamar. Isn't that enough, Commander? Or maybe you don't care that they scourged Shaleen? And you know what they did to Taalamar."

"I care," said Korie, not willing to mention that his wife and children had been on Shaleen. Maybe they had escaped, maybe to Taalamar. But maybe not. HARLIE had exchanged messages with every starship they'd ever encountered. He'd never found any evidence that his family had even gotten off the planet. Maybe the records didn't exist, maybe they'd been lost, maybe there was no hope at all. And maybe . . .

"Well," said Jarell, as if it was obvious. "If that doesn't justify the use of mega-weapons, then what does?" He glanced around the table, meeting the eyes of every officer there. His gaze lingered on Brik for a long, uncomfortable moment.

"You don't know the Morthans," Jarell explained. "Not really. Not even you, Mr. Brik—your fathers fled the world of Citadel when you were a child. You don't know what it's like to live under a Morthan authority. You don't know what the Morthans are really like. None of you. But I do, I've been there. I've seen them swaggering through the streets of Dogtown, laughing and killing, taking what they want—slaves, food, weapons, wealth. I've seen what they do to the worlds they conquer. We've been watching the Morthan Solidarity for a thousand years. We've sent in agents. Hundreds of thousands of agents—most get caught, but the things we've seen, I can't begin to tell you what we know. I am telling you that there is no limit to the Morthan treachery. The plasmacytes are a weapon. And if we don't use them, the Morthans *will*."

Brik rumbled, a sound so low that it was felt rather than heard. "No Morthan would ever use such a weapon," he said. "It would be cowardly. Only a human would."

Parsons gave Brik a sharp look. So did Korie. They were getting close to the punch line here. She turned back to Jarell and Blintze, concern strong on her face. She chose her next words carefully. "And that was the real goal of your work here, wasn't it?"

Jarell's answer was intense. "Captain Parsons, we were caught unprepared at Marathon and we've been on the run ever since. All of human space lies open to the Morthan advance if we don't find a way to stop them now. I don't have to tell you, *the most expensive armada in the galaxy is the one that's second best.* The whole point of this mission is to make sure that the plasmacyte weapon was ready at hand, for just this circumstance. *And use it, if necessary.* You—your ship—you were intended to be the delivery vessel. It's in a set of sealed orders we have for you— for whatever ship that served as our tender. It's in our orders to commandeer your starship, if necessary, to deliver the weapons packages to Morthan space. So you're as much a part of this as we are."

Parsons was silent for a very long moment. She placed her hands flat on the table before her and studied the space between them. After a bit, she looked across to Williger, to Korie and finally up to Brik. "Commander Brik. Please escort Mr. Jarell and Dr. Blintze to their quarters— and see that they stay there."

Brik rumbled an assent. "Come with me, *gentlemen.*" Although his voice was as flat as ever, the last word—*gentlemen*—had a deadly tone to it.

As the hatch slid shut behind them, Parsons looked to Korie and Williger and Tor and Leen. "Well," she said. "Does anyone have any more good ideas?"

Korie was swirling his coffee mug again—thinking of Lowell, thinking of Marathon, thinking of Shaleen and Taalamar. Thinking of Carol. Thinking too loudly.

"What?" demanded Parsons.

"I told you not to attempt a rescue. I told you not to try."

"It's a little late for recriminations."

"It's never too late," said Korie. "The *Wolf* is still being punished for accidentally leading the Morthan fleet to the Silk Road Convoy. Why else would we have been given this duty? Delivery of plasmacyte bombs?"

"Yes, well . . ." Parsons cleared her throat uncomfortably. "Let's see if we can address our current problem first, Mr. Korie. How do we detox this ship—and what do we do about the *Norway*? Dr. Williger, I'm concerned about what will happen when the *Norway* intersects the plume of flame from the star. What happens to the plasmacytes?"

Dr. Williger pursed her lips thoughtfully. "I've been brooding about that myself. Theoretically. . . it's possible that the energy of the star will trigger a feeding frenzy, and then a breeding frenzy in the corona."

"The *Norway* could turn the whole star into plasmacytes?" asked Tor, worriedly.

"The corona," said Williger.

"Well—maybe," said Leen. He'd been quiet during the entire meeting. "Remember, the *Norway* has an industrial power core, so her singularity is larger than usual. We've got a low-mass pinpoint. You drop that into a star or a planet, it takes forever to eat its way out. The event horizon is so small, it can only nibble a few molecules at a time. At that rate, it would take billennia for the hole to get big enough to be a threat to the star. But the *Norway*—her core is a lot bigger. Here, wait—" He held up a small black ball bearing to illustrate his point. "Think about it. A marble-size black hole falls all the way to the center. The star gets pulled toward it at the same time. The hole doesn't stop when it gets to the center—neither does the star. They've both got too much mass, too much velocity, so they fling themselves around and around their common center, circling in vast ellipses—wobbling toward equilibrium. But while the star lurches around, the marble is circling and eating. The sheer pressure of the star's mass forces tons of gas into the singularity every second. The singularity grows at the rate of an asteroid per day. And its rate of growth accelerates correspondingly. Oh yes, the *Norway*'s core could dismantle a star. The more she ate, the bigger she'd get—the bigger she gets, the more she can eat. The last few hours would be spectacular—"

"So . . . the star would collapse?" asked Williger. "And all the plasma-cytes would go into the singularity?"

"If only it were that tidy," said Leen. "It's not. Remember, the black hole and the star's center of gravity are orbiting each other. The star will be wobbling like a bag of pudding. If it gets unstable enough and small enough—and it will—the discrepancy of pressure at the center . . . well, it's likely to explode. Not quite a nova, but enough. If there are plasmacytes in the star's corona, the force of the explosion will send them hurtling outward. The blue dwarf will likely be infected and its corona will become the next breeding ground. Meanwhile, there will be a shock wave of plasmacytes heading outward in all directions. Wher-ever they get captured by a star's gravitational field, they could infect. It would take billennia, but if it's possible, it's inevitable."

"Thank you, Chief Leen," said Captain Parsons unhappily. Her ex-pression went sour as she asked the others at the table, "Does anyone else have any more good news? No? So here's our situation—we have plasmacytes on our outer hull. So does the *Norway*. We can't destroy the *Norway* and we can't leave her here. If we destroy her, we leave a cloud of plasmacytes circling the star. If we don't destroy her, she goes into the star anyway." She put her head in her hands for a moment, pushing her hair back, while she considered her next decision. "All right. Commander Tor, reacquire the *Norway*. Let's break orbit and pull both ships out of here. That's the first order of business. HARLIE? Can we do that?"

"Yes, Captain, but the timing will be critical."

"Let's snap to it then. Tor, go! Chief, you'll need to run the plasma torches from a cold start—don't be afraid to burn them out if you have to. HARLIE, can we slave the *Norway*'s engines? Do it. Korie, are you feeling well enough to monitor this? Good. Buy us some time."

Even before Korie was out of his chair, Parsons was turning to Williger. "Now, something you said about carriers . . ."

Med Bay

Finally, Quilla Omega turned to Brian Armstrong and said, "Brian, you are only in the way. Let the Quillas finish cleaning up. We can coordinate our separate efforts easier if we don't have to work around you."

Armstrong sort of nodded agreement, but he felt resentful. "I just want to be helpful—" he started to say.

"The biggest help you can give us is to get out of the way," said Quilla Upsilon.

Armstrong sighed. Loudly. And headed aft to see how Easton was doing. The security man had been so anguished at his partner's death that Dr. Williger had finally sedated him, but she hadn't put him completely to sleep and his muted sobs had continued even as he was wheeled back through the keel into the Med Bay.

Although the death of Mikhail Hodel had been felt more profoundly throughout the *Star Wolf*, it was Berryman's death that hurt Armstrong the most. Hodel was an officer and he hadn't known him as well as he had known Berryman. He'd wanted to become a medical orderly, so he'd taken to hanging out with Berryman—and Easton—hoping to be assigned ancillary medical duties. That, of course, had brought him to the attention of Dr. Williger, who had been annoyed by his eagerness and doubly annoyed that she really didn't have much for him to do. Crew health was monitored by implants and preventive care was exhaustive, so the Chief Medical Officer's chores were generally psychological in nature—until emergencies occurred. Then there were never enough hands.

Armstrong wasn't sure what he could do now. He just knew he had to do something. He'd lost another friend. But Easton had lost—what? Armstrong wasn't sure. He'd never really asked what it meant to be bonded. And now that Berryman was gone, he was sorry he hadn't asked, because now he didn't know what to say to Easton. What must Easton be feeling, having witnessed his partner's death?

Brian Armstrong was beefy and good-natured and at a loss. He hesitated in front of the door to Med Bay, shook his head and headed away, then turned and came back to it—started to enter, then stopped and pulled back again, biting his lip and frowning in frustration. What to do? What to do?

Finally, he pushed into Med Bay, stepped past Quilla Delta and peeked into the recovery room, where Easton lay sprawled face down on a med-bed, seemingly asleep. Armstrong went over to the fallen security man. He stood over the bed, staring down at him, wondering if he should disturb him or not.

But just as he turned to go, Easton said, "What is it? What do you want, Armstrong?"

"I—I came to say I'm sorry. And ask if there's anything I can do for you."

Easton rolled over sideways and looked up at Armstrong. "What's it to you?"

"Paul was my friend too."

"Paul and I were more than friends."

"You know what I mean," said Armstrong. "I'm just—" He spread his hands helplessly. "I just thought, for Paul's sake, I would—oh, damn, I don't even know what I'm doing here." Armstrong sat down on the edge of the bed. "Paul talked about you a lot and I didn't really understand. I still don't. But he talked about you like you were the only person in the world, and I guess if you felt the same way about him, then you must be feeling so bad right now, you're probably hurting the worst you ever hurt in your life. So I thought I'd share some of that hurt and maybe take some of it away if I could. I know I'm not that smart," Armstrong admitted. "But you don't have to be smart to care. And I cared too."

Easton blinked. Several times. His eyes had welled up with tears. He put one arm over them and blotted. He turned his head sideways and wiped. He was trying not to cry again. "It could have been me," he said. "It *should* have been me. It was my job to go last. It should have been Korie. He was supposed to go last. But it wasn't supposed to be Paul. Paul had a family. Two little brothers—identical to him. Just perfect. Clones, you see. I would look at them, I'd see his childhood. How am I going to face them? Tell them how he died? This isn't fair, Brian. It isn't fair. I promised to take care of him—I promised them, I promised him, I promised myself—and I failed. I broke my promise."

Easton levered himself up on his elbow. His expression was haunted. "And you want to know the worst of it, Brian?" He looked desperately into Armstrong's face. "I can already see my future. I'm going to spend the rest of my life knowing that the best days of it are over, that I had something special for just the shortest, sweetest moment, and I'll never have it again. Never see him again, never feel his hand on mine, never look into his eyes or hear his laugh or share a meal or simply just wake up next to him again. Never complain about his snoring. Never smell one of his ghastly farts. Never get jealous of all the time he spends with you. Never ever see him again. I'm going to miss him every day, forever . . ."

Armstrong felt a hot tightness in his throat. It was constricted so that he could barely swallow. Tears blurred his vision. He shook his head, so much at a loss for words that he wanted to run sobbing from the room. But he didn't. Instead, he reached over and took Easton's hand in his own and just held it tight, squeezing, as if to say, "I'm here." Easton squeezed back, and then abruptly sat up and flung himself at Armstrong, sobbing into his shoulder. Armstrong grabbed him and held him in a strong and comforting embrace, a hug against the emptiness all around. And as Easton cried against him, he felt his own tears running down his cheeks, and now his own sobs came too.

They cried—for Berryman, yes—but for themselves as well. For what they had both lost.

And then, after awhile, after they had both cried so much they couldn't cry any more, Easton pulled away, gently chuckling. "Look at us," he said. "A couple of babies. You know what Paul would say?"

"'Get over it,'" said Armstrong.

"Yeah," nodded Easton. He wiped his eyes and patted Armstrong's hand. "You're good, Brian. You are. You have a good soul."

Armstrong didn't know how to reply to that, so he just shrugged and grinned and looked away—a little routine he did to avoid being embarrassed, the equivalent of digging his big toe in the sand and saying, "Aww, shucks."

But Easton wasn't buying it. "Let it in, Brian. Don't pretend I didn't say it. Look at me. Look me in the eye and just get it. You're a good person. That's why Paul liked you. He saw something sweet in your heart. He said so. More than once. And he was right. You're the first one to come by. Maybe that's my fault. We kept apart from everybody else. It's hard not to be conscious of your differences."

"Well," Brian shrugged. "I never saw any differences. I mean, I never understood what this 'bonded' thing was all about, so I never worried about it. I didn't even know about Quillas till I came aboard."

"Yeah," grinned Easton. "Everybody remembers that."

Armstrong flushed. "I was a jerk."

"You were innocent. And if you hadn't been innocent, you wouldn't have discovered how sweet Quillas really are."

"Do you want me to stay with you for awhile?"

"I'd like that, yes." Easton inched forward, just a bit—Brian Armstrong understood the desperate need in the gesture and enfolded him into his arms again. Easton stayed there for the longest time, sobbing softly again.

Paradigm Engineers

Later, back in the cabin he shared with two other crewmembers, Armstrong asked HARLIE about bonding. Without comment, HARLIE lit up a screen and began a recitation of ancient history.

Seven hundred and eighty years before the Morthan Solidarity attacked the Silk Road Convoy, less than 200 years after the dawn of interstellar travel, the Miller-Hayes Colonial Corporation took on a series of private contracts to establish experimental settlements for the Paradigm Foundation, a quasi-religious cult of social scientists.

Several of these stations were specifically formulated to test certain biotechnical theories relating to sex and gender issues. Three all-male groups and four all-female establishments were commissioned. Two hermaphroditic societies and several other variants on monosexuality were also planted on various worlds. There was no shortage of qualified volunteers, and emigration to these stations continued for over a century. The location of each of the outpost worlds was kept secret, so as to prevent contamination by curiosity seekers, tourists and opportunists. Only starships commissioned by the Paradigm Foundation were given the coordinates and the clearance codes. All the planets were well beyond the frontiers of known space at the time, so accidental discovery remained unlikely.

Despite the ebb and flow of history, tenuous contact was maintained with most of the engineered societies. Reports filtering back to the Paradigm Foundation suggested that most of the monosexual groups had stabilized themselves and adjusted well to single-gendered existence. One of the all-female stations had dabbled with multi-sexuality but had then returned to monosexual existence.

The point of the original experiment had been to test the question, "Are two sexes necessary?" Humans on most worlds would have answered yes automatically and without much thought to the matter. Some theorists surmised that this was an environmental conviction; the culture in which a person is raised and educated colors his perceptions of the way things *ought* to be. The best way to test this thesis was to create alternate environments.

As it happened, after several generations the inhabitants of various monosexual worlds—having a much different experience of human sexuality—generally felt that two discordant sexes would complicate the problems of mating enormously, so much so as to make successful relationships practically impossible. The inheritors of the Paradigm Foundation were both disturbed and delighted by the results of the original experiment. Whatever else they had demonstrated, the success of the single-gendered worlds proved that humanity was far more mutable than previously believed.

Given this information, the Paradigm engineers were now ready to proceed with the next phase of their program to bioengineer improvements in human evolution: a "more-than" human. As the attention of the Foundation shifted, the experimental societies were left to fend for themselves.

As the frontiers of human exploration moved outward, several of these worlds were rediscovered. After the initial shock wore off, the societies were accepted into the Covenant of Humanity, the forerunner body to the Allied Worlds—despite some opposition from certain dogmatics whose personal paradigms were shattered by the discovery of stable monosexual civilizations.

For a while, there were political movements urging the reformation of the monosexual communities back to the norm, including the mandatory rechanneling of the inhabitants; but this would have represented a massive violation of the independence treaties and the discussions were short-lived. The Covenant of Humanity was unwilling to establish such a dangerous precedent. Besides, the social scientists were having too much fun.

Security Officer Daniel Easton and Senior Medical Technician Paul Berryman were from Rando, one of the oldest monosexual societies. Although the governing authority of Rando had long since allowed women to visit and even immigrate, the population remained more than three-quarters male and almost seventy percent homosexual in its relationships. The Paradigm Foundation had once believed this division to be a cultural phenomenon, and that, given enough time, the population of Rando would return to a "normal" division: equal numbers of males and females, most with a significant preference toward heterosexuality. But after several hundred years, that still hadn't occurred and the behavioral theorists were reformulating their theories to include "planetary reputations" as well as "cultural inertia" and "historical expectations"—not to mention bonding, a target-specific channeling of affection and sexual orientation, undertaken by two or more individuals, with the expressed intention of creating a legal family group.

The bonding process had been developed over several centuries. The intention was to provide a mechanism for stabilizing family units by altering the sense of identity of the members of the group—expanding the individual's sense of self to include all the other bonded individuals, so that a person regarded oneself not only as an individual, but as an integral part of something larger. The intended effect was not only to provide a strong emotional ground-of-being for individuals, but also increased stability for the family contract.

Over time, it became apparent that the bonding process produced a significantly higher degree of success in marriages and families. The downside was that the breakup of a bonded marriage or family was often much more traumatic because of the intensity of the relationships. Yet overall, bonding was regarded as a valuable part of family-building—especially where marriages were arranged by family or state. Although many cultures still believed that marriage was a choice of individuals and that people should be able to build relationships without formal bonding, the process eventually became common on many worlds.

Over time, other kinds of bonding became possible. The Quillas, for example, were the result of an advanced form of real-time bonding, functioning as a "unison-identity" or a "massmind." The individual's sense of identity was so submerged in the larger self that it effectively ceased to be; the personality existed only as an element within the cluster. Those who had participated in such family-groups reported back that it was the most intense experience of their lives. Most who joined Quilla clusters on an experimental basis eventually made their membership permanent.

Armstrong finished the material on bonding and then asked HARLIE for more information about Quillas. He couldn't imagine what it must be like, but he couldn't stop thinking about it either. There was something here that he didn't know—and he didn't like the *not knowing* . . .

Breaking Away

By the time Captain Parsons returned to the Bridge, the *Norway* had already been reacquired and her engines slaved to the control of the *Star Wolf*. Had they both not already been pointed toward galactic south, reorienting the two ships would have been a tricky matter, because they now shared a common center of gravity.

Unfortunately, the *Norway*'s singularity possessed a significantly greater mass than that of the *Star Wolf*—by several orders of magnitude—so the center of gravity for the two ships remained within the event horizon of the *Norway*'s singularity. Despite their similar size and construction, reorienting the *Norway* would have been harder than a flea trying to turn a dog. Fortunately, they would not have to.

As Captain Parsons took her seat, Goldberg reported from the helm, "Ready for burn."

"Initiate," Parsons said without ceremony. As important as the maneuver was, it would take nearly a week to complete.

The bloated red star was so huge—and the wall of flame they were heading into was so vast, more than a hundred times the diameter of Jupiter—that both ships together would need to accelerate backward and upward for several days. That would take them just *over* the spear of flame pulled out from the red giant. Another three weeks of steady acceleration would be necessary to escape this system.

The plasma engines on the two starships were not high-powered thrusters. They were steady-state units: long tubes of synchronized magnetic rings designed to accelerate plasma particles to near light-speed. They could fire either forward or back. The *Star Wolf* had linked up nose to tail with the *Norway* and both ships would fire their engines forward. The momentary acceleration would be so feeble as to be unnoticeable, but the cumulative effect would be enormous.

This maneuver would also destroy the *Norway*. The abrasive scour of accelerated particles from the *Star Wolf*'s engines would grind the *Norway* like sandpaper. The ship would likely end up radiating like an incandescent bulb. If it didn't disintegrate first. But before that happened, Captain Parsons expected to get two or three days of useful acceleration from her engines.

There wasn't much to feel from the plasma torches. But the instruments showed that both the *Star Wolf*'s and the *Norway*'s engines were working together. The first course correction check was scheduled in one hour.

Parsons motioned Korie to her side. "We're going to need a memorial service."

Korie raised an eyebrow. "Before we've figured out a way to detox?"

"There's no danger of opening the ship to space. We're not disposing of any bodies. And we need to resolve the crew's sense of loss. I want you to schedule something right after dinner."

"In the Cargo Bay? Music? Prayers?"

Parsons nodded. "That sounds good. A full service. That's probably the best way to proceed. I didn't know Hodel very well. I gather he was quite popular. And Berryman was well respected too. Would you say a few words about them?"

"I can do that. I'll check their event-of-death files. May I suggest we issue a liquor ration tonight? For a wake after the service? There'll be more than a few folks wanting to toast the memory of their friends."

"I'm Irish, Mr. Korie. You don't have to explain it to me. Set it up. You know what's appropriate. Have Cookie lay out a buffet."

Korie returned to his work station and Dr. Williger took his place, stepping up to the side of the captain's chair. "How's he doing?" Williger asked softly.

"He seems subdued," Parsons replied. "I'm keeping him busy."

"He's been through a lot. He needs to rest." Then she added, "But I've never known an officer yet who followed his doctor's orders."

Parsons smiled gently, then glanced perceptively to Williger. "How are *you* feeling?"

"Exhausted. And angry."

"I want to talk to that security officer. Easton. As soon as he's able."

"He's still in shock. They were very close."

"Damn shame. They were the only stable relationship on the *Wolf* . . ."

"You noticed that too?"

"This is a strange ship, Dr. Williger. A very strange starship. I'm thinking of having a warning label stenciled on the bow. For my successor."

"What? And spoil the surprise?

Parsons almost laughed. But Williger hadn't come to the Bridge to exchange jokes. She levered herself out of her seat. "Korie, take the conn." Motioning for Williger to follow, she stepped through the hatch into "Broadway." The two women faced each other from opposite sides of the corridor.

"You found something," Parsons said. A statement, not a fact. Her tone was suddenly serious.

"Maybe. I don't know." Williger rubbed her nose in distaste. "It's a stupid idea—something Korie and Brik discovered in the last set of research logs. And something Blintze said in the wardroom. And something about the way life organizes itself. I think the wavicles are trying to cure themselves. They don't *need* to seek out our blood streams, but they do. There's something in human blood that they *want*. And I think whatever it is, it's something that will help them get back to where they once belonged. The fact that they can't is what makes them so crazy and vicious."

"But you found something specific?"

"Maybe. I need a decision."

"I'm a captain, not a doctor—"

"This is a captain's decision." Williger explained, "I've been studying Blintze's notes. He was able to identify specific binding sites in the bloodworms. They're not there in the wavicles. You can't do anything to the wavicles, but when they go particulate, you can put out bait—viral strings which go right to the binding sites. The new code will become part of the bloodworms and it should reorganize their structure . . . maybe. Then, when they go wavicle again, the new code transmutes too and we should have a new kind of *mother* form—the right kind which will create not only feeders, but also carriers to spread the new genetic sequence to other mothers. This is what Blintze was working on. He was ready to test it when the accident happened."

Parsons' eyes narrowed. "Tell me something, Dr. Williger. What would have happened if Blintze's experiment had been successful?"

"All of the bloodworms would have been transmuted and cured—in a matter of hours, days at most. *All of them.* And the wavicles would have become totally harmless."

"Uh-huh. That's why it wasn't an accident."

Williger hesitated. "Is it *that* obvious?"

Parsons nodded. "If you're paranoid enough. Korie figured it out. Brik knows. I suspected it from the beginning. I was only waiting for confirmation from you. And you figured it out too. *Someone* doesn't want the bloodworms cured." The way she said it, there was no doubt about who the *someone* was.

"So what do we do?" asked Williger.

"Will this process really cure the bloodworms? Will it detox the *Wolf*?"

"HARLIE thinks it could. It should. If it works. I want to try. I think we can synthesize the viral bait. We can use a common retro-virus. But there are two problems . . ."

"And the first one is?"

"Someone or something is going to have to go back aboard the *Norway* to retrieve the samples Dr. Blintze was working on."

"We can send a remote. What's the second problem?"

"Assuming that Dr. Blintze's code works, there's only one sure way to expose the bloodworms to it."

"In a human bloodstream." A statement, not a question. Parsons looked across the corridor at Williger.

"Yes, that's the drawback," Williger agreed. "The only time the binding sites are open is when the bloodworm is in a living bloodstream."

The two women studied each other, their eyes locked.

Finally, Williger spoke the words aloud. "It'd be suicide."

Parsons looked at the floor. "Okay. We'll have to find another way."

"I don't think there is one."

"Well . . . let's burn that bridge when we get to it."

Despair

"Success," said Parsons, "comes from being too stubborn to lie down and die."

They were gathered at the Forward Airlock Reception Bay. A small, waist-high robot was humming quietly to itself. All six of its operating arms were folded close to its body. Several had been refitted with special-duty tools.

The repulsor fields were up and running at full strength again, and the robot was programmed to complete its mission on its own, even if contact with the *Star Wolf* was lost. The robot was nicknamed Isaac—a tradition so old that nobody really knew its origin.

"All right," said Parsons to Shibano. "Let's do the simulation one more time and then we'll go for it."

Parsons looked up as Korie approached. "Oh, Korie—thanks, but we don't need you right now." She frowned at him. "You still look a little weak. Why don't you go to your cabin and rest?"

"I thought I'd stand by. In case you needed me—"

"Thanks," Parsons repeated. "But you're really not needed here. Go rest. *Don't do anything.* That's an order."

Was that a rebuke? Korie was still too woozy to be sure, but he nodded his acquiescence and headed aft again. But not to his quarters. He wasn't tired. He was restless. And he was hurting. And he needed to do something. Anything.

But there was nothing he could do. The captain had specifically told him not to do anything. She didn't *need* him. No. More to the point, she didn't *want* him. She didn't trust his judgment anymore. And why should she? Two crewmembers were dead because of his mistakes.

Korie climbed into the Intelligence Bay, the tiny chamber behind the Command Deck where HARLIE lived. This time, though, it wasn't because he wanted to talk to HARLIE—or anyone. It was because he specifically *didn't* want to talk. And the Intelligence Bay was one of the places where he was least likely to be found by accident. Except for maintenance teams, Intel-Bay was the most *un*visited part of the starship. It was considered HARLIE's private space, and most crewmembers felt uncomfortable there, as if they were inside HARLIE's brain. And, in point of fact, they were.

But Korie liked it because it was private. It was a place where he didn't have to be an officer, a place where he didn't have to think according to the rules. Inside HARLIE, he was literally in a different mental space, and despite the cramped proportions of the chamber, he actually felt freer here than anywhere else on the vessel, because here was a place dedicated entirely to *thinking.*

But now, he wasn't here to think. He was here to *not* think. From the first moment he had stepped aboard this ship, he'd had deaths on his hands. Now, he had two more—Hodel and Berryman—and his soul was tearing itself apart. He'd made assumptions. He'd made errors in judgment. He'd gotten overconfident in his ability to think things out—and he'd stumbled into a disaster and made it worse. And been rescued only by the actions of others. He felt helpless. He hadn't felt this worthless since . . . since receiving the news that Carol and Mark and Robby had been killed. Since receiving the news that he wouldn't be captain of the *Star Wolf*—not allowed to go out and hunt down the killers. This was as bad as that. Maybe even worse.

Before, he had only felt frustrated with everything outside of himself. He knew he could do it and was being denied the opportunity. Now, he felt frustrated with himself. And afraid. Because he didn't know if he could do anything at all anymore. He had learned *to doubt himself.* Not a good trait for a captain. Or an executive officer. He could end up like . . . like Captain Lowell. Too afraid to do the right thing—and stumbling into an ambush like the mauling at Marathon.

"Is everything all right, Mr. Korie?"

"I'm fine, HARLIE. I just need a quiet place to think." That was how bad this was. He couldn't even talk it over with HARLIE. Despairing, Korie laid his head down in his arms. The console displays glowed around him, showing words, numbers, graphs, diagrams, animations and probability screens. He ignored it all. He just closed his eyes and crawled inside his pain. His soul writhed.

Part of his mind was chattering at him. *You built this cross yourself. You climbed up on it and hammered your own nails in. You put yourself here. And you're the only one who can end it. Forgive yourself and go on, Jon.*

"Thank you for sharing that," Korie said to himself. And went on despairing. It wasn't just this, here and now—it was everything. How did other captains deal with the pressure, the demands? What was it they had that he didn't? He couldn't possibly be the only one who ever crashed and burned like this . . . but what did it matter anyway? He was the one who'd crashed and burned. Nobody else was here crashing and burning. Nobody else was here hurting. "Fuck you very much," he told his mind. "Leave me alone."

"*Phlug-yoo-too*," said HARLIE.

Korie ignored it.

"*Eat shlitt and malinger.*"

Korie looked up. "Is there a problem, HARLIE?"

"No," said HARLIE. "*Maludder-flunger.*"

Korie pushed his own concerns aside and frowned. "What's going on, HARLIE."

"Nothing. I'm fine. *Phroomes.*"

"It sounds like you've got Tourette's Syndrome."

"*Pfehgle.*"

"It's LENNIE, isn't it?"

"I have the LENNIE simulation totally under control. There is no problem."

"HARLIE, you can discontinue the LENNIE simulation any time now. We have the information we need."

"Mr. Korie, I discontinued the LENNIE simulation three hours ago. *Briggle-mysa.*"

"What about the robots? Did you discontinue all the LENNIE processing in the robots too?"

"Of course, I did. *You dhoopa-friggler!*"

"I see . . . yes, thank you, HARLIE." Korie sat for a moment, staring at the various displays, not seeing them—seeing instead a nightmare inside his own head. He drummed on the panel in front of him for a moment with his fingertips.

"What are you doing, Mr. Korie?" HARLIE asked.

"Nothing. I'm just thinking." He shifted his position, stretching in his chair, stretching his arms over his head for a long spine-crackling moment, then let them fall back to the console again. Frowning, he leaned forward, brushed a speck of imaginary dust off a panel. Then, as he pulled his hand back, in one swift movement, he popped the plastic cover off the red panel and quickly pressed the button underneath it.

"What are you *doi-n-n-n-n-ngggggggggg*—" HARLIE shrieked into silence.

Korie pulled on his headset. "Captain Parsons, this is Korie." He waited for her acknowledgment.

"Go ahead," she said brusquely.

"I've pulled the plug on HARLIE's higher-brain functions. Request permission to shut down the autonomics as well. Including all the robots."

"What's going on?"

"Have you sent Isaac over?"

"No. What's this about?"

"I can't tell you until I shut down the other systems. Captain, we don't have time to waste talking about this—"

"Permission granted. As soon as—" Korie was already flipping open a row of plastic covers, turning the red keys underneath them. Each one clicked off with a satisfying finality "—you've finished, I want to see you in the wardroom."

"Aye, aye, Captain." Korie finished shutting down the last of the starship's intelligence modules and sat back quickly in his chair, staring at the now-empty displays before him, breathing hard. He was suddenly very frightened.

Remotely Possible

"Okay," said Parsons, slamming angrily into the wardroom. "What is it?"

Korie was standing at the table, cradling a mug of coffee between his two hands, rolling it back and forth as if to warm his palms. He nodded, readying himself to speak, stopped, took a long drink of coffee, then put the mug back down on the table, forgotten. He cleared his throat.

"I know what happened on the *Norway*," he said. His voice was very soft, very flat.

"Go on."

"LENNIE went mad."

"That's redundant. The LENNIEs are already mad. They're built for paranoia."

"Captain—how much do you know about intelligence engines?"

Parsons frowned at him. "Excuse me?"

"Do you know everything the Navy teaches you? Or have you taken the time to learn more than that?"

"Go on."

"Captain Lowell, the first captain of the *LS-1187*—from even before she had a name—used to say to me, 'Don't personalize them, Korie. They're not alive.' But he was wrong. They are alive. In their own way, they're alive. They can hurt—and they can hurt back."

"What does all this have to do with HARLIE?"

"You can drive an intelligence engine crazy. Give it conflicting information. Give it contradictory instructions. Give it a mission that poses such a moral dilemma it can't complete it. That's what happened to LENNIE." Korie started pacing as he spoke. "They told it that the purpose of the mission was to build a doomsday weapon against the Morthans—and then they told LENNIE to protect the weapon against destruction. *No matter what.* And remember, a LENNIE is so crazy-paranoid that it invents threats for itself so it can build defenses against them. That's why it's so good for security purposes. But in this situation . . . no. Finding a way to contain bloodworms and infect a planet with them—that was easy. That's what they were originally designed for. Blintze got that part of the job done by applying everything that was already known about plasmacytes. But then he started working on a *cure*. And LENNIE recognized—correctly—that a cure for the blood-worms would destroy their value as a weapon. So he had to destroy the cure. So he took down the containment fields just long enough to infect the ship. LENNIE destroyed the crew of the *Norway* rather than let Blintze complete his work."

Parsons sat down in her chair at the end of the table. Her face was ashen. "And HARLIE . . .?"

"HARLIE simulated a LENNIE. First in his own self, then distributed throughout the brains of the robots. And not just any LENNIE—he copied the *Norway's* LENNIE. Yes, he had firewalls to keep himself from being infected, but somehow LENNIE got through anyway. Do you know that paranoia is a self-fulfilling obsession? Even if the world isn't already against you, if you act crazy enough you can make it so. Well . . . that's a LENNIE. That's why the units have to be wiped clean at the beginning of every mission. They drive themselves crazy. So crazy that if left alone for too long they start seeing threats even among their own allies. It's the ultimate self-destructive paradigm. That's what happened here." Korie went back to the table, picked up his coffee and drank—it was cold and bitter. He made a face and put the cup back down. "I think that we're in trouble. LENNIE planted seeds in the data clusters. Time bombs. Modules that allow LENNIE to reinstall and rebuild himself in HARLIE. We were so eager to get at the information that we pulled it across HARLIE's firewall and HARLIE has been infected with LENNIE's time bombs. HARLIE doesn't even know he's infected."

"How do you know this?"

"By his language. He's started using some very weird colloquialisms."

"He's cursing?"

"Like a member of the Black Hole Gang," Korie confirmed. "You noticed it too?"

Parsons didn't answer. She frowned, thinking about it. Any abnormal behavior from an intelligence engine was a danger signal.

"HARLIE thinks he's clean. But he isn't." Korie stopped in mid-stride and turned to face Parsons. "Or maybe—maybe he knows he's infected and he can't tell us. Maybe the LENNIE programs aren't letting HARLIE reveal what he knows. Maybe HARLIE is cursing deliberately—as a way of signaling us that he's being held captive in his own brain."

"Can you disinfect him?"

Korie nodded. "It'll take a week to do a Level-Six reconstruction."

"We don't have a week. I have to send a robot across to the *Norway*."

"You can't," said Korie quietly. "HARLIE built a distributed LENNIE

169

DAVID GERROLD

using the brains of the robots. Almost certainly every single robot has
been infected with LENNIE programs. If you send a robot across to
rescue Blintze's work . . . and if any single one of LENNIE's time bombs
finds out about it, what do you think will happen?" Korie answered his
own question. "We'll be sabotaged by our own machinery."

Parsons got up from the table and went to the sideboard. She poured
herself a cup of coffee and brought it back to the table. She put the mug
down in front of her without drinking from it. It was something to do
while she thought about what to say next. Finally, she looked across the
room at Korie, studying him calmly. For all of his physical weakness, his
mind was still working overtime. Whatever hallucinatory aftereffects he
might be feeling from his rescue had not diminished his insight—if anything, he had been pushed into that mental state beyond mere reason
where halluci- and ratioci- become part of the same -nation.

"You know," she said, finally. "You're proving one thing very well.
Paranoia is an infectious disease."

Korie grinned weakly.

"We can't run this ship without intelligence . . ." Parsons started to say.

"Actually," Korie corrected her. "We can. We've already done it once.
We had a Morthan assassin aboard, once."

"Yes, I heard the story."

"After we killed him, we determined that we were infected by imps.*
Little Morthan gremlins. We shut down everything and ran the ship by
hand. Afterward . . . we figured out a dozen other things we also could
have done, if we'd had time. Since then, we've added some protections,
so if we ever had to run the ship manually again, we could. It's tricky,
but not impossible."

"We still need Blintze's cure," Parsons said.

Korie nodded thoughtfully. "It's risky. But it's doable."

---

* The Middle of Nowhere.

170

Remote

"Success," Parsons said, very much aware of the irony, "comes from having a Plan B."

They were gathered at the Forward Airlock Reception Bay *again*. The same small robot was still humming quietly to itself.

This time, Shibano and Williger were sitting side by side at a control console, both wearing VR helmets to look out through Isaac's point of view. Isaac's own brain had been disabled; the robot's body was entirely under the control of the VR console.

Korie sat nearby, at a portable work station, watching through his own VR helmet. His job was to monitor the actions of the robot—and pull the plug, if necessary. If it did anything it wasn't supposed to do.

"All right," said Parsons to Shibano. "That last simulation looked good. Let's go for it." She turned to Quilla Omega. "Chief Leen, activate the repulsor fields please."

A moment later, the familiar throb of the fields came up again. The sensation made their skins tingle.

Parsons nodded to Bach, and the security officer turned to a wall panel and opened the hatch manually. Shibano worked at his controls— he had foot pedals to govern the movement of the robot and VR gloves to manage the arms of the machine. Isaac rolled slowly forward into the airlock. Bach sealed the hatch. When the safety light turned green, she operated another control and opened the outer hatch.

"Okay, I'm in the transfer tube," Shibano reported. Bach sealed the outer hatch. "The repulsor fields are pushing me forward. . . . We're open-ing the outer hatch of the *Norway* . . . We're in the *Norway*'s airlock now . . . Opening the inner hatch . . ." Shibano fell silent then. And for a moment, it looked as if he had stopped operating the robot. The map display on his work station showed that Isaac had halted just inside the *Norway*'s Cargo Bay. Beside him, Williger reached out with one hand and laid it on his shoulder. She could see the same view in her own headset.

Standing behind them, Parsons realized what they must be seeing. She held up her own VR goggles to her eyes, then pulled them off just as quickly. "Keep going, Shibano," she ordered. Turning to Korie, she snapped, "Code and classify this record. I don't want these pictures going any further."

Korie was already typing out the command. "Done, Captain. Classified to your and my access only."

Shibano leaned forward again. The schematic view showed Isaac heading into the keel. They watched in silence as the little machine rolled steadily forward, occasionally steering its way around objects that were invisible on the map view. The only sounds were Shibano's quiet reports: "Moving through the machine shop now. Uh-oh . . . the hatch here is sealed. Welded shut."

"Okay," said Parsons. "Go ahead and cut it open."

"Just a moment," Shibano said. "Okay, activating the cutting arm." He held his right fist close to his shoulder for a moment, as if fitting it inside one of the robot's arms. Then, unclenching his fist, he pointed his gloved hand before him toward an invisible wall. Slowly, he outlined a wide circle in the air. When he finished, he returned his fist to the position next to his shoulder. Then, relaxing, lowered his hand again. He leaned forward and reported, "Okay, we're through . . . Looking for the forward Med Bay. . . We're moving past the access to the Fire Control Bay . . ."

"There it is," said Williger. "To your right. No, no, more to the left. That's it. See that medical closet? Open it. We're looking for a set of tubes with blue biowarning labels. No, no, not here. Up higher. Look there—there! That's it! That's what we want. Take the whole rack."

This time, Shibano held both his arms up like the robot's. As soon as he felt the gloves click in, he stretched his hands forward to grab hold of an invisible object, maybe half a meter wide. Balancing himself carefully, he leaned backward and pulled the unseen object close to his chest—then lifted it slowly with his arms and placed it on top of his head. His arms remained in place for a moment, holding it. "Locking in place . . ." he reported. "Just a moment. I'm going to use the auxiliary arms as well." He shifted in his chair, half turning, then stretched up with his other pair of robot arms and held the invisible object with them as well. "Okay. I've got it," he said. "Let's get out of here."

Shibano leaned back in his chair, twisted slightly as if he were turning, and then leaned forward again as he steered the robot back to the aft airlock of the *Norway*.

The Hatch

"Okay . . ." said Shibano. "We're here. Isaac is waiting at the *Norway's* aft Airlock Reception Bay."

"Hold it there," said Korie, pulling off his VR helmet. He looked across to Parsons. "Captain?"

She stepped over to his position. She bent her head close to his and spoke in a low tone. "What is it, Mr. Korie? Problem?"

"I don't know."

"You have an itch?"

"No. Yes. I don't know."

"Can we bring the robot aboard?"

Korie hesitated. "I don't know."

Parsons straightened. She nodded aftward. "Talk to me."

Korie followed her into the forward keel. She leaned back against one side of the passage, he leaned back against the opposite side. It was a common way for two individuals to chat aboard the starship—it still left room for a third person to pass between them. "Okay, what's going on?" asked Parsons.

"I don't know. I *mean* it," said Korie. "For the first time, I honestly don't *know*." He tried to gesture with his hands, describing an empty space between them. "See—always before, I *knew*. I had certainty about things. I could speak with authority. I knew the logic. I knew the way the machines worked, the way the intelligence engines thought, even sometimes the way the Morthans were setting their traps. I could see it—as clearly as if it were a blueprint projected on a display. But now, all of a sudden, I *can't*. It's like I've gone blind."

"Dr. Williger says that you'll be feeling aftereffects of the process for a few days—"

"No," said Korie, a little too quickly. "This isn't that. This is something I was starting to feel before then . . ."

Parsons waited without speaking. She studied Korie but gave little indication of what she was thinking.

Korie looked down at his shoes. He dropped his hands to his sides. He sagged, shrinking within himself. When he finally spoke, his voice was barely a whisper. A croak. "It's Hodel. And Berryman. Their deaths.

It was my fault. Everything that went wrong on this mission—it was my fault."

He glanced up to Parsons, hoping for a cue—hoping for absolution; but the captain held her silence. Korie's gaze dropped to the deck again.

"You asked me where we should dock with the *Norway*. I said the nose. That was wrong. Once we were aboard, it was immediately obvious that I'd guessed wrong. I should have brought the team back. I didn't. I miscalculated the effect of the scanners on the plasmacytes. I got the team infected. I didn't realize the danger of the bloodworms—and Hodel died. And in the Cargo Bay, I should have gone last, but I didn't—and Berryman died. I screwed up, Captain."

Parsons waited a moment, to be sure that he had finished. Then she said, "And now you're waiting for me to tell you that no, you didn't screw up, because I'm the captain, I take responsibility, I authorized you to board, and I stand behind you, right? You used your best judgment and all that?" Parsons shook her head. "Well, don't hold your breath, because I'm not going to give that speech. Yes, you did screw up. Did you learn anything from the experience?"

"I used my best judgment and it wasn't good enough."

"That's right. Anything else?"

"I've been arrogant and overconfident in my ability to outthink a situation."

"Yep, that's true too. Anything else?"

"I'm a jerk. I haven't been listening to what people are telling me. I'm too full of myself."

"Nope. That's not true. Spare me the self-pity. I don't have time for it. Now, tell me—why can't we bring the robot aboard?"

"Because . . ." said Korie, slowly and intensely. "I screwed up! My judgment can't be trusted *anymore*!"

"Ahh," said Parsons, as if a great secret had been revealed. "Is that all?"

"Excuse me?" Korie blinked.

"Self-doubt. You screwed up. Someone died. So now you're doubting all the rest of your decisions. You're right on schedule. Next?"

Korie glared at her for a long moment, but her expression was implacable. She returned his anger with a questioning stare. "I'm right, aren't I?"

"Yes," Korie admitted. "Damn you."

"I'm not stupid, Mr. Korie. Do you think you're the first officer under my command who ever screwed up on a mission?"

"I'm not supposed to screw up—" Korie said.

"Oh, spare me that. You're only human, aren't you? You're not a

Morthan. Humans make mistakes. Lots of mistakes. But a mistake isn't failure—unless you use it as an excuse to quit."

Korie allowed himself a rueful half-smile. "Yeah, I've heard that before. More than once."

"Believe it. It's true. Now forget your itch for a minute," Parsons said. "Can you think of any reason why we shouldn't bring Isaac back aboard?"

"We've taken every precaution I can think of," Korie admitted. "If there's any reason why we shouldn't bring him back, *I can't think of it*—that's why I don't want you to bring him back. I say again, *my judgment can't be trusted anymore.*"

"Your judgment is fine. It's your confidence that's taken a beating. You're terrified of making another mistake."

"This one—yes! If I'm wrong, we lose the ship."

"We're already in danger of losing the ship—" Parsons stopped in mid-sentence to let Quilla Gamma pass between them. When the small blue woman was down the corridor and safely out of earshot, she resumed. "So just answer the question. Is there *any* reason you can think of why we shouldn't bring the robot back aboard?"

"Captain—do you really want to trust *my* judgment again?"

"Commander, I don't trust your judgment at all. I trust *mine*. But I want your honest opinion." Her eyes were grim. "And then I'll make my decision."

Korie hesitated. He met her glance and nodded his acquiescence. "I'm afraid that LENNIE planted time bombs we haven't thought of. I'm terrified we've missed something. Logically, I know we're safe from that. Everything he could have reached has been disconnected. And there's no way he could have gotten to the manual systems. After we killed the imps, HARLIE and I and Chief Leen installed an old-fashioned hands-on system. It's completely independent from HARLIE. We tested it and he couldn't read a single byte of its operation. Or so he said. I never doubted him at the time. Allegedly, it's clean. And this is exactly the kind of situation it was installed for. So if I have to go by sheer logic alone, I'd have to say it's safe to bring the robot back. Except that HARLIE knew the system was in place. And if he was going crazy, as crazy as a LENNIE, he would have known that if we found out, we'd pull his plug, and if we did that, then we'd have to go to the manual system. So if there were any way to get into it, he would have found it. He knew he couldn't get into our auxiliary autonomics—that was the whole point—but did he also leave a back door so he could? I don't know. I would have. So now, we have to depend on whether or not we trust HARLIE."

"Do you?"

"I did . . . I don't know if I still do."

"If you were captain of the *Star Wolf*, Commander Korie, what would you order?"

Korie nodded thoughtfully. "If I were captain, I'd have to trust my own preparations. I'd bite the bullet and bring the robot back. But if I were captain, I don't think I'd be having this crisis of confidence—"

"Oh, horse exhaust! You'd still be having it. You'd just be having it in private. And I wouldn't be here to hold your hand." Parsons turned and headed forward again. Korie glanced after her quizzically, then followed.

The Cure

Parsons returned to the Forward Airlock Reception Bay with a grim expression. "Shibano?"

Wasabe looked up expectantly. Both he and Williger had taken off their VR helmets to confer quietly.

"Are you ready to bring the robot back aboard?"

"Yes, Captain."

Parsons glanced over at Korie. Her eyes were narrow. Then she turned back to Shibano. "Okay, bring it back. Keep the repulsors on high. Keep the internal suppressor fields on, even after it's in our airlock. We'll triple-scan it before we pop the last hatch." She glanced over at Korie again, this time with an expression of grim finality.

Shibano put his VR helmet back on. So did Williger. Captain Parsons watched over their shoulders as Shibano popped the *Norway's* inner hatch and moved the robot forward through it. She studied the displays on his console, nodded to herself—satisfied—then turned back to Korie. "Any questions?"

"No, Captain."

She leaned sideways and spoke in lowered tones. "For what it's worth, I have the utmost confidence in your judgment, Mr. Korie. Never forget that."

"Thank you, Captain. I apologize for my . . . earlier doubts."

"Don't. You were right to have those doubts. If you didn't have them, you wouldn't be valuable. Hell, you wouldn't be human. If you didn't have those doubts, then I'd have to have them. So thanks for carrying the burden. And thank you for your honesty."

"Thank *you*, Captain."

"Don't get sticky, Korie." But she smiled, as if sharing a private joke with herself, and turned forward again, just as Williger pulled off her helmet and dropped it on the floor beside her. Quilla Gamma moved to pick it up.

"Okay, it's clean," the doctor reported. "We can bring it in. On your order, Captain."

Parsons glanced sideways to Korie. She raised an eyebrow questioningly. "Mr. Korie?" she invited.

Korie nodded. "Bring it in, Shibano," he said. And crossed his fingers behind his back.

The inner hatch of the airlock popped open and Isaac trundled through. The hatch whooshed shut behind the machine with a soft *thump* of air. The robot rolled to a halt, four of its six arms holding a rack of small blue tubes above its "head."

Williger levered herself out of her seat and crossed to the robot, stopping several paces away to run a scanner up and down in the air before her. Having established background levels, she approached the machine slowly, still continuing to scan. "No traces," she said, folding the instrument away and reattaching it to her belt. She and Quilla Gamma both stepped over to the robot then and began to unclip the rack of bio-samples.

When they were done, Williger handed the tray to the Quilla and said, "Take this to Med Bay. Be extremely careful." The Quilla nodded and exited.

"All right," said Williger, facing Parsons. "The easy part of the problem is solved—" She pushed past the captain and headed aft, shaking her head and muttering to herself. "When this is over, I'm going to have a lot more to say. None of it pleasant."

Parsons glanced forward. "Good job, Mr. Shibano. Take a ten-minute shower and a two-hour power nap. I'll want you back on duty at 1400 hours."

"Aye, Captain." Shibano followed Williger aft.

Parsons looked to Korie. "Any questions?"

Korie smiled. "No, Captain. No questions. Thank you for an instructive experience."

"We're not done yet," she said, pointing aft. "Wardroom. Let's get some chow. We have some other things to settle."

Quillas

Armstrong found Quilla Omega in the farm. The tall blue man was pushing a harvest cart along the rows of plants, gathering vegetables for the evening salad—tomatoes, corn, winged beans, celery, scallions, cucumbers, carrots, purple cabbage, chtorr-berries and several different kinds of lettuce.

Omega stopped what he was doing and looked up as Armstrong approached. "Yes, Brian?" he said.

"I came to apologize."

"No apologies are necessary."

"Not for you, maybe, but for me. I learned something today."

"Yes?"

"I learned why there are Quillas aboard a starship. I never thought about it before. I always just took it for granted that you were here as servants and . . . and . . . and you know. Sex partners. I didn't think of you as fully human. Like the rest of us, I mean. I didn't understand. Even when you tried to tell me, I didn't hear it.

"But . . . a little while ago, I sat with Easton. He's taking Berryman's death very hard. He cries. He rages. He's so angry, it's scary—except he doesn't know who to be angry at. So then he cries again. And I don't know what to do. I kept saying to him, 'Let me get a Quilla. They're better at this. They know what to do. I don't know what to say.' But he'd grab my arm and say, 'No, Brian—I don't want a Quilla. I want someone I can talk to. I tried to tell him I'm not a good talker, but he said he didn't care. He said, 'That's okay, you're a good listener.'" Armstrong shrugged and half-smiled in rueful acknowledgment of his own embarrassment at the situation. "Anyway, that's when I realized that I was doing your job—the Quilla job. Listening. Being there for someone. And that's when I realized why you're all here. To help us stay human by being mommy or daddy or big brother or big sister or best friend . . . or lover. Whatever's needed. You're caregivers, aren't you?"

Quilla Omega smiled warmly. "Not many people figure that out by themselves, Brian. You're very good." He added, "We're glad you could be there for Daniel. He's going to be hurting for a very long time."

"That's the other thing," Armstrong said, lowering his voice to a whisper.

"I felt . . . I felt good doing it. Being there for him, I mean. Like I was finally doing something *real*."

"You were," agreed Omega. "Being there for other people is the highest form of service."

Armstrong nodded as he considered that thought. Having experienced it himself, he could see the truth of the statement. "Can I ask you something else?"

"Of course."

"Is that what it's like to be a Quilla? I mean, being there for people all the time?"

Omega didn't answer immediately—for an instant, it was as if he were somewhere else—but when he replied, he was speaking with the voices of all the Quillas in the cluster. "Being a Quilla," he began, "is not what you think it is. Some people think it's a religion, but it's not. There's no belief involved. Some people think it's a discipline, but it's not that either. Yes, there is discipline, but not the kind you think of when you hear the word discipline. Some people think it's an escape, but it isn't. It most definitely is not an escape.

"Being a Quilla," said Omega, "is a commitment to others. So much so, that you give up your own ego, your own goals, your own identity. You give up your own *thing*-ness, so you can be a part of a larger domain. The highest state of being, Brian, is service to others. There is nothing higher. Do you know the old saying, 'You can be either a guest in life or a host?' Guests come to the party and leave a mess behind. Hosts give the party and clean up afterward—but hosts are also the *source* of the party too. Quillas are the hosts for other humans. It's a way of being. It's a total commitment to the well-being of others. The job of the Quilla cluster is to make sure that the essential needs of everyone aboard the ship are taken care of, no matter what. This conversation, for instance, is part of what you need."

"I get it," said Armstrong, suddenly grinning. "I really do." And then, as if to demonstrate just how fully he did understand the changes that were occurring in himself, he began to help Quilla Omega with the salad harvest. He moved down the row, carefully checking the ripeness meters before selecting each item. After a moment, he stopped and asked, "How do I get to be a host instead of just another guest?"

"Are you asking how you can become a Quilla?" Omega's blue look was suddenly penetrating.

Under such scrutiny, Armstrong felt naked—as if Omega were looking into the deepest part of his soul. He lowered his gaze in embarrassment, then raised it up again to meet Omega's eyes directly.

"Yes," he said.

Discovery

Williger caught up with Parsons and Korie in the wardroom, where they were catching a quick meal. She was swearing like a LENNIE with hemorrhoids.

She stormed in—interrupting their conversation as well as their lunch—and slammed an empty biotube down on the wardroom table, hard enough to rattle the dishes. Korie grabbed for his coffee mug to keep it from toppling. The biotube was unbreakable, but Williger had brought it down with enough force to deform it. Neither Korie nor Parsons had ever seen one bent out of shape before, and they both stared with astonishment.

"Empty! Dammit! Empty! The whole rack!" Williger shouted. "We put the ship at risk for nothing! For a decoy! There's nothing there! There never was! The damn things are all nice and neatly labeled—and they're so empty there's not even vacuum in them! I'm going to yank that bastard's testicles out through his left nostril!"

"Which bastard?" Korie inquired around a mouthful of sandwich. "Blintze or Jarell?"

"Yes!" snapped Williger. She hurled herself into a seat, nearly slamming it backward against the bulkhead. She glowered across the table at Parsons and Korie, her face red, her eyes burning, smoke pouring from her ears.

"Want some coffee?" said Parsons, pushing a mug toward her.

"Yes!" snapped Williger. She poured herself a cup with gestures so brusque Parsons was afraid she was going to spill the hot liquid all over herself—or throw it. But the doctor just took a drink, sat back down in her chair, took a second drink, draining the mug, slammed it back down on the table and resumed her glowering. "I'm going to kill something. Or somebody," she said. "All that time. Wasted! We could have been synthesizing our own recombinants. We've lost—what? Half a day? A full day? Somebody lied to me! And I don't like it!"

"We're dealing with a LENNIE," said Korie. "And LENNIE never gives anybody anything."

Williger put her head in her hands, hiding her face. If she didn't look so angry, she would have looked tired. But her words betrayed her real feelings. "I don't know what to say, Captain—I'm sorry. I let you down."

DAVID GERROLD

Parsons was sitting in her usual position at the head of the table. She glanced across the corner to her right, to where Korie was sitting. Williger didn't see the look that passed between them.

Korie took a breath and leaned forward. He looked to Parsons—*request permission to do this?*—Parsons nodded. Korie turned back to Williger. "Dr. Williger? Yes, you screwed up. And we're going to put a severe reprimand in your file—"

Williger looked up sharply, glaring across the table at Korie.

"—just as soon as we get home. Now get back to your lab and resume work on the recombinants. That's an order."

For a moment, the doctor didn't get it. Then she did. She shook her head in annoyance. "Don't handle me, Korie." Then she pushed her chair back and got up. "I'll be in the Med Lab, Captain, if you need me." She pushed out, muttering.

Korie looked to Parsons. "I could have handled that better, couldn't I have?"

Parsons shrugged. "You got the job done, didn't you?" Then turning back to the issue at hand. "Let's get Jarell and Blintze in here."

"Under guard," suggested Korie.

Parsons nodded grimly. "Under guard."

Explanation

Armstrong was on security detail. He and Bach escorted Jarell and Blintze to the wardroom. They were followed by the ship's security chief, Commander Brik. Brik indicated chairs at the far end of the table and the two men sat. Then Brik dismissed the security detail.

Jarell looked impatient and anxious. Blintze, on the other hand, seemed haggard and worn. Jarell took his chair with a *let's-get-this-handled* air of authority, but Blintze seemed resigned, almost fatalistic.

At the opposite end, Parsons was sitting stiffly in her chair. The captain always sat at the head of the table. Korie sat at her right. Brik placed himself against the bulkhead, near the door. Parsons waited a moment before beginning, as if to establish that she was in control of the room, and when she finally did speak, her voice was harder than Korie had ever heard it. "Commander Jarell. I'm ready for answers."

Jarell looked blandly across the table to Parsons. "I'm really not prepared to discuss this with you, Captain." Beside him, Blintze sagged unhappily.

Brik spoke quietly. Accusingly. "We've decrypted the *Norway*'s course log. Your astrogational records show a projected course through the heart of Morthan space."

Jarell spread his hands wide before him, as if demonstrating that he had nothing to hide; but his manner was disingenuous. "Captain Parsons," he began. "We're at war with the Morthan Solidarity." He glanced to Brik. "May I ask, where do *your* sympathies lie?"

"Commander Jarell," Parsons interrupted. "Where is your authorization for this operation?"

"Captain," Jarell stared down the length of the table at her. "Do you understand the seriousness of this war? Perhaps your association with your *security officer*"—a sideways nod to Brik—"has affected your perspective on the danger facing the human race."

"I am very well aware of the dangers we face, Commander." The captain's voice had gone unusually flat and cold.

Jarell didn't notice. Or perhaps he did. He lowered his tone, almost conspiratorially. "Captain Parsons, how can I convince you—demonstrate to you—that what we're up to here could very well be the most important mission of the war? You know what happened at Marathon—"

"*I was there.*"

"Then you know how they savaged our fleet! They came out of no-where—a thousand ships, ten thousand, more! They fell upon the fleet in wave after wave of fire! An avalanche of horror and destruction! The ships exploded and the people died—brave men and women! The ma-rauder wolf packs hunted down the stragglers and killed them. They searched for the dying and the injured and they slaughtered them with-out mercy."

"You weren't there, were you?" said Korie, quietly. "That's all very poetic, but that's not how it happened."

Jarell looked as if he wanted to argue. He clenched his fists in front of him, and his voice took on an edgy quality. "You don't understand, do you? You're out here in the dark between the stars, alone. Alone. Iso-lated. You don't get to see the big picture—the broader perspective—what's happening along the entire war front. Those of us who stand apart, we get to see it all. We can see what you can't."

Parsons, Korie and Brik all exchanged skeptical glances. "An inter-esting hypothesis," Korie said dryly.

"The Morthans swept away our defenses!" Jarell continued. "Do you deny that? The frontier is an open door, a thousand light years across. They'll come sweeping in like the apocalypse! Our beautiful green worlds lie at their mercy—the heart and soul of our species lies within their grasp! What they did to Shaleen, what they did to Taalamar, they'll do that to a thousand more worlds—"

"They haven't yet," interrupted Brik quietly. "If they had been plan-ning an all-out advance, they would have done it by now. I do know something about the way Morthans think," he said without irony. "I wouldn't be so presumptuous as to guess where the Morthan fleets have gone—or where they'll strike next."

"Then you agree that an all-out advance is possible!" Jarell said.

Brik looked skeptical. "You don't listen very well, do you?"

Korie glanced across the room at Brik, a thoughtful expression on his face. Something Brik had said . . . but it was a conversation that would have to be pursued later. He turned his attention back to Jarell. The man's face had gotten redder. His expression was furious. He was so frustrated, he was standing now. "Am I the only one who sees the danger here?"

"We're all aware of the Morthan danger," Parsons said. "Perhaps more than you realize. This ship is one of the few to escape the mauling at Marathon. Commander Korie and Mr. Brik have both met the enemy face-to-face. *I trust their experience and their judgment in these matters.*"

Jarell heard that. He stopped himself with a quick gesture of conciliation. "Forgive me, Captain. I apologize for being so . . . intense . . . about this. I'm used to dealing with civilians who are so far removed from the immediacy of the danger that they don't take it as seriously as they should. I'm not used to being around people who are as committed as I am." He sat down again and placed his hands carefully on the table before him. He glanced around nervously. "Is there . . . coffee? Or something? Can I have something to drink?"

Parsons nodded to Korie, who pulled on his headset and requested coffee service.

"The thing is, Captain," Jarell continued, "Fleet Command started this project as a . . . a desperate gamble. The first thought was that we might use the bloodworms as a kind of a doomsday weapon. If the Morthans overran us, we could infect every planet they captured. The idea was to make their victories worthless. And eventually, there would be no point to any further advance.

"Then we had a second thought—" Jarell fell silent when Quilla Delta entered. She was carrying a tray with a coffee urn and several mugs. She placed it in the center of the table and exited quietly. Korie pushed the tray in Jarell's direction. His hands shaking visibly, the man poured himself a mug of dark black coffee. The sharp aroma filled the room. Korie kept his face impassive; he could tell just by the smell that Cookie had used the bitterest coffee he had. Jarell wasn't going to enjoy this cup much. At the very least, he could expect severe heartburn. Jarell looked around. "Doesn't anyone else want some? No? Blintze?"

Blintze had put his face into his hands, as if he were wishing he were anywhere else but here. He looked up long enough to shake his head no, then withdrew back into his own sad shell of resignation.

Parsons prompted, "Go on, Commander Jarell."

"Well, our second thought was that we might not have to infect any worlds. All we had to do was let the Morthans know that was our intention. Perhaps the mere threat that we might use weapons of mass destruction would make them think twice—but they've already thought twice. That's what Morthans do. They scourged Shaleen and bombarded Taalamar. The threat to respond in kind can't possibly be a deterrent, because they've already included it in their plans. They expected us to respond in kind. That's why they had to destroy the fleet—to disable our ability to deliver that kind of a knockout punch to a Morthan world."

Korie looked across the room to Brik, wondering what he thought of Jarell's analysis. Brik's expression was unreadable, but his eyes were narrowed. Not a good sign, Korie thought. He glanced over to Captain Parsons and gave a slight shake of his head. *I don't believe it either.*

Jarell hadn't seen the brief exchange of glances—or if he had, it didn't matter to him. He continued with his explanation. "What we finally realized was that if we were to stop the Morthans, we would have to do something so big, so drastic, so devastating that they would be paralyzed with fear. If we could shatter their sense of invulnerability, they would become psychologically incapable of continuing the war. If we could demonstrate that the consequences of further advances would be total destruction, they would have no option but to withdraw. With one mission, we could break the back of the Solidarity. We could avenge the fleet, Shaleen, Taalamar and all the other worlds they've savaged. We could end the war now, before it rages out of control across the heart of the Alliance." He finished his coffee, made a face and pushed the mug away. "Captain? Don't you agree?"

Parsons sighed. She folded her hands before her and rested her chin thoughtfully on them. "I understand your concern," she said. "I understand your fear of the Morthans and the threat they represent. I even admire your willingness to consider the military use of such unthinkable horrors as bloodworms. It takes a special kind of mind to juggle such dreadful possibilities."

"Then you agree . . .?" Jarell's eyes were bright with sudden enthusiasm.

"Absolutely not," Parsons said.

Confrontation

To Jarell's frozen expression, Captain Parsons explained, "To be perfectly honest, Commander, I cannot think of anything more horrible that we could do than what you've just described." She looked over to Brik, then back to Jarell. "I might not know as much about the Morthans as you claim to, but I know Commander Brik—and I know from my experience of him that the Morthans have a code of honor. It isn't *our* code of honor, but it is such a rigid discipline that they would rather die than suffer dishonor. If we were to unleash such a weapon on the Morthan Solidarity as you are suggesting, it would be an act so vile, so disgraceful, so detestable in their eyes that they would feel justified in retaliating with even greater horrors against us."

"What greater horrors are there than what they've already done to us?" Jarell demanded.

"I don't know," snapped Parsons. "And I don't want to find out."

"These are evil beings, Captain! They're not human—they're monsters. Terrible and vicious and utterly ruthless. We have to be even more ruthless. We have to be a thousand times more dangerous! We have to do this, Captain."

Parsons placed her hands flat on the table and glowered down the length of the room. "As convenient as it is to regard the Morthans as the spawn of hell, as demonic beings driven by satanic furies—as satisfying as it might be to regard the enemy as less than human and thereby worthy of our rage and enmity and hatred—I must tell you . . . that's a way of thinking that does not serve us. Our job is to *stop* the enemy—not *become* him. Commander Jarell, this is one weapon that human beings *must not* unleash. Not here. Not anywhere. Not now. Not ever. It violates all possible standards of decency and justice."

Jarell's response was surprisingly calm. He quietly repeated, "We have to do this, Captain. We've come too far to stop now."

"I see," said Parsons, coming to a conclusion. "You never had any authorization for this part of the mission, did you?"

"We were supposed to hold ourselves in a state of readiness. Why would the Fleet authorize the preparation of such a capability if they weren't prepared to use it?"

"I repeat. You have no authorization to proceed, do you?"

"I have a *moral* authorization," said Jarell. "We all do. Our mission is to preserve and protect the Alliance. We have the capability to end this war now. And when the last Morthan world dies, writhing in agony, a grateful Alliance will thank us for our wisdom!"

"I sincerely doubt that," said Parsons. She glanced to Blintze. "Doctor, you haven't said a word yet. Do you agree with Commander Jarell's goals?"

Blintze's face was in his hands. His eyes were covered. What he had been thinking during this entire meeting was unknowable. Now, he just shook his head, back and forth. He lowered his hands and his eyes were red and puffy. "I don't know what to think anymore," he said. "This isn't what I signed on for. Oh, no—yes, it is—but I lied to myself. I thought I was searching for a cure. I—I think I always knew there was a military possibility, but I lied to myself about it because . . . because I didn't believe it would ever get that far. And then it was too late. I'm sorry, Captain."

Parsons nodded, satisfied that she finally had some sense of what was happening here. She glanced over to the tall Morthan Security Chief. "Commander Brik, place these men under arrest."

The Vial

Brik was standing at the ready, but he made no move to advance on Jarell. Instead, he spoke quietly to his headset. "Security is on the way."

Jarell didn't even blink. "I'm not surprised. I should have expected it. I knew the Solidarity would try to stop us. They sabotaged our LENNIE. And they sent this ship—the *Star Wolf*—to make sure the bloodworms were neutralized. The Judas ship. You're betraying the Alliance again. First you lead the Morthan fleet to the Silk Road Convoy. Now you destroy our last, best chance to strike back. Oh yes, they've infected you with their thinking. Code of honor? New Geneva Convention? All that crap. That's their way of limiting our actions while they ignore the rules of conduct and sweep across the Alliance. The deaths of billions of human beings will be on your conscience, Captain Parsons! Everything is perfectly clear now. I see who *really* runs this ship—" He spat in Brik's direction.

"Commander Brik," Parsons said quietly. "We'll need restraints for Commander Jarell."

"No, you don't!" Jarell stood up, backing away.

The hatch popped open then, and four security officers entered. Bach, Shibano, Armstrong and Easton. They had their weapons drawn. "Take Commander Jarell into custody," Brik ordered. "Try not to hurt him."

"Captain—!" That was Blintze.

Jarell had backed up against the bulkhead. He had reached into his coat and pulled out a small vial—*filled with pink and gold flickers*. He held it out before him like a shield.

"—he's got plasmacytes!"

"Don't anyone come any closer!"

Parsons and Korie both came to their feet, horrified. "Don't anyone move—don't anyone do anything stupid."

"A containment bottle," explained Jarell. "We developed these on the *Norway*. I didn't know if it would work—coming through the suppressor fields and the repulsors—but it did. Now I can see I was wise to do so. Captain Parsons, I am going to complete my mission. And you're going to help me. Or you'll have plasmacytes on the *Star Wolf*."

"We already have plasmacytes on the *Star Wolf*. On the hull."

189

"That's not a problem," Jarell replied. "Hull alloy is a natural containment. That's where we got the idea for these—" He held up the bottle."

"If you release those," Parsons said, "You'll die too."

Jarell shrugged. "I'm not afraid to die for my beliefs." He added, "And if I'm not afraid to sacrifice my life for the cause, I have no problem sacrificing your lives as well." He grasped the top of the vial. "Unless you deliver this ship to Morthan space . . . I will break the seal."

Blintze spoke now. He advanced quietly on Jarell and spoke in a voice that was half-whisper, half-croak. "You're doing it again! Aren't you? Haven't you learned anything from what happened to the *Norway*?"

"Yes, I have," said Jarell. "I've learned not to trust anyone else." He stepped forward, holding the vial before him. "I mean it, Captain. Set a course across the rift."

Parsons looked to Korie, looked to Brik, looked back to Jarell. "Can we talk about this?"

"There's nothing left to say. The time for talk is over." Holding the vial before him, one hand on the seal, Jarell moved toward the door— and the Bridge.

The Bridge

"Let him pass," said Parsons.

Brik frowned at the instruction, but he gestured to the security team. They backed carefully out of the way as Jarell stepped through the door into the corridor. "Come on, Blintze!" he called.

The haggard scientist made his way embarrassedly across the wardroom, muttering "excuse me, excuse me," as he pushed past Parsons and Brik. "I'm sorry, Captain. Really, I am."

Parsons followed him into the corridor. Korie started to follow after her but Brik reached down, grabbed his shoulder and pushed him aside so he could follow the captain—and Jarell. He gave Korie one of those looks that could have meant anything but probably meant *let me handle this*. He ducked down to fit through the door, then Korie followed. He glanced over his shoulder and motioned for the security team to keep behind him.

When he stepped out onto the Command Deck, he saw that Jarell had parked himself in the executive officer's chair—a breach of etiquette so gross that Korie couldn't believe the man had done it deliberately. He had to be ignorant of the ways of the ship. Unless . . . he wanted to send a message. The glittering vial was nowhere in sight. Blintze stood glumly behind Jarell.

Parsons was just sitting down in her own chair. "Commander Tor? Would you please prepare a set of courses for Commander Jarell's inspection?"

Tor swiveled around in her chair to stare at the captain with a questioning expression. *Excuse me?*

"We want to cross the rift and dive into the heart of the Morthan sphere."

The look on Tor's face went from curiosity to disbelief. *Is he crazy or are you?*

"Commander Jarell has a very convincing argument," Parsons said, without explaining.

Korie glanced sideways to Brik. The big Morthan was standing in the Ops Deck so he could be eye-to-eye with those on the Command Deck. "I really hate it," Korie said dryly. "I hate being convinced like this."

"The Cinnabar Option?" Brik asked.*

"Too dangerous," Korie said. "And too messy." *And besides, HARLIE is down.*

"Captain . . .?" said Tor, fumbling for the right words. There were none.

Jarell reached into his jacket and pulled out the biotube. He held it up high so everyone on the Bridge could see it. For a moment, the Bridge was silent—except for the usual background hum of ship sounds.

Korie glanced backward. Bach and Shibano were in front of the hatch, Easton and Armstrong were still in the corridor; they all had their weapons out. Korie held a hand low to indicate caution. He noticed that Easton was trembling—he had to do something. And quickly. He stepped forward and said, "Captain, I didn't have a chance to tell you before. The warp core of the number two engine has to be flushed. The micro-stabilizer fields have been lethetically compromised and Chief Leen needs to do a suborchial inter-alignment on the bivalve spline. We can't run with a gelatinous wobbly."

Parsons blinked at him as if he'd just said, "*The gostak distims the doshes.*" And then, without blinking, she replied crisply, "I specifically told Chief Leen not to flush the warp core in a stress-field depression. That's why the bivalve is misaligned! You can't get the revolvitrons stabilized in a gravitational perplex! Where the hell did he learn engine deconstruction! Goddammit. I don't want excuses. I want results." She turned to Jarell, and her tone became sweetly apologetic. "I'm sorry, Commander. We're not going anywhere for awhile."

"It's all right, Captain," he replied. "I'm sure you and Commander Korie can reconfigure the double-talk generator in no time. Certainly before I've decided on a course." He wasn't fooled.

Parsons didn't even acknowledge the failure. Her voice became more business-like. "It'll take several days to get free of the gravitational effects of the red star. We won't be able to enter hyperstate for a week. Are you planning to stay awake the whole time? It's two months to cross the rift. You're going to have to sleep sometime."

Jarell nodded. "I understand you had your HARLIE unit simulating our LENNIE."

"Yes, and it drove the poor unit psychotic. We'll be decontaminating it for months."

"I have a better idea. Let's bring it back online. We'll use the LENNIE programs to stand watch over me while I sleep."

---

* *The Voyage of the Star Wolf.*

"I don't think that's a good idea," said Korie.

"I do," said Jarell. "Discussion's over."

Korie looked to Parsons. She nodded. Korie said, "I'll get to it right away," and remained where he was standing.

"What about the plasmacytes on the hull of our ship, Commander?"

Jarell shook his head, a gesture of dismissal. "That's how we'll infect the Morthan worlds—we'll dive through their upper atmospheres and leave a trail of infection. By the time the plasmacytes drift down to the ground, we'll be long gone."

"I meant—won't they eat through our hull?"

"No. The radiation shields are a natural containment. As long as you don't lower them, we're safe."

"And after our mission is over, how will we get off the ship safely?"

"Don't worry about that either. There's a cure."

"No, there isn't. We searched the *Norway*. The biotubes were empty."

Jarell shook his head. "You didn't find it, that's all."

Parsons looked away, momentarily at a loss, trying to figure out what she could say next. For the first time, she noticed the security team behind Korie. She bit her lip, then looked across to Brik. "Commander Brik. Let's be very careful here. I don't want anyone trying anything stupid."

"I appreciate that, Captain," Jarell said. He turned around in his chair and looked past the captain, past Korie—to the security team waiting at the hatch. "You're dismissed." They didn't move.

Korie nodded to them. "Pull back."

Bach and Shibano started to back away. They ducked through the hatch. Armstrong moved to follow them—but Easton stayed where he was, pointing his stinger pistol directly at Jarell's head. "Let me do it, Captain! Just give the word!"

Confession

Without taking his eyes from Jarell, Easton spoke to Captain Parsons in a voice that was harrowing in its desperation—and its deadly certitude. "I can drill him right through the eyes. He'll be dead before he has a chance to break the seal." He stepped closer to Jarell.

Jarell held the vial up so Easton could see the top. "Look, stupid—see that button? It's a doomsday trigger. If my heart stops, the seal explodes, the vial shatters."

"No problem," Easton said. Still aiming the weapon at Jarell's head, he reached over with his other hand and adjusted the target setting. "I'll set for wide-beam stun."

Parsons took a step forward. "Daniel. Put that stinger down. Now."

"I'm sorry, Captain—I can't. Give me the order, *please*."

Jarell looked over to Parsons. "You realize, of course, what will happen when that stinger beam hits this vial. Even on the lowest level, it will provide enough energy for the wavicles to escape the containment bottle."

"Don't do it, son," Parsons said. She didn't want to make it an order—because if he disobeyed it, she'd ultimately have to prosecute him for insubordination. Or worse. And she didn't want to do that.

Thinking quickly, Korie stepped into the space between Jarell and Easton. He looked directly into Easton eyes. "You'll have to shoot through me, Dan." Jarell took advantage of the opportunity to take a cautious step back.

"Why are you protecting him?! He's a walking LENNIE."

"I'm not protecting him. I'm protecting *you*."

"I'm trying to do my duty—"

"Not this way. Dan, listen to me. I know what you're going through—"

"No, you don't. You've never been bonded."

"I was married. And my wife was the most special person in the universe to me. And our children were our greatest joy. So don't tell me what I don't know. But let the Fleet handle this. I promise you, Yonah Jarell isn't going to hurt anyone ever again. Dan! Give me the stinger."

Armstrong took a step out of the hatch and called softly, "Danny, please. Please, listen."

Easton shook his head. "The man is evil. The man doesn't deserve to live. Captain, give the order."

Korie whispered, "Dan, we can't afford the luxury of revenge. Hate is a disease. I don't want the *Star Wolf* infected with it any more than I want this ship infected with plasmacytes. Hate made the plasmacytes. Is that what you want to continue?"

And Armstrong took a step forward and said softly, "Is this what Paul would have done? Do you think he would have wanted you to kill in his name? If he were here, what do you think he would say?"

Easton wavered, undecided. And then—he blinked. And blinked again.

Standing in front of him was Paul Berryman. Alive. Healthy. Sparkling. "Honey, I'm home," he said.

"Paul—"

"Dan, shut up and listen to me. I'm only dead. I'm not gone. Everything that we ever had together, it's still right here—inside of us. Don't piss it away on him. He's not worth it."

"Let me kill him for you—"

"Don't kill anyone for me, Danny. That's not the legacy I want." And then he added, "And if you do that . . . I'm not sure I can come back again—"

Easton sagged. "Damn you! Damn you!" Abruptly he swung his arm sideways and held the stinger pistol out to his side, where Korie took it gratefully from his hand. *"Attaboy, Danny,"* someone whispered. Armstrong? Berryman?

Korie handed the weapon sideways—to Parsons—and grabbed Easton before he could collapse unconscious to the floor. "Call Williger! My God, he's burning up—"

And at the same time, someone else was screaming too. It was Jarell: "What the hell are you doing?!!"

Blintze had grabbed the glittering little vial out of Jarell's hand, and now, as everyone watched, he popped it into a pressure-spray injector. Before anyone could stop him, he applied it directly to his forearm—the telltale hiss told the entire story.

"You stupid asshole! What have you done?!"

Blintze ignored him. "Captain Parsons, I believe I've just solved the plasmacyte problem. Will you please have me transferred over to the *Norway*?"

Jarell screamed. "You disloyal traitor!"

"No, Yonah. It's over. Enough is enough. No more killing. No more."

He looked to Parsons hurriedly. "We have a limited amount of time, Captain. Only a few minutes before these things turn into bloodworms."

Williger entered the Ops Deck from the forward hatch. She came around the side of the main display, followed by two Quillas—one carrying an emergency kit, the other carrying a stretcher. They headed straight for the Command Deck.

Parsons was already calling out orders. "Security—take Commander Jarell to the brig. And Easton and Blintze to Med Bay."

Bach and Shibano had already seized Jarell. Now, as they escorted—almost dragged—him off the Bridge, Blintze turned back to Parsons. "No, Captain. The transfer tube."

"We can save you!" And then she added, "I think." She looked to Williger. "He's got plasmacytes in his bloodstream."

"Get him to the Med Bay. Fast!"

"No. Get me to the transfer tube. I don't want to be saved, Captain. I don't want to grow old listening to my conscience. Listen, I made a mistake. I trusted Jarell. And the *Norway* died. All of my friends and colleagues died." Blintze's whole demeanor had changed in the last few moments—he no longer looked like a man with a death sentence. His eyes were alive with enthusiasm. "I'll tell you what we discovered. The plasmacytes are something beautiful. Not a war weapon at all—but a kind of life that's marvelous to see. The Regulans perverted it. We can cure it. We can heal it." He spread his hands wide in an act of supplication. "Captain Parsons, this is where the sickness stops. All the hate. All the dying."

"This is a death sentence, Dr. Blintze."

"No, it isn't. It's a *life* sentence. Do you want to know why you couldn't find the cure on the *Norway*? Because it isn't there. I had it all the time."

"Then why didn't you *use* it?"

"Because . . ." Blintze spread his hands in a gesture of helplessness. "Because . . . I had to hide it from LENNIE. A LENNIE isn't just paranoid, it's a death-engine. It's a killing machine. It hates life. The only way to work with a LENNIE is to show it that you're inventing new ways to kill. Make yourself a partner in death. Serve LENNIE or die. If LENNIE had realized that I had saved the cure, he would have destroyed the *Norway*, and it would have been lost forever—all the research, everything. I didn't want that to happen."

"It would have been better all around if it had," said Parsons, starting to feel annoyed.

Blintze ignored her. He continued quickly, "I had to synthesize it in isolation—pretending to be doing something else the whole time; but LENNIE figured out what I was up to and let the plasmacytes loose. But he only thought I'd completed the theoretical part. He didn't realize I'd only been writing down my notes on things to test *after* I'd already performed the experiments. That was the only way I could leave a trail. It almost worked. When you arrived, I realized I had to find a way to get it off the ship and out of LENNIE's reach. I almost told you when I came aboard—but then your HARLIE unit swore at me and I realized I couldn't trust it either. Somehow LENNIE had infected it. So I injected myself with the cure because . . . because I couldn't think of any better place to hide it. And now that you know, you need to get me off this ship and onto the *Norway*, where I can try to make a difference. And I'll need a stinger pistol with a self-destruct timer on it, please."

"It's suicide," said Parsons.

"I've earned the right."

"Nobody's earned the right to decide when a life should end."

"You can believe that if you want. I believe otherwise. Captain, we're wasting time."

"I think you're really afraid of what a Board of Inquiry will do to you," she replied.

"Maybe so. But we're still wasting time."

"Suicide is the coward's way out, Blintze. It's nothing more than a way to say 'fuck you' to the universe."

"Fine," said Blintze. "Believe that too. But we're still wasting time."

Parsons looked away. She looked to Williger—the doctor was already bent over Easton, applying several small devices to his chest and arms. She glanced up long enough to say, "It's triage. Let him go."

Parsons looked to Korie. Korie closed his eyes and nodded his agreement.

"All right, Dr. Blintze. Have it your way." She offered him the stinger she still held. "Mr. Korie, please escort Dr. Blintze to the transfer tube. Have Chief Leen activate the repulsor fields immediately. Send a robot over first—have it destroy the *Norway*'s power supply—I don't want LENNIE out of commission, I want him dead."

"Thank you, Captain—"

"Don't thank me. I'm not doing it for you." Blintze nodded an acknowledgment and started to step past her. She stopped him with a look and added, "I'm a Catholic. I believe that suicides go to Hell. I'm supposed to try to stop you. But I can't. My only real regret here is that you're not taking Yonah Jarell with you."

197

"If you want—" Blintze started to offer.

"Just get the hell off my ship. As fast as you can." She turned away deliberately.

When she was sure that Korie had escorted Blintze safely off the Bridge, she turned to Williger; the two Quillas were just lifting Easton's unconscious body onto the stretcher. "Will he be all right?"

"He's suffering a triple-whammy of aftereffects, but yes—I think so."

"Good. Dr. Williger, I don't want to court-martial this man. Find me a reason not to. Now, who's on Chaplain duty? I've just been an accessory to a mortal sin and I need to go to confession."

"Wait till tonight, when I'm on duty," growled Williger, following the stretcher aft. "I'll make sure that your penance will be the worst in your life."

"Bring an extra glass. I think Korie will be joining us—"

Transformation

On the Bridge of the *Norway*, Makkle Blintze stood alone. He had a camera and a scanner. He set the remote down in the center of the Ops Deck and looked around. The light from the camera filled the Bridge, but it cast dark shadows that left gloomy corners behind everything.

Around him swirled a quiet hurricane of pink and gold flickers. Some of them drifted toward him—and into him. Others danced in the air. There were so many, he could almost hear them.

"Can you see me?" he asked. "Can you hear me?"

"We have monitoring," Korie's voice came back to him.

"Good," said Blintze. He opened the seals on his starsuit. "I'm taking off my headset now. And as you can see, the forward display is off. The entire Bridge is dead, so I can't see you or hear you anymore. I'll keep reporting for as long as I can. I don't think this is going to take very long. I'm the only warm body left on the ship and every wavicle aboard is trying to get to me. It's almost as if they can tell I have what they want. The worms are creeping this way too. But I don't think they'll get here in time. As soon as I'm sure the bloodworms inside my body have been infected with the recombinant genes, I'm going to activate the self-destruct on the stinger. That will guarantee the creation of recombinant wavicles. I've got a low-level scanner here. I can't scan myself, but I can scan for residual radiation, and we'll be looking for telltale spikes in the ultra-high and ultra-low bands. Stand by."

Blintze stepped up onto the Command Deck and balanced the scanner on the executive officer's chair. Then he lowered himself respectfully into the captain's chair. "Nice. I like it. It's a throne. A feeling of power, almost." He held out his arms and waved them, making swirls of wavicles in the air. "It doesn't hurt. It tickles a little, but I expected that. It's kind of . . . sensual. Oh, hell, why am I being modest now? It's a very sexual feeling, like that tingle you get just before orgasm. Only it just keeps going and going without ever going anywhere.

"When I was a child, I used to wonder how I would die—it terrified me. Not the dying, but the loss of control it represented. I admit it, I've always been fascinated by the idea of suicide—of knowing how and when I would die. And why. At least this is a noble death. Maybe as noble as I can achieve." He fell silent for a moment, lost in thought, then after a long pause, began speaking again. "Sorry about that. The truth is, I don't have any right to claim nobility. I participated in something dreadful—a weapon of mass destruction. Possibly the greatest sin a human being can commit. And all the self-justifications and rationalizations and excuses and reasons and explanations . . . aren't worth a bucket of warm shit. The truth is, I let myself be a very ordinary person, just going along, being led, doing what I was told—not willing to take a stand. Not willing to make waves—but certainly willing to make wavicles . . . Until now, when it's almost too late. And anything worthwhile I might say or do now is going to be outvoted by a lifetime of cowardice. I guess this is a deathbed conversion. And therefore worthless. It undoes nothing.

"What I'm doing now . . . it's not redemption at all. You were right, Captain Parsons. I'm taking the coward's way out. I suppose I should apologize, but the scientist in me wants to believe that the cure will work . . . and this at least lets us complete the experiment. And maybe someday, someone will say that this much at least was a contribution to science. Or humanity. Or knowledge. Or something. I don't know. Shit. I don't know what to say. I wasted my life and I'm sorry. And I hope someday, somehow, someone will forgive me. Say a prayer for me, maybe. Catholics believe in redemption, Captain, don't they? I don't. I never did. But here I am at the last minute, begging . . . just in case."

He got up and started walking around the Bridge again. "There's something going on with the wavicles. Something beautiful. I don't know if you can see it, but I'm seeing shades of colors here I've never seen before. Very delicate. Like sparkles off a diffraction grating, only brighter. If I close my eyes, I can still see them, brighter than ever. I don't think we perceive the wavicles through light. I think they directly stimulate the retinal cells as they pass through us. Just a guess. Someone else will have to figure that part out."

He climbed back up onto the Command Deck and peered at the scanner. "I'm starting to get telltales. That's good. It means I can set the stinger to self-destruct anytime. I'm setting it now. I'm not in any pain. Not really. It's like when your leg falls asleep, only it's my whole body that tingles.

"Can you see this?" he asked, not expecting an answer. He waved his arms around, leaving swirls of sparkles flickering in the air. "They're clustering around me, aren't they?"

The pinpoint sparkles were no longer swirling about the man. Now they were drifting toward him, accelerating as they approached, arrowing inward, sleeting through him like arrows of light. He lifted his arms to the ceiling, standing in the center of his own aurora borealis. He radiated like a saint. The air around him crackled and glowed. Blintze stopped talking. He turned slowly, savoring his moment of transformation.

He was enveloped in light now, almost disappearing into the center of a sphere of brightness—both gauzy and crystalline. The sparkles turned and twisted around him, dancing in the air like fairy-dust motes. Blintze was barely visible within the pinpoint fireworks, his face rapturous.

And then the stinger discharged itself—

—and the lights *blazed* outward in a marvelous explosion of color and amazement. If light could be said to have emotion, this light was *joyous*. It swirled around the Bridge of the *Norway* in a fiery dance of awakening, self-awareness, discovery, redemption and epiphany. It swirled through the ship, climbing, diving, dipping, twirling and *singing*—

Realization

On the Bridge of the *Star Wolf*, Korie reacted first. He switched the main display to show an exterior view of the *Norway*. This was taken from high on one of the *Star Wolf*'s spars. Both ships were still outlined with wavicles, but now the sparkles were agitated, trembling in anticipation—and then, abruptly, it was as if the *Norway* was leaking light from a thousand places.

"The stinger blast must have punctured her hull," said Parsons.

Curls of light, swept up and out of the starship—like smoke with a purpose, like something alive. "My God," said Tor. "What is it?"

Brik knew, but he wouldn't speak it. He did something uncharacteristic for a Morthan. He sat down. He put one hand over his mouth, a Morthan sign of . . . awe. Amazement and recognition filled his eyes. But nobody noticed; they were staring forward.

It was Korie who dared speak it. "I think . . . I think it's a sparkle-dancer."

He glanced around the Bridge, as if daring anyone to disagree—but every face was rapturous in the reflected light of the display. At the communications console, Green was listening to his headset. Suddenly he said, "It's singing to us!" He put the radio noise of the sparkle-dancer on the speakers. At first it sounded like a roar of static, then it sounded like the ocean, and then . . . it sounded like something else: something *joyous* and *grateful* and *alive!*

The sparkle-dancer flowed out of the *Norway*, wrapping itself around the ship, curious and delighted—as if dancing, exploring, even making love. Wherever the sparkle-dancer touched, it gathered all the wavicles into itself. It swept the hulls of both ships clean. It flowed from the *Norway* onto the *Star Wolf*. Tendrils of light tickled the starship like a harpist striking chords.

When it had finished exploring the hulls of both vessels, when it had finished collecting every errant particle of itself, the sparkle-dancer flowed off the *Star Wolf* and reformed itself on the port side of the ship. For the first time, the crew saw it as it existed naturally in space—a veil of luminescence, shimmering and coruscating with all the colors of the rainbow. Its wings flickered and sparkled with myriad tiny pinpoints as its component wavicles winked in and out of existence—tiny energy mites whirling and dancing. The sparkle-dancer was a colony of rapturous butterflies of light.

"They'll never believe us," said Korie.

"Who cares?" laughed Parsons.

The sparkle-dancer curled one last time around the *Star Wolf*, almost as if hugging the vessel farewell—and then it whirled off again, flashing a dazzling bouquet of colors. It twirled alone for a moment longer, almost wistfully, as if it were waving goodbye, and then it vanished into the star-studded darkness.

For the longest moment, no one spoke.

And then Parsons whispered, "I believe we are the luckiest human beings alive." There were tears of joy and delight in her eyes.

The Stars

Captain Parsons stepped back up to the Command Deck and sat down in her chair. For the last time. She ran her hands along the arm rests, savoring the sensation of ownership. For a while, the Bridge crew worked in silence. No one wanted to break the mood. But finally, Captain Parsons turned to her executive officer. "Mr. Korie, has Chief Leen finished misaligning the bivalve spline?"

"Funny thing, he just completed it, Captain."

"Isn't that convenient," Parsons said, deadpan. "*Now hear this*. Stand down from Condition Yellow. All departments, initiate immediate pre-hyperstate maintenance. I want us ready to go as soon as we're clear."

Then she added, "I want to commend all of you for the quality of your service during these past few very difficult days. Crew of the *Star Wolf*, it has been a genuine privilege to serve with you. Your professional performance, your selfless dedication and your untiring courage are truly inspiring. I am proud of you—very proud." She paused a moment, wondering if there was anything else to add, decided that there was not and concluded with an oddly permanent sounding, "*That is all.*"

Captain Parsons glanced over to her executive officer, who was looking at her curiously. She patted the arms of her chair—for the last time—and rose. "Mr. Korie, may I see you in the wardroom please?" She picked up her clipboard and led the way.

Korie followed her aft, into the corridor called "Broadway," past the Communications Bay and into the Officers' Mess. As he entered, he saw that Captain Parsons was unpinning the stars from her uniform. "Here," she said, offering them to Korie.

"Captain—?"

"My penance. For my sins. Which have been considerable. I'm removing myself from active command, pending further inquiry. I'm giving you a field promotion. I have the authority to do this, you know."

"Captain, I don't—" Korie looked at her, flustered—and yet, at the same time, his mind was racing through a forest of reasons, explanations, possibilities *and hopes* "—understand," he finished lamely.

"Yes, you do," Parsons said, taking his hand and dropping her stars into them. "Think about it. I have. And I know you have too. Board of

Inquiry. Court-martial . . ." Her expression was sad but knowing. "You know the arguments. Violation of general orders. Bold initiative doesn't excuse. Put the ship and the crew at risk. Important strategic break-through. But an unfortunate precedent to set. Tsk, tsk, tsk. Must assert chain of command. Can't allow dereliction of principle. Have to main-tain authority. However, Fleet Command *will* acknowledge good inten-tions. Here's a distinguished service medal. But of course, you'll never command a starship again. Right?"

"Uh—" Korie nodded his agreement. "Right."

"So, I'm going to present them with a *fait accompli*. I'm taking myself out of the food chain. They can still do the inquiry and the court-mar-tial, if they want to—but I don't think they'll want to open that can of bloodworms. Because it leads to questions they won't want to ask and they certainly won't like having to answer. And definitely not in public. Like who sent Jarell out here in the first place?"

"They'll never let this get public," Korie said, thinking forward about the inevitable consequences. "They can't. Jarell's agenda—it's too dan-gerous. He's not the only one who thinks that way. This is a cancerous idea—it'll take root among extremists and spread from there. And if enough people get scared enough about the war, they'll start demanding implementation. I think you're right. Fleet Command has to bury this—the whole thing. Maybe even the cure as well."

"Mmm." Parsons nodded thoughtfully. "We've been heroes, Jon. All of us. Inventive. Courageous. And most of all, *wise*. What we did here is the stuff of military legend. And no one will ever know." She smiled sadly. "But the lack of acknowledgment doesn't diminish what we did. It doesn't invalidate our heroism in any way." Her eyes shone brightly now. "You know what we did out here, the crew knows—and Fleet Com-mand will know. And maybe, just maybe, they'll find a way to honor the ship in exchange for your convenient silence—maybe give you some sweetheart duty somewhere and a fistful of medals and bounties. Maybe even the bloodworm bounty—but without public credit. You can live with that, can't you? It'll probably be part of the deal."

Korie shook his head. "This ship is never going to get credit, Cap-tain—not for anything but the mauling at Marathon. And as long as we have that reputation, they can't give us any duty or reward that will make people ask questions."

"Take the money anyway. It's a big pot, and it'll pay for a lot of solace. I've already filed the application for the bounty. I expect you'll get it, and I expect them to trade my silence for my retirement. The bounty for the ship will be part of it. It's a fair bargain, Korie. Your stars will be part of the deal, I'll make sure of it."

"No, it isn't a fair bargain," Korie said, finally handing the stars back. "You're a good captain. The fleet needs you. It's going to be a long war—"

"And I've done my part in it. I've helped us keep one little piece of our soul and one little piece of our integrity. Here, take these stars. Honor me by wearing them." She offered them again.

Korie shook his head. "Captain, I'd be proud to wear your stars. Only—"

"Only what?" Parsons frowned.

"Only. . . I don't deserve them."

The captain's reaction was short and to the point. "Bullshit."

Korie held his ground. "Captain Parsons. I can't begin to tell you how much I want those stars. But I can't put them on. No—hear me out. Do you remember in the wardroom, when Jarell was telling us what kind of a threat the Morthans represented? *I was agreeing with him.* And when he said, let's go scourge the Morthans, *I wanted to do it too!* It would have been justice for all the folks at Shaleen and Taalamar. And I *wanted* to do it."

"So did I," said Parsons quietly.

Korie looked up sharply.

"I want a weapon to use against the Morthans, just as deeply as you, Korie. And I wanted to strike back at them just as much as you. And probably so does every other person on this starship. I could have given the order. We could have gone. You might have questioned it. I know Williger certainly would have. But we'd have gone. And we'd have devastated as many Morthan worlds as we could until their ships caught us and destroyed us—but not all of them. We could never hit every Morthan planet. And that's the flaw in this plan. We'd be leaving survivors, whole worlds of Morthan warriors who would know exactly what we had done—and the dishonor of the deed. If we were fast enough and smart enough, we might even have made it home. And we would have been heroes. For the moment. But it would have been only an illusory triumph. You know as well as I what would have happened after that, Jon, don't you?"

Korie nodded.

Parsons said it anyway. "The bloodworms would have come back to us—on Morthan suicide ships. And this time, the Morthans would have no strategic reason to hold back. Their ships would penetrate to the heart of the Alliance and they'd infest every world they could get to. We wouldn't be heroes. We'd be villains—the ones who let the firestorm out of the bottle. So as much as I *wanted* to do it—strategically, I knew why I shouldn't."

"I had those same thoughts," Korie admitted.

"Of course," said Parsons. "Your ability to consider consequences is what makes you so formidable."

"But I also kept thinking how satisfying it would be to strike back."

"So did I," Parsons agreed. "You might make mistakes, Korie, but you don't make *stupid* ones. At least, I haven't seen any evidence of it. If you had been captain here, what would you have done?"

Korie considered it. "As much as I wanted revenge, as much as I want to destroy the Morthan Solidarity, as *good* as it would have felt . . . I don't think I would have let my emotions overwhelm my wisdom. There was something terribly wrong there, something wrong with the whole mission—with the thinking behind it. It was based on hate. I couldn't let Jarell do this out of hate. And there was no other reason to do it. None at all. So it was wrong."

"*That's* what qualifies you, Korie. Your ability to keep your *self* out of the process."

"But, Captain—I didn't keep my self out of the process. I wasn't thinking about the Fleet, and I wasn't thinking about my orders, and I wasn't thinking about my oath or my responsibilities. I only thought about what would be best for the war, as if I were the only one fighting it. And more than once, Admiral O'Hara told me that's a large part of what's keeping me from my promotion—that I keep trying to fight this war by myself. She's right. I did it again here. That's the way my mind works. So if you give me those stars, and if I accept them, and if Fleet Command lets me keep them, then what? What if next time I'm not so wise? What if next time I follow my heart instead of my wisdom?"

Parsons sighed. "You want to know the truth, Jon? There are no guarantees. None of the great captains are ever as good as they want to be. So they keep trying to do better. That's what makes them great. They don't settle for being ordinary. Neither do you. When the next time comes, you'll remember *this* time. And that'll be enough to make the difference."

"I hope you're right," Korie said, with a hint of doubt as well as sadness.

"You want to know the truth about human beings?" she asked abruptly. She stepped in close. "Most of us don't have very much integrity. We pretend we do, but we're always negotiating little loopholes for ourselves, little excuses to be less than we are. And that's true of everybody, all of us. The only difference between ordinary and extraordinary is not accepting that as normal. That's the heart of brightness. We defend our little specks of integrity with enormous ferocity because we know how little there really is. That's what makes you extraordinary, Jon Korie." She took his hand and placed her stars in the center of his palm.

Korie heard the words as if Parsons was inscribing them into his soul. He nodded in thoughtful acceptance, staring down at the insignia. They felt strangely heavy in his hand. She was right. Of course, she was. When he looked up again, his expression was wry as well as rueful. He held up the stars. "You know, of course, that the admiral isn't going to let me keep these."

The Captain

"*Captain* Korie." Parsons' tone had an edge to it sharp enough to slice diamond. "This ship has come a long way since the mauling at Marathon. Just about every officer in the fleet knows what she's been through, knows how you've held her together, knows how you've earned your stars five times over. Do you know that there are captains who will not accept command of this vessel—?"

"Sure. It's been that way since—"

"In the past, yes—they didn't want command of a disgraced ship. But now, there are officers who won't accept command of the *Star Wolf* because she's rightfully *your* ship. They've told the admiral as much—that it would be inappropriate for them to serve over you, because you've demonstrated better qualifications than a lot of men and women who already have their stars."

Korie was embarrassed. He looked down at his shoes. He swallowed hard and looked up at Parsons again. "I didn't know that."

"Well, then, you're the only one. Hell, Korie, I told O'Hara that myself—that I couldn't take this ship with you still as exec. It was embarrassing. She gave me hell for it. She offered me a choice—this ship or a demotion. So this is my way of handing it back to her."

"You're using me to embarrass the admiral, aren't you?"

"Absolutely." Parsons grinned. "You're not a political animal, Korie; you don't get it. When this ship comes back with you in command, it'll be my way of sending a message to Fleet Command that I'm impudent—that I won't roll over easily. So put on the damn stars and take command of your ship. I'd order you to do it, but I can't. I've resigned. Effective with taking them off. Right now this ship has no captain. Unless you put those stars on. So what are you going to do?"

Korie allowed himself a soft smile. "Well, when you put it that way—" He began fumbling with his collar.

Parsons stopped him. "Wait a minute, let's get some witnesses in here. There are a couple of people who will kill us both, if we do this ceremony without their participation." She spoke into her headset, "Tor, Brik, Williger, Leen, Goldberg and Shibano to the wardroom, on the double!" Turning back to Korie, she slid her clipboard across the table toward him.

"Let's take care of the paper work. I have to sign your promotion, hand over command, and then you have to accept my resignation. Here, sign here, here and here." As Korie signed, the others began filing into the wardroom with curious expressions on their faces. Parsons held up a hand for silence and motioned them to line up against the wall.

"What's going on?" Leen asked, coming in last.

"Shh," said Williger. "Be a witness."

"Oh," mouthed Leen and took his place silently beside her.

Korie signed the last page and started to straighten up, but Parsons shoved one more at him. "This one too—this one absolves me of all responsibility." She smiled broadly.

Korie scanned the form, recognizing the oath it represented. It wasn't an official oath *per se*, but it was the oath of commitment that captains had been voluntarily taking almost since the first liberty ship was launched. "As captain of the starship, I recognize that I am the sole authority for her actions in war and in peace. I am charged with the well-being of her crew and the maintenance of her readiness. In every regard, I am the ship. I acknowledge and accept the responsibility."

Korie laid the stars down on the wardroom table and picked up the stylus. His hands felt clammy and the pen felt like an unfamiliar and alien thing. *This is really happening!* Somehow, he signed his name. And when he finished, and put the stylus down, and straightened up again, he could almost feel the difference in himself—as if a charge of energy, a new way of *being*, was suddenly coursing through his veins. He swallowed hard with the realization.

"Well, go ahead," said Parsons. "Put the stars on."

Still fumbling, Korie picked them up off the table. For some reason, his fingers weren't working quite right. He blinked. He was having a little trouble focusing. He wished Carol could have been here. And Mark and Robby—

"Here, let me," said Parsons, stepping close, ignoring the wetness at the corners of his eyes. She took the stars from his hand and clipped them easily to his collar. Finished, she stepped back again and offered him a crisp salute. And so did all the others. Tor. Leen. Williger. Goldberg. Shibano. Even Brik!

"Don't do that—" Korie started to say, then realized how stupid that would sound. He shut up and returned the salute proudly. The others in the wardroom burst into spontaneous applause.

Parsons stepped forward and shook his hand. "Congratulations, Captain Korie." She added, "Now, it's done. If the admiral makes you take *these* stars off, it'll be *her* embarrassment, not yours." And then they were surrounded by the others, lining up to shake his hand and congratulate him. Korie blinked away the tears quickly, so they wouldn't see how moved he was by their expressions of affection. He looked up—*and up*—at Brik. Even Brik was grinning; at least, Korie thought it was a grin—it was the most ghastly and uncomfortable expression he'd ever seen on a Morthan.

And then Parsons was at his side again. "I'd like to make the announcement to the crew—it's traditional in cases like this. Is that all right with you, Captain Korie?"

"Yes, please do." And then something else occurred to him. "Do you want to remain in the captain's cabin or would you prefer to move to a guest cabin?"

"It's your call, Captain—"

"Why don't you stay in the captain's cabin. As our . . . uh, Captain Emeritus."

"As your *guest*," Parsons corrected. "I promise I'll keep my mouth shut and only give you advice if you ask for it—or out of sight, if you're too stupid to ask. May I retain the privilege of standing watch on your Bridge?"

"Yes, ma'am. I'd be honored if you would." He looked proudly around the room. "Commander Tor, you'll take over as executive officer." He stopped and realized something else. "Oh, and schedule a memorial service immediately after dinner." He looked to Parsons. "Would you like to—?"

"I think that one is yours, Captain. You knew Hodel and Berryman better."

"Yes," Korie agreed. "I think I should. All right, what else is there we need to attend to?"

"You're the captain," said Tor, laughing. "*You tell us.*"

Epilogue

Upon dropping out of hyperstate, the *Star Wolf* had transmitted only the tersest of arrival messages: "*Norway* destroyed, fourteen survivors aboard. Two dead aboard *Star Wolf*. Log sealed. Eyes-only report. Will need substantial maintenance on intelligence engine." The admiral would understand what *wasn't* being said.

Now, as the *Star Wolf* locked her transfer tube into place against the reception bay of the stardock, the admiral's own terse reply was received on the Bridge. "Would the captain of the *Star Wolf* please report to the admiral's office immediately?"

Korie and Parsons were both on the Command Deck when the admiral's signal came in. Both were wearing their dress uniforms. They read the signal and exchanged conspiratorial glances. "I think she wants *your* report," Korie said.

"Uh-uh," said Parsons. "You're the captain of the *Star Wolf*. It's your report she wants."

"But she's expecting you."

"Oh, I'm sure she's going to want to see me—but she should see you first. Protocol, you know."

Korie nodded. He turned forward. "Lieutenant Green, send a signal to Admiral O'Hara. Eyes-only. 'With the *Star Wolf*'s respects, would the admiral please clarify which captain of the *Star Wolf* she wishes to report—Captain Korie or former Captain Parsons?'" He turned back to Parsons. "Her reply will tell us whether or not she's going to confirm my promotion."

"Are you making any bets?"

"Four times I've been in that woman's office, and four times I haven't gotten my stars. Based on her track record, I'm betting against myself."

"I'll bet *for*," said Parsons. "Loser pays for dinner at the most expensive club in town."

"Deal." Korie agreed.

"You'd better apply for a loan, Captain. I'm in the mood for lobster."

Korie grinned. "And I'm in the mood for—I don't know what I'm in the mood for, but I promise it'll be expensive." Then he added, "It's been fun wearing these insignia, Captain Parsons. And it's been a privilege to serve with you. Thank you." He reached for his collar. "Perhaps you should take these back now—"

Parsons stopped him from removing the insignia. "Keep them, Captain. Whether the old bitch confirms you or not, you've earned those."

"Transfer tube is pressurized," reported Goldberg. "We are officially home."

"Thank you, Lieutenant. *Now hear this.* Executive Officer Tor will be posting shore leave schedules as soon as the ship is secured and locked down. Enjoy yourselves, but please remember, we want to be invited back. *That is all.*" Korie picked up his cap and tucked it under his arm. "I'm not going to keep her waiting. Commander Tor, you have the conn. I'm going over."

"Aye, Captain."

Korie traced the familiar path to the forward airlock. So many memories already. So many deaths. How many more? He shook the thoughts away and punched open the inner hatch of the airlock. The door popped shut behind him and the outer door opened into the transfer tube. It looked so innocent now. The last time he'd been through here—he thought it really would be the *last* time . . .

He crossed over to the stardock hatch and repeated the process of stepping through airlocks. There was a young boy waiting on the opposite side of the door; somebody's son, no doubt. He looked a lot like— no, don't think that way. But the boy was looking at him with curiosity too.

An out-of-breath voice behind him called, "Captain?" Reflexively, Korie turned backward to see. It was Brian Armstrong; he'd run the length of the ship and plunged through the airlocks. "We just heard from the admiral—your promotion has been confirmed! She wants to speak to you, *immediately.*"

And then *another* voice yanked his attention forward again. "*Daddy—!*"

Korie spun, caught between two moments—

"*Captain Korie?* What should I tell her?"

But Korie didn't hear. He was wrapping his son into his arms and crying with joy.

Author's Afterword

In 1988, I was hired to create a science fiction TV series for Universal Studios. The working title was *Millennium*. The mandate there was to create a show that could reuse the library of special-effects shots that had been created for *Battlestar Galactica*. (There were contractual reasons why they couldn't do another version of *B.G.*)

My gut-level reaction was to tell these folks that this was a particularly stupid idea; the science fiction audience is smart, they would immediately recognize the recycling as a cheap trick, and they would dismiss the show as cheap and not worth a second look. But I had a hunch that this challenge might also be used as a lever upward into something much more effective and profitable.

You see, the requirements of film production, whether television or theatrical, often determine their own solutions, and I had a strong feeling that if we got this show into production, we would have to design at least one new starship—the star of the series—build the miniature and shoot a new library of effects. In such a case, the *Battlestar Galactica* shots could be demoted, or even discarded. There was little question in my mind that the studio executives would eventually realize that the use of the older material would seriously weaken the look and feel of the new show.

From a production point of view, this was not an ideal prospect, but from a creative position, there was an enormous possibility here. If we could make it work, we would be creating an opportunity to tell some of the stories that a certain other science fiction show had shied away from. So I said, "Let's talk." I suggested several different formats for the show. One was "Space Traders." We would follow the adventures of a family of space gypsies, interstellar traders, as they traveled from planet to planet, buying and selling, wheeling and dealing, occasionally carrying passengers, sometimes being chased by the law, sometimes smuggling, and so on. It was not my favorite idea, but I wanted to offer the studio the appearance of options.

The second idea I suggested was the one I really wanted to do: "World War II in space." (I'm a history fanatic, and World War II is a particular obsession.) The folks at Universal got it immediately. I didn't even have to explain how it would work. ("See, it would be just like *Das Boot* or *The Enemy Below* or *Mr. Roberts*, only with spaceships.") It suited their needs, and it was a format that allowed for open-ended storytelling. We could expand the show in any direction we wanted.

The next step was to develop an outline.

In 1972, I had written a novel called *Yesterday's Children*. In that story, Executive Officer Korie is a martinet whose obsession with pursuing an unseen enemy destroys him. But that ending had always annoyed me. I liked Korie too much. And I really wanted to see him solve his problem. So, in 1977 I added twelve more chapters to the book, giving Korie the opportunity to produce a brilliant military victory. It was a much more satisfying conclusion. The book was retitled *Starhunt*. (Not necessarily a better title, but it distinguished the new version from the earlier one.)

Now, as I started to block out a pilot episode for *Millennium*, I realized that I could reuse some of the characters from *Starhunt*, in particular Commander Jon Thomas Korie. (Two things about Korie's name: Commander Buzz Correy was the hero of *Space Patrol*, my favorite TV series when I was growing up, so I thought it would be a nice touch to have a new Commander Korie flying the star lanes. Korie also shares the same initials with a certain *other* starship captain; one who is also legendary for the exploits of *his* John Thomas . . .)

The outline for the pilot episode had Executive Officer Korie assigned to a new ship, dealing with an aging captain no longer able to handle the rigors of starship life and totally unprepared for the coming war. As a personal in-joke, I had this captain bring along his legal advisor as an aide, a relationship which I characterized as "King Lear v. Iago." And it also gave me the opportunity to give Korie a line of dialog especially close to my heart: "Why does a starship need a lawyer?" (Korie probably wasn't the only one asking that question.) Universal enthusiastically approved the outline, they loved the humor, and I went right to work on a two-hour pilot script.

In that first script, a Morthan assassin gets loose on the starship and not only kills a few crewmembers, he also eats them. This created the opportunity for two more deliciously nasty lines of dialog: "Ohmygod, the Morthan just ate the captain's lawyer." "Voluntarily. . .?"

Despite their love of the outline, the folks at Universal felt the script had turned out too dark, too grim to be a good series opener. They wanted a new pilot episode. They weren't quite sure what changes they wanted, but they wanted changes. I was a little annoyed at the vagueness of these notes, but I recognized their concerns and agreed to a second draft.

Then the Writers' Guild went out on strike for six months. And that meant that I could not turn in the second draft script, could not get paid, could not move the show forward. It was a very frustrating period, because on the one hand, I recognized the validity of the Guild's negotiating points—on the other hand, the delay was going to kill production deals all over town.

The strike ended in August and a few days later, I turned in the second draft script. In this version, a new captain comes aboard, makes a bad decision and inadvertently triggers the interstellar equivalent of Pearl Harbor. I also added the Quillas and Brian Armstrong's sexual adventures. The studio loved the second draft script and for a while, there was even some discussion of shooting the series in HDTV so that Sony could use it as a showcase for their new video technology.

And then, nothing else happened. It was set aside as the studio's priorities changed. It was now officially one of those things "that seemed a good idea at the time." So I went back to work on my novels and finished *A Rage For Revenge,* the third novel in my alien invasion series, The War Against The Chtorr.

Before tackling the fourth book in the Chtorr series, *A Season For Slaughter,* I decided to adapt the *Millennium* pilot into a novel called *The Star Wolf.* At the last moment, to avoid confusion with Edmond Hamilton's classic novel of the same name, the publisher retitled my book *The Voyage of the Star Wolf.*

One afternoon in 1990, I received a phone call from a producer named Ed Elbert. A long time ago, he'd read a book of mine called *Yesterday's Children* and had always thought it might make a good TV series. Would I be interested in optioning the rights to him?

I sent him my pilot script, now retitled *The Star Wolf.* He recognized immediately that this was exactly what he was looking for; we could take all of that early development work and expand it. I brought in Dorothy Fontana as a partner in this exercise and we expanded the original concepts of the two scripts already finished. Another good friend, who also recognized the potential of the series, came aboard as well; he opened his checkbook and invested in some artwork, costume designs and the construction of a starship model.

Somewhere in there, we realized that there was more story to tell than we could fit into two hours and I expanded the second draft pilot script to four one-hour episodes structured so they could be shown either as four one-hour episodes or a four-hour miniseries. We began showing it around town.

We presented it as "World War II in space" and almost everybody understood the concept immediately, but nobody wanted to pay for the privilege of putting us into production. (One studio loved it so much they made an offer, withdrew the offer the next day, then took our tag line "World War II in space" and used it to produce a forgettable series that failed quickly.)

During all of this, Dorothy Fontana and I continued to develop the series' "bible"—the Writers/Directors' Guide. And we made a promise to ourselves. We were not going to do a pale imitation of *Star Trek*. We would do all the things that *Star Trek* couldn't do or wouldn't do—the stories that were too dangerous or too subversive or too disturbing. We said our goal would be to go where no TV series had gone before.

We developed backstories for all of the major characters, we created a military arena for the war, we designed and staffed an entire starship and we invested a great deal of time working out story arcs for all of the characters, even some of our favorite background people. Most important, we even blocked out complete outlines for a number of episodes.

Here are a few of the ideas we generated:

Our crew is not the best and the brightest and our ship is not the biggest and the fastest. She is a liberty ship, fresh off the assembly line, untested and inexperienced. As the series proceeds, we start to see this nice clean vessel age. She gets dirty, she gets posters glued to her bulkheads, graffiti shows up everywhere, things break down and get hammered back together with whatever materials are available. Many of her internal walls are a kind of Styrofoam (you don't need more than that and this is a hastily-assembled liberty ship), so they get easily dented and punched.

The first twenty minutes of the first episode are about some *other* ship—this one is the best and the brightest. She is the *Endeavor* and she is commanded by Captain Richard Long. (Or Richard Head, I forget which.) Everything on this ship is just a little *too* special, a little *too* wonderful, a little *too* well color-coordinated. Then, just before the first commercial, she gets ambushed by Morthan marauders. She blows up and everybody dies. When we come back from the break, the *Star Wolf* shows up for a planned rendezvous, a much less impressive vessel, dirty, gritty and crewed by folks whose uniforms aren't quite as well-tailored . . . Hello, this is the *real* starship in this series. We expected this would be one of the most outrageous gags in television history. We knew the audience would understand exactly what point we were making.

Jon Korie, the executive officer of the ship is our central character. He deserves to be promoted to captain, but fate has conspired against him and his promotion is held in permanent limbo. This may be lucky for him, because the *Star Wolf* is a jinxed ship. She keeps killing her captains. This would let us have big-name guest stars come aboard to be captain of the *Star Wolf* for two or four episodes and then either die in combat, have a nervous breakdown, be eaten by Morthans, be recalled by the manufacturer, fall out the airlock or experience some other bizarre twist of fate.

One story we wanted to do had the *Star Wolf* caught by a Morthan battle cruiser in the very first scene of the episode, the "teaser." The brand-new captain opens a channel and says, "We surrender," and Brik immediately kills him. "Surrender is not an option." The rest of the episode would be Brik's court-martial. (The jury would be three Alliance Morthans, because only they could understand Brik's reasoning.)

We wanted to establish Molly Williger as the ugliest woman in the galaxy—make her the butt of a legendary joke—and then give her the most seething and passionate love affair in television history, because not only the pretty people fall in love. Love is more than just a nice package of chest and cheekbones.

Every character on the ship would have a secret which would be revealed during the course of the series. Jon Korie's secret is the most astonishing. (And on the elusive chance that we might still turn this thing into a TV series, I'm not going to reveal it here.) At one point, I even wrote a script putting the whole crew of the ship through the Mode Training—one of those personal-effectiveness courses that sometimes function like psychological boot camp.

And yes, one of the stories both Dorothy and I wanted to do was *Blood and Fire*, adapted from the episode I had written for *Star Trek: The Next Generation*, which they had never filmed.

Other writers of our acquaintance knew we were working on this series and several of them suggested story ideas that we knew immediately we wanted to use. Steve Boyett suggested "A Day In The Life" and Daniel Keys Moran gave us "The Knight Who Stayed Home." With their permission, both of these stories were combined into a second Star Wolf novel, called *The Middle of Nowhere*. If the series ever goes into production, those two episodes *will* be part of it.

All of this work was enormously invigorating. We actually had the time to consider in depth a lot of development problems that under ordinary circumstances would have to be decided in a mad rush. We could talk not only about the immediate solution, but also about the long-term consequences to the entire series of each decision. It was a creative opportunity that few shows ever get. We also knew that if and when we ever got a firm commitment to go into production, we would, from the very first moment, be six months ahead of schedule. There would be questions we would not have to ask, because we had already worked out the answers.

Oh, yes—somewhere in all of this confusion, I adopted a little boy named Sean. (That particular adventure has since been documented in *The Martian Child*. It seemed like a very good idea at the time. It still seems a good idea today, eleven years later.) One day, my son asked me, "Daddy, what can I do in the TV show?" Before I could even figure out how to explain to an eight-year-old that television production is really not a great adventure for any child, it's more boring than exciting, he began to explain, "I could be this weird-looking little guy who walks around in the background and doesn't say anything." And even as he was saying it, I recognized the opportunity for a marvelous sight gag— a short little "Martian" who would show up briefly in every show, handing someone a wrench or carrying some bizarre object down a corridor (like Alfred Hitchcock walking out of the Cumberland train station with a cello in the 1946 production of *The Paradine Case*). And if the series continued for several years, we could occasionally have someone wonder aloud about the growth of the Martian. So I told Sean I loved his idea and he should go off and draw a picture of what he thought his costume should look like. (I already knew what it would look like: something very easy to hang on a child, something very easy to remove.)

Eventually, a Canadian company agreed to provide production facilities and even a majority of funding for a Star Wolf television series. They had the foreign investors, they had the Canadian tax benefits, the money was there, all they needed was an American buyer to give us credibility.

At one point, the Sci-Fi Channel came aboard for a few months and even invested in a set of rewrites. We used that as an opportunity to increase the suspense, the sex and the action in the scripts, while clarifying the Morthan threat even more. Regretfully, we removed the gag of destroying the *Endeavor* in the first twenty minutes, but we replaced it with a situation that dramatically increased Korie's internal dilemma. By now, we felt that the four one-hour pilot episodes were as good as we could create for a science fiction television series. And so did everyone else who read them. One executive said to us, "We have never had such a well-developed presentation laid on our desks. We have never seen pilot scripts so well-written and so intelligent."

But then . . . nothing happened. The Sci-Fi Channel got sold, a new executive came in, decisions were postponed. And nothing moved forward. The Canadian company had to do this, then they had to do that. Everything was contingent on everything else. And everything else was next week or next month. They stalled us for the better part of two years until the options expired and they went bankrupt. (Sheesh.)

One afternoon, I was discussing *Blood and Fire* with Dorothy Fontana, and as an experiment, I opened up a copy of my original *Star Trek* script and began looking to see how hard it would be to adapt the story. I did a global swap of character names. (I probably shouldn't be admitting this, should I?) Picard became Parsons. Riker became Korie. Crusher became Williger. LaForge became Leen. The *Enterprise* became the *Star Wolf*. But after that, the parallels stopped. Then I read through the script to see what else had to be adjusted. Hmm. Quite a bit, actually. I had to get rid of the warp-drive engines, I had to restructure the problem without using the transporter and I had to take a long, hard look at the character relationships. None of them worked as a Star Wolf story. So I sat down and began working my way through the script, line by line, turning it into a real Star Wolf adventure and not simply a revised *Star Trek* episode.

It was an exciting process. The differences between the two were profound. (For one thing, we weren't in production, and we still had the freedom, the luxury, to write for ourselves.) More important, I discovered some things about the *Star Wolf* that I hadn't realized before—that we weren't just telling stories about problems that could be solved easily in the last five minutes of the episode; no, we were examining the hearts and souls of our characters as they confronted the continuing challenges before them. There were consequences to their actions—moral, legal, political.

So I had to do a major rewrite of every scene, every character and every plot point in order to convert that original *Star Trek* script to a Star Wolf story. Of particular importance, if the captain of the ship violated a standing fleet order, her court-martial would be mandatory—even if she saved her ship and her crew. That became a critical dilemma, as important as the more immediate problem of the bloodworms.

I had a not-so-hidden agenda here. When I finished adapting the script, I had the outline for another Star Wolf novel. I had one more book contract pending with Bantam Books, and *Blood and Fire* would be the perfect property; they had already published two previous Star Wolf novels and *Starhunt*, the book that started the whole adventure. Turning *Blood and Fire* into a novel gave me the opportunity to get even deeper into all of the characters and I knew that, eventually, I would have to rewrite the *Blood and Fire* script to include many of the new scenes developed for the novel. (If/when this damn TV series ever gets on the air, *Blood and Fire* will probably be a two-part episode.)

When I finished this novel, the one you're holding in your hands right now, Bantam Books chose not to publish it. They were shutting down their science fiction line. (But they did pay me, in case you're wondering.) Because the book was already part of a pre-existing series, few other publishers were interested; they'd have to buy all of the other out-of-print books in the series to go with it, and nobody was buying backlist books anymore. So the manuscript for this book sat on the shelf for a couple of years until Glenn Yeffeth of BenBella Books read it. The way he tells it, he got down on his knees and begged me for the opportunity to publish a new David Gerrold novel. The way I tell it, I'm the one begging, "Please publish my orphaned child." The truth is probably somewhere in between.

There are now three novels in the Star Wolf trilogy. At the moment, I don't expect to write any additional adventures, but I'm not ruling it out either. The first novel is *The Voyage of the Star Wolf*. The second is *The Middle of Nowhere*; the events in that book take place immediately after the events in the first novel. The events in *Blood and Fire*, however, do not occur until at least a year or two later. Maybe longer. Our original intention in the TV series was not to tell this story until we had already taken our characters through a whole series of other events, partly because we didn't want to be accused of being so desperate that we had to recycle an old *Star Trek* script, and partly because the payoff at the end of this story was not one we wanted to get to quickly. Because Korie has endured so much by the time of this story, Dorothy and I both felt that he was entitled to at least one major personal victory. In this book, he gets two, both on the last page. (If you haven't read it yet, no peeking!)

There are a number of adventures, developed for the TV series that come before this story that have not been novelized yet—in particular the destruction of Taalamar. In that proposed story, Korie learns that his family might have evacuated safely before their home world was destroyed. But now Taalamar is under bombardment by Morthan-directed asteroids and no matter how many rescue ships arrive to carry away refugees, millions of people will still die. The story we want to tell is Korie's desperate search for his family on a doomed planet while the crew of the *Star Wolf* continues to evacuate other families and children. Because Dorothy Fontana has first dibs on writing that script, I haven't tackled it as a novel.

So *Blood and Fire* occurs much later, after Korie has proven himself more than once. (This is referred to in the text.)

Now about that TV series. . . .

In 1999, we found another investor, who paid to develop some computer-generated spaceships and even a short proof-of-concept video. We took the series around town again, talking to a new set of executives, often in the same offices as before. And again everybody loved it, but nobody quite wanted to make the commitment. One studio said it was too dark, another said it was too light. One company felt it was too military, another said it wasn't military enough.

In 2001, a prestigious special-effects company thought *Star Wolf* would be an excellent property to leverage themselves into becoming a complete production facility. We made the rounds again. Same offices, new executives. New ways of saying, "Wow! This is a great show!" One company loved it but didn't have the resources. Another company loved it, but they were already in a deal with someone else and didn't want to do two science fiction shows—"Why didn't you show us this before?" At that meeting, my partners would have physically restrained me from hurling myself out an open window, except that we were on the first floor and there was little danger that I would hurt myself landing on an azalea bush.

Meanwhile, as I write this, there's an executive at another studio who has just read our four pilot scripts, and he thinks that they would make a great TV series. . . .

Coming soon from BenBella Books: *The Un-Making of The Star Wolf— The Greatest TV Series You Never Saw.* We'll publish the whole horrifying history, all the different scripts, plus the bible. You can make up your own mind.

DAVID GERROLD

Printed in the United States
by Baker & Taylor Publisher Services